THE DRAGON MURDER CASE

THE DRAGON
MURDER CASE

S. S. Van Dine

FELONY & MAYHEM PRESS • NEW YORK

All the characters and events in this work are fictitious.

THE DRAGON MURDER CASE

A Felony & Mayhem mystery

PRINTING HISTORY

First edition (Scribner's): 1933
Felony & Mayhem edition: 2020

Library of Congress Cataloging-in-Publication Data

Names: Van Dine, S. S., author.
Title: The dragon murder case / S.S. Van Dine.
Description: Felony & Mayhem edition. | New York : Felony & Mayhem Press,
   2020. | Series: Philo Vance ; 7 | "A Felony & Mayhem mystery." |
   Summary: "A guest at a Manhattan estate dives into a swimming pool and
   disappears, and Philo Vance is on hand to sort out both the murder and
   the mythological references brought up by the crime"-- Provided by
   publisher.
Identifiers: LCCN 2019045247 | ISBN 9781631942020 (trade paperback) |
   ISBN 9781631942105 (ebook)
Subjects: GSAFD: Mystery fiction.
Classification: LCC PS3545.R846 D73 2020 | DDC 813/.54--dc23
LC record available at https://lccn.loc.gov/2019045247

Sometime we see a cloud that's dragonish.
—*Antony and Cleopatra.*

The icon above says you're holding a copy of a book in the Felony & Mayhem "Vintage" category. These books were originally published prior to about 1965, and feature the kind of twisty, ingenious puzzles beloved by fans of Agatha Christie and John Dickson Carr. If you enjoy this book, you may well like other "Vintage" titles from Felony & Mayhem Press.

————◆◆◆————

ELIZABETH DALY
Unexpected Night
Deadly Nightshade
Murders in Volume 2
The House without the Door
Evidence of Things Seen
Nothing Can Rescue Me
Arrow Pointing Nowhere
The Book of the Dead
Any Shape or Form
Somewhere in the House
The Wrong Way Down
Night Walk
The Book of the Lion
And Dangerous to Know
Death and Letters
The Book of the Crime

NGAIO MARSH
A Man Lay Dead
Enter a Murderer
The Nursing Home Murder
Death in Ecstasy
Vintage Murder
Artists in Crime
Death in a White Tie
Overture to Death
Death at the Bar
Surfeit of Lampreys
Death and the Dancing Footman
Colour Scheme
Died in the Wool
Final Curtain
Swing, Brother, Swing
Night at the Vulcan
Spinsters in Jeopardy
Scales of Justice
Death of a Fool

For more about these books, and other Felony & Mayhem titles, or to place an order, please visit our website at:

www.FelonyAndMayhem.com

THE DRAGON MURDER CASE

CHAPTER ONE

The Tragedy
(Saturday, August 11; 11.45 p.m.)

THAT SINISTER AND terrifying crime, which came to be known as the dragon murder case, will always be associated in my mind with one of the hottest summers I have ever experienced in New York.

Philo Vance, who stood aloof from the eschatological and supernatural implications of the case, and was therefore able to solve the problem on a purely rationalistic basis, had planned a fishing trip to Norway that August, but an intellectual whim had caused him to cancel his arrangements and to remain in America. Since the influx of post-war, *nouveau-riche* Americans along the French and Italian Rivieras, he had forgone his custom of spending his summers on the Mediterranean, and had gone after salmon and trout in the streams of North Bergenhus. But late in July of this particular year his interest in the Menander fragments found in Egypt during the early years of this century, had revived, and he set himself to complete their translation—a work which, you may recall, had been interrupted by that amazing series of Mother-Goose murders in West 75th Street.*

However, once again this task of research and love was rudely intruded upon by one of the most baffling murder mysteries in which Vance ever participated; and the lost comedies of Menander were again pigeon-holed for the intricate ratiocination of crime. Personally I think Vance's criminal investigations were closer to his heart than the scholastic enterprises on which he was constantly embarking, for though his mind was ever seeking out abstruse facts in the realm of cultural lore, he found his greatest mental recreation in intricate problems wholly unrelated to pure learning. Criminology satisfied this yearning in his nature, for it not only stimulated his analytical processes but brought into play his knowledge of recondite facts and his uncanny instinct for the subtleties of human nature.

Shortly after his student days at Harvard he asked me to officiate as his legal adviser and monetary steward; and my liking and admiration for him were such that I resigned from my father's firm of Van Dine, Davis and Van Dine to take up the duties he had outlined. I have never regretted that decision; and it is because of the resultant association with him that I have been able to set down an accurate and semi-official account of the various criminal investigations in which he participated. He was drawn into these investigations as a result of his friendship with John F.-X. Markham during the latter's four years' incumbency as District Attorney of New York County.

Of all the cases I have thus far recorded none was as exciting, as weird, as apparently unrelated to all rational thinking, as the dragon murder. Here was a crime that seemed to transcend all the ordinary scientific knowledge of man and to carry the police and the investigators into an obfuscous and unreal realm of demonology and folk-lore—a realm fraught with dim racial memories of legendary terrors.

---

*   *The Bishop Murder Case.*

The dragon has ever entered into the emotional imaginings of primitive religions, throwing over its conceivers a spell of sinister and terrifying superstition. And here in the city of New York, in the twentieth century, the police were plunged into a criminal investigation which resuscitated all the dark passages in those dim forgotten times when the superstitious children of the earth believed in malignant monsters and the retributive horrors which these monsters visited upon man.

The darkest chapters in the ethnological records of the human race were reviewed within sight of the skyscrapers of modern Manhattan; and so powerful was the effect of these resuscitations that even scientists searched for some biological explanation of the grotesque phenomena that held the country enthralled during the days following the uncanny and incomprehensible death of Sanford Montague. The survival of prehistoric monsters—the development of subterranean Ichthyopsida—the unclean and darksome matings of earth and sea creatures—were advanced as possible scientific explanations of the extraordinary and hideous facts with which the police and the District Attorney's office were faced.

Even the practical and hard-headed Sergeant Ernest Heath of the Homicide Bureau was affected by the mysterious and incalculable elements of the case. During the preliminary investigation—when there was no actual evidence of murder—the unimaginative Sergeant sensed hidden and ominous things, as if a miasmatic emanation had arisen from the seemingly commonplace circumstances surrounding the situation. In fact, had it not been for the fears that arose in him when he was first called to take charge of the tragic episode, the dragon murder might never have come to the attention of the authorities. It would, in all probability, have been recorded conventionally in the archives of the New York Police Department as another "disappearance," accounted for along various obvious lines and with a cynical wink.

This hypothetical eventuality was, no doubt, what the murderer intended; but the perpetrator of that extraordinary crime—a crime, as far as I know, unparalleled in the annals of violent homicide—had failed to count on the effect of the sinister atmosphere which enveloped his unholy act. The fact that the imaginative aboriginal fears of man have largely developed from the inherent mysteries enshrouded in the dark hidden depths of water, was overlooked by the murderer. And it was this oversight that roused the Sergeant's vague misgivings and turned a superficially commonplace episode into one of the most spectacular and diabolical murder cases of modern times.

Sergeant Heath was the first official to go to the scene of the crime—although, at the time, he was not aware that a crime had been committed; and it was he who stammered out his unidentifiable fears to Markham and Vance.

It was nearly midnight on August 11. Markham had dined with Vance at the latter's roof-garden apartment in East 38th Street, and the three of us had spent the evening in a desultory discussion of various topics. There had been a lackadaisical atmosphere over our gathering, and the periods of silence had increased as the night wore on, for the weather was both hot and sultry, and the leaves of the tree-tops which rose from the rear yard were as still as those on a painted canvas. Moreover, it had rained for hours, the downpour ceasing only at ten o'clock, and a heavy breathless pall seemed to have settled over the city.

Vance had just mixed a second champagne cup for us when Currie, Vance's butler and major-domo, appeared at the door to the roof-garden carrying a portable telephone.

"There is an urgent call for Mr. Markham," he announced; "and I took the liberty of bringing the telephone… It's Sergeant Heath, sir."

Markham looked nettled and a bit surprised, but he nodded and took the instrument. His conversation with the Sergeant was a brief one, and when he replaced the receiver he was frowning.

"That's queer," he commented. "Unlike the Sergeant. He's worried about something—wants to see me. He didn't give any hint of the matter, and I didn't press the point. Said he found out at my home that I was here... I didn't like the suppressed tone of his voice, and told him he might come here. I hope you don't mind, Vance."

"Delighted," Vance drawled, settling deeper into his wicker chair. "I haven't seen the doughty Sergeant for months... Currie," he called, "bring the Scotch and soda. Sergeant Heath is joining us." Then he turned back to Markham. "I hope there's nothing amiss... Maybe the heat has hallucinated the Sergeant."

Markham, still troubled, shook his head.

"It would take more than hot weather to upset Heath's equilibrium." He shrugged. "Oh, well, we'll know the worst soon enough."

It was about twenty minutes later when the Sergeant was announced. He came out on the terrace garden, wiping his brow with an enormous handkerchief. After he had greeted us somewhat abstractedly he dropped into a chair by the glass-topped table and helped himself to a long drink of the Scotch whisky which Vance moved toward him.

"I've just come from Inwood, Chief," he explained to Markham. "A guy has disappeared. And to tell you the truth, I don't like it. There's something phony somewhere."

Markham scowled.

"Anything unusual about the case?"

"No—nothing." The Sergeant appeared embarrassed. "That's the hell of it. Everything in order—the usual sort of thing. Routine. And yet..." His voice trailed off, and he lifted the glass to his lips.

Vance gave an amused smile.

"I fear, Markham," he observed, "the Sergeant has become intuitive."

Heath set down his glass with a bang.

"If you mean, Mr. Vance, that I've got a hunch about this case, you're right!" And he thrust his jaw forward.

Vance raised his eyebrows whimsically.

"What case, Sergeant?"

Heath gave him a dour look and then grinned.

"I'm going to tell you—and you can laugh all you want to... Listen, Chief." He turned back to Markham. "Along about ten forty-five tonight a telephone call comes to the Homicide Bureau. A fellow, who says his name is Leland, tells me there's been a tragedy out at the old Stamm estate in Inwood and that, if I have any sense, I better hop out..."

"A perfect spot for a crime," Vance interrupted musingly. "It's one of the oldest estates in the city—built nearly a hundred years ago. It's an anachronism today, but—my word!—it's full of criminal possibilities. Legend'ry, in fact, with an amazin' history."

Heath contemplated Vance shrewdly.

"You got the idea, sir. I felt just that way when I got out there... Well, anyway, I naturally asked this fellow Leland what had happened and why I should come. And it seems that a bird named Montague had dived into the swimming pool on the estate, and hadn't come up—"

"Was it, by any chance, the old Dragon Pool?" inquired Vance, raising himself and reaching for his beloved *Régie* cigarettes.

"That's the one," Heath told him; "though I never knew the name of it till I got there tonight... Well, I told him that wasn't in my line, but he got persistent and said that the matter oughta be looked into, and the sooner I came the better. He talked in a funny tone—it sorta got to me. His English was all right—he didn't have any foreign accent—but I got the idea he wasn't an American. I asked him why he was calling up about something that had happened on the Stamm estate; and he said he was an old friend of the family and had witnessed the tragedy. He also said Stamm wasn't able to telephone, and that he had temporarily taken charge of the situation... I couldn't get any more out of him; but there was something about the way the fellow talked that made me leery."

"I see," Markham murmured non-committally. "So you went out?"

"Yeah, I went out." Heath nodded sheepishly. "I got Hennessey and Burke and Snitkin, and we hopped a police car."

"What did you find?"

"I didn't find anything, sir," Heath returned aggressively, "except what that guy told me over the phone. There was a week-end house-party on the estate, and one of the guests—this bird named Montague—had suggested they all go swimming in the pool. There'd probably been considerable drinking, so they all went down to the pool and put on bathing suits..."

"Just a moment, Sergeant," Vance interrupted. "Was Leland drunk, by any chance?"

"Not him." The Sergeant shook his head. "He was the coolest member of the lot. But there was something queer about him. He seemed greatly relieved when I got there; and he took me aside and told me to keep my eyes open. I naturally asked him what he meant, but right away he got casual, so to speak, and merely said that a lot of peculiar things had happened around those parts in the old days, and that maybe something peculiar had happened tonight."

"I think I know what he meant," Vance said with a slight nod. "That part of the city has given rise to many strange and grotesque legends—old wives' tales and superstitions that have come down from the Indians and early settlers."

"Well, anyway,"—Heath dismissed Vance's comments as irrelevant—"after the party had gone down to the pool, this fellow Montague walked out on the spring-board and took a fancy dive. And he never came up..."

"How could the others be so sure he didn't come up?" asked Markham. "It must have been pretty dark after the rain: it's cloudy now."

"There was plenty of light at the pool," Heath explained. "They've got a dozen flood-lights on the place."

"Very well. Go on." Markham reached impatiently for his champagne. "What happened then?"

Heath shifted uneasily.

"Nothing much," he admitted. "The other men dove after him and tried to find him, but after ten minutes or so they gave up. Leland, it seems, told 'em that they'd all better go back to the house and that he'd notify the authorities. Then he called the Homicide Bureau and spilled the story."

"Queer he should do that," ruminated Markham. "It doesn't sound like a criminal case."

"Sure it's queer," agreed Heath eagerly. "But what I found was a whole lot queerer."

"Ah!" Vance blew a ribbon of smoke upward. "That romantic section of old New York is at last living up to its reputation. What were these queer things you found, Sergeant?"

Heath moved again with uneasy embarrassment.

"To begin with, Stamm himself was cock-eyed drunk, and there was a doctor from the neighborhood trying to get him to function. Stamm's young sister—a good-looker of about twenty-five—was having hysterics and going off into faints every few minutes. The rest of 'em—there was four or five—were trying to duck and making excuses why they had to get away *pronto*. And all the time this fellow Leland, who looks like a hawk or something, was going round as cool as a cucumber with lifted eyebrows and a satisfied grin on his brown face, as if he knew a lot more than he was telling.—Then there was one of those sleezy, pasty-faced butlers, who acted like a ghost and didn't make any noise when he moved…"

"Yes, yes," Vance nodded whimsically. "Everything most mystifyin'… And the wind moaned through the pines; and an owl hooted in the distance; and a lattice rattled in the attic; and a door creaked; and there came a tapping—eh, what, Sergeant?… I say, do have another spot of Scotch. You're positively jittery." (He spoke humorously, but there was a shrewd, interested look in his half-closed eyes and an undercurrent of tension in his voice that made me realize that he was taking the Sergeant far more seriously than his manner indicated.)

I expected the Sergeant to resent Vance's frivolous attitude, but instead he wagged his head soberly.

"You got the idea, Mr. Vance. Nothing seemed on the level. It wasn't normal, as you might say."

Markham's annoyance was mounting.

"The case doesn't strike me as peculiar, Sergeant," he protested. "A man dives into a swimming pool, hits his head on the bottom, and drowns. And you've related nothing else that can't be explained on the most commonplace grounds. It's not unusual for a man to get drunk, and after a tragedy of this kind a hysterical woman is not to be regarded as unique. Naturally, too, the other members of the party wanted to get away after an episode like this. As for the man Leland: he may be just a peculiar officious character who wished to dramatize a fundamentally simple affair. And you always had an antipathy for butlers. However you look at the case, it doesn't warrant anything more than the usual procedure. It's certainly not in the province of the Homicide Bureau. The idea of murder is precluded by the very mechanism of Montague's disappearance. He himself suggested a swim in the pool—a rational enough suggestion on a night like this—and his plunge into the pool and his failure to come to the surface could hardly be indicative of any other person's criminal intent."

Heath shrugged and lighted a long black cigar.

"I've been telling myself the same things for the past hour," he returned stubbornly; "but that situation at the Stamm house ain't right."

Markham pursed his lips and regarded the Sergeant meditatively.

"Was there anything else that upset you?" he asked, after a pause.

Heath did not answer at once. Obviously there was something else on his mind, and it seemed to me that he was weighing the advisability of mentioning it. But suddenly he lifted himself in his chair and took his cigar deliberately from his mouth.

"I don't like those fish!" he blurted.

"Fish?" repeated Markham in astonishment. "What fish?"

Heath hesitated and contemplated the end of his cigar sheepishly.

"I think I can answer that question, Markham," Vance put in. "Rudolph Stamm is one of the foremost aquarists in America. He has a most amazin' collection of tropical fish—strange and little-known varieties which he has succeeded in breeding. It's been his hobby for twenty years, and he is constantly going on expeditions to the Amazon, Siam, India, the Paraguay basin, Brazil and Bermuda. He has also made trips to China and has scoured the Orinoco. Only a year or so ago the papers were full of his trip from Liberia to the Congo..."

"They're queer-looking things," Heath supplemented. "Some of 'em look like sea-monsters that haven't grown up."

"Their shapes and their colorings are very beautiful, however," commented Vance with a faint smile.

"But that wasn't all," the Sergeant went on, ignoring Vance's æsthetic observation. "This fellow Stamm had lizards and baby alligators—"

"And probably turtles and frogs and snakes—"

"I'll say he has snakes!" The Sergeant made a grimace of disgust. "Plenty of 'em—crawling in and out of big flat tanks of water..."

"Yes." Vance nodded and looked toward Markham. "Stamm, I understand, has a terrarium along with his fish. The two often go together, don't y' know."

Markham grunted and studied the Sergeant for a moment.

"Perhaps," he remarked at length, in a flat, matter-of-fact tone, "Montague was merely playing a practical joke on the other guests. How do you know he didn't swim under water to the other side of the pool and disappear up the opposite bank? Was it dark enough there so the others couldn't have seen him?"

"Sure it was dark enough," the Sergeant told him. "The flood-lights don't reach all across the water. But that explanation is out. I myself thought something of the kind might have happened, seeing as how there had been a lot of liquor going round, and I took a look over the place. But the opposite side of the pool is almost a straight precipice of rock, nearly a hundred feet high. Across the upper end of the pool, where the creek runs in, there's a big filter, and not only would it be hard for a man to climb it, but the lights reach that far and any one of the party could have seen him there. Then, at the lower end of the pool, where the water has been dammed up with a big cement wall, there's a drop of twenty feet or so, with plenty of rocks down below. No guy's going to take a chance dropping over the dam in order to create a little excitement. On the side of the pool nearest the house, where the spring-board is, there's a concrete retaining wall which a swimmer might climb over; but there again the floodlights would give him dead away."

"And there's no other possible way Montague could have got out of the pool without being seen?"

"Yes, there's one way he might have done it—but he didn't. Between the end of the filter and the steep cliff that comes down on the opposite side of the pool, there's a low open space of about fifteen feet which leads off to the lower part of the estate. And this flat opening is plenty dark so that the people on the house side of the pool couldn't have seen anything there."

"Well, there's probably your explanation."

"No, it isn't, Mr. Markham," Heath asserted emphatically. "The minute I went down to the pool and got the lay of the land, I took Hennessey with me across the top of the big filter and looked for footprints on this fifteen-foot low bank. You know it had been raining all evening, and the ground over there is damp anyway, so that if there had been any kind of footprints they would have stuck out plain. But the whole area was perfectly smooth. Moreover, Hennessey and I went back into the grass a little distance from the bank, thinking that maybe the guy might have climbed up on a ledge of the rock and jumped over the muddy edge of the water. But there wasn't a sign of anything there either."

"That being the case," said Markham, "they'll probably find his body when the pool is dragged... Did you order that done?"

"Not tonight I didn't. It would take two or three hours to get a boat and hooks up there, and you couldn't do anything much at night anyway. But that'll all be taken care of the first thing in the morning."

"Well," decided Markham impatiently, "I can't see that there's anything more for you to do tonight. As soon as the body is found the Medical Examiner will be notified, and he'll probably say that Montague has a fractured skull and will put the whole thing down as accidental death."

There was a tone of dismissal in his voice, but Heath refused to be moved by it. I had never seen the Sergeant so stubborn.

"You may be right, Chief," he conceded reluctantly. "But I got other ideas. And I came all the way down here to ask you if you wouldn't come up and give the situation the once-over."

Something in the Sergeant's voice must have affected Markham, for instead of replying at once he again studied the other quizzically. Finally he asked:

"Just what have you done so far in connection with the case?"

"To tell the truth, I haven't done much of anything," the Sergeant admitted. "I haven't had time. I naturally got the names and addresses of everybody in the house and questioned each one of 'em in a routine way. I couldn't talk to Stamm because he was out of the picture and the doctor was working over him. Most of my time was spent in going around the pool, seeing what I could learn. But, as I told you, I didn't find out anything except that Montague didn't play any joke on his friends. Then I went back to the house and telephoned to you. I left things up there in charge of the three men I took along with me. And after I told everybody that they couldn't go home until I got back, I beat it down here... That's my story, and I'm probably stuck with it."

Despite the forced levity of his last remark, he looked up at Markham with, I thought, an appealing insistence.

Once more Markham hesitated and returned the Sergeant's gaze.

"You are convinced there was foul play?" he queried.

"I'm not convinced of anything," Heath retorted. "I'm just not satisfied with the way things stack up. Furthermore, there's a lot of funny relationships in that crowd up there. Everybody seems jealous of everybody else. A couple of guys are dotty on the same girl, and nobody seemed to care a hoot—except Stamm's young sister—that Montague didn't come up from his dive. The fact is, they all seemed damn pleased about it—which didn't set right with me. And even Miss Stamm didn't seem to be worrying particularly about Montague. I can't explain exactly what I mean, but she seemed to be all upset about something else connected with his disappearance."

"I still can't see," returned Markham, "that you have any tangible explanation for your attitude. The best thing, I think, is to wait and see what tomorrow brings."

"Maybe yes." But instead of accepting Markham's obvious dismissal Heath poured himself another drink and relighted his cigar.

During this conversation between the Sergeant and the District Attorney, Vance had lain back in his chair contemplating the two dreamily, sipping his champagne cup and smoking languidly. But a certain deliberate tenseness in the way he moved his hand to and from his lips, convinced me that he was deeply interested in everything that was being said.

At this point he crushed out his cigarette, set down his glass, and rose to his feet.

"Really, y' know, Markham old dear," he said in a drawling voice, "I think we should toddle along with the Sergeant to the site of the mystery. It can't do the slightest harm, and it's a beastly night anyway. A bit of excitement, however tame the ending, might help us forget the weather. And we may be affected by the same sinister atmospheres which have so inflamed the Sergeant's hormones."

Markham looked up at him in mild astonishment.

"Why in the name of Heaven, should you want to go to the Stamm estate?"

"For one thing," Vance returned, stifling a yawn, "I am tremendously interested, d' ye see, in looking over Stamm's collection of toy fish. I bred them myself in an amateur way once, but because of lack of space, I concentrated on the color-breeding of the *Betta splendens* and *cambodia*—Siamese Fighting Fish, don't y' know."*

Markham studied him for a few moments without replying. He knew Vance well enough to realize that his desire to accede to the Sergeant's request was inspired by a much deeper reason than the patently frivolous one he gave. And he also knew that no amount of questioning would make Vance elucidate his true attitude just then.

After a minute Markham also rose. He glanced at his watch and shrugged.

"Past midnight," he commented disgustedly. "The perfect hour, of course, to inspect fish! Shall we drive out in the Sergeant's car or take yours?"

"Oh, mine, by all means. We'll follow the Sergeant." And Vance rang for Currie to bring him his hat and stick.

---

*   At one time Vance had turned his sun-parlor into an aquarium and
      devoted several years to breeding these beautiful veil-tailed fish. He
      succeeded in producing corn-flower blue, deep maroon, and even black
      specimens; and he won several awards with them at the exhibitions of
      the Aquarium Society at the Museum of Natural History.

CHAPTER TWO

A Startling Accusation
(Sunday, August 12; 12.30 a.m.)

A FEW MINUTES LATER we were headed up Broadway. Sergeant Heath led the way in his small police car and Markham and Vance and I followed in Vance's Hispano-Suiza. Reaching Dyckman Street, we went west to Payson Avenue and turned up the steep winding Bolton Road.* When we had reached the highest point of the road we swung into a wide private driveway with two tall square stone posts at the entrance, and circled upward round a mass of evergreen trees until we reached the apex of the hill. It was on this site that the famous old Stamm residence had been built nearly a century before.

It was a wooded estate, abounding in cedar, oak, and spruce trees, with patches of rough lawn and rock gardens.

---

*   *This is not to be confused with Lower Bolton Road, otherwise known as River Road, which turns off Dyckman Street near the New York Central Hudson River railroad tracks and passes below the Memorial Hospital.*

From this vantage point could be seen, to the north, the dark Gothic turrets of the House of Mercy, silhouetted against a clearing sky which seemed to have sucked up the ghostly lights of Marble Hill a mile distant across the waters of Spuyten Duyvil. To the south, through the trees, the faintly flickering glow of Manhattan cast an uncanny spell. Eastward, on either side of the black mass of the Stamm residence, a few tall buildings along Seaman Avenue and Broadway reached up over the hazy horizon like black giant fingers. Behind and below us, to the west, the Hudson River moved sluggishly, a dark opaque mass flecked with the moving lights of boats.

But although on every side we could see evidences of the modern busy life of New York, a feeling of isolation and mystery crept over me. I seemed infinitely removed from all the busy activities of the world; and I realized then, for the first time, how strange an anachronism Inwood was. Though this historic spot—with its great trees, its crumbling houses, its ancient associations, its rugged wildness, and its rustic quietude—was actually a part of Manhattan, it nevertheless seemed like some hidden fastness set away in a remote coign of the world.

As we turned into the small parking space at the head of the private driveway, we noticed an old-fashioned Ford coupé parked about fifty yards from the wide balustraded stone steps that led to the house.

"That's the doctor's car," Heath explained to us, as he hopped down from his machine. "The garage is on the lower road on the east side of the house."

He led the way up the steps to the massive bronze front door over which a dim light was burning; and we were met by Detective Snitkin in the narrow panelled vestibule.

"I'm glad you're back, Sergeant," the detective said, after saluting Markham respectfully.

"Don't you like the situation either, Snitkin?" Vance asked lightly.

"Not me, sir," the other returned, going toward the inner front door. "It's got me worried."

"Anything else happen?" Heath inquired abruptly.

"Nothing except that Stamm has begun to sit up and take notice."

He gave three taps on the door which was immediately opened by a liveried butler who regarded us suspiciously.

"Is this really necessary, officer?" he asked Heath in a suave voice, as he reluctantly held the door open for us. "You see, sir, Mr. Stamm—"

"I'm running this show," Heath interrupted curtly. "You're here to take orders, not to ask questions."

The butler bowed with a sleek, obsequious smile, and closed the door after us.

"What are your orders, sir?"

"You stay here at the front door," Heath replied brusquely, "and don't let any one in." He then turned to Snitkin, who had followed us into the spacious lower hallway. "Where's the gang and what are they doing?"

"Stamm's in the library—that room over there—with the doctor." Snitkin jerked his thumb toward a pair of heavy tapestry portières at the rear of the hall. "I sent the rest of the bunch to their rooms, like you told me. Burke is sitting out on the rear doorstep, and Hennessey is down by the pool."

Heath grunted.

"That's all right." He turned to Markham. "What do you want to do first, Chief? Shall I show you the lay of the land and how the swimming pool is constructed? Or do you want to ask these babies some questions?"

Markham hesitated, and Vance spoke languidly.

"Really, Markham, I'm rather inclined to think we should first do a bit of what you call probing. I'd jolly well like to know what preceded this *alfresco* bathing party, and I'd like to view the participants. The pool will keep till later; and—one can't tell, can one?—it may take on a different significance once we have established a sort of social background for the unfortunate escapade."

"It doesn't matter to me." Markham was plainly impatient and skeptical. "The sooner we find out why we're here at all, the better pleased I'll be."

Vance's eyes were roving desultorily about the hallway. It was panelled in Tudor style, and the furniture was dark and massive. Life-sized, faded oil portraits hung about the walls, and all the doors were heavily draped. It was a gloomy place, filled with shadows, and with a musty odor which accentuated its inherent unmodernity.

"A perfect setting for your fears, Sergeant," Vance mused. "There are few of these old houses left, and I'm trying to decide whether or not I'm grateful."

"In the meantime," snapped Markham, "suppose we go to the drawing-room... Where is it, Sergeant?"

Heath pointed to a curtained archway on the right, and we were about to proceed when there came the sound of soft descending footsteps on the stairs, and a voice spoke to us from the shadows.

"Can I be of any assistance, gentlemen?"

The tall figure of a man approached us. When he had come within the radius of flickering light thrown by the old-fashioned crystal chandelier, we discerned an unusual and, as I thought at the time, sinister person.

He was over six feet tall, slender and wiry, and gave the impression of steely strength. He had a dark, almost swarthy, complexion, with keen calm black eyes which had something of the look of an eagle in them. His nose was markedly Roman and very narrow. His cheek-bones were high, and there were slight hollows under them. Only his mouth and chin were Nordic: his lips were thin and met in a straight line; and his deeply cleft chin was heavy and powerful. His hair, brushed straight back from a low broad forehead, seemed very black in the dim light of the hallway. His clothes were in the best of taste, subdued and well-cut, but there was a carelessness in the way he wore them which made me feel that he regarded them as a sort of compromise with an unnecessary convention.

"My name is Leland," he explained, when he had reached us. "I am a friend of long standing in this household, and I was a guest tonight at the time of the most unfortunate accident."

He spoke with peculiar precision, and I understood exactly the impression which the Sergeant had received over the telephone when Leland had first communicated with him.

Vance had been regarding the man critically.

"Do you live in Inwood, Mr. Leland?" he asked casually.

The other gave a barely perceptible nod.

"I live in a cottage in Shorakapkok, the site of the ancient Indian village, on the hillside which overlooks the old Spuyten Duyvil Creek."

"Near the Indian caves?"

"Yes, just across what they now call the Shell Bed."

"And you have known Mr. Stamm a long time?"

"For fifteen years." The man hesitated. "I have accompanied him on many of his expeditions in search of tropical fish."

Vance kept his gaze steadily upon the strange figure.

"And perhaps also," he said, with a coldness which I did not then understand, "you accompanied Mr. Stamm on his expedition for lost treasure in the Caribbean? It seems I recall your name being mentioned in connection with those romantic adventures."

"You are right," Leland admitted without change of expression.

Vance turned away.

"Quite—oh, quite. I think you may be just the person to help us with the present problem. Suppose we stagger into the drawing-room for a little chat."

He drew apart the heavy curtains, and the butler came swiftly forward to switch on the electric lights.

We found ourselves in an enormous room, the ceiling of which was at least twenty feet high. A large Aubusson carpet covered the floor; and the heavy and ornate Louis-Quinze furniture, now somewhat dilapidated and faded, had been set about the walls with formal precision. The whole room had a fusty and tarnished air of desuetude and antiquity.

Vance looked about him and shuddered.

"Evidently not a popular rendezvous," he commented as if to himself.

Leland glanced at him shrewdly.

"No," he vouchsafed. "The room is rarely used. The household has lived in the less formal rooms at the rear ever since Joshua Stamm died. The most popular quarters are the library and the vivarium which Stamm added to the house ten years ago. He spends most of his time there."

"With the fish, of course," remarked Vance.

"They are an absorbing hobby," Leland explained without enthusiasm.

Vance nodded abstractedly, sat down and lighted a cigarette.

"Since you have been so kind as to offer your assistance, Mr. Leland," he began, "suppose you tell us just what the conditions were in the house tonight, and the various incidents that preceded the tragedy." Then, before the other could reply, he added: "I understand from Sergeant Heath that you were rather insistent that he should take the matter in hand. Is that correct?"

"Quite correct," Leland replied, without the faintest trace of uneasiness. "The failure of young Montague to come to the surface after diving into the pool struck me as most peculiar. He is an excellent swimmer and an adept at various athletic sports. Furthermore, he knows every square foot of the pool; and there is practically no chance whatever that he could have struck his head on the bottom. The other side of the pool is somewhat shallow and has a sloping wall, but the near side, where the *cabañas* and the diving-board are, is at least twenty-five feet deep."

"Still," suggested Vance, "the man may have had a cramp or a sudden concussion from the dive. Such things have happened, don't y' know." His eyes were fixed languidly but appraisingly on Leland. "Just what was your object in urging a member of the Homicide Bureau to investigate the situation?"

"Merely a question of precaution—" Leland began, but Vance interrupted him.

"Yes, yes, to be sure. But why should you feel that caution was necess'ry in the circumstances?"

A cynical smile appeared at the corners of the man's mouth.

"This is not a household," he replied, "where life runs normally. The Stamms, as you may know, are an intensely inbred line. Joshua Stamm and his wife were first cousins, and both pairs of grandparents were also related by blood. Paresis runs in the family. There has been nothing fixed or permanent in the natures of the last two generations of Stamms, and life in this household is always pushing out at unexpected angles. The ordinary family diagrams are constantly being broken up. There is little stabilization, either physical or intellectual."

"Even so"—Vance, I could see, had become deeply interested in the man—"how would these facts of heredity have any bearing on Montague's disappearance?"

"Montague," Leland returned in a flat voice, "was engaged to Stamm's sister, Bernice."

"Ah!" Vance drew deeply on his cigarette. "You are inferring perhaps that Stamm was opposed to the engagement?"

"I am making no inferences." Leland took out a long-stemmed briar pipe and a pouch of tobacco. "If Stamm objected to the alliance, he made no mention of it to me. He is not the kind of man who reveals his inner thoughts or feelings. But his nature is pregnant with potentialities, and he may have hated Montague." Deftly he filled his pipe and lighted it.

"And are we to assume, then, that your calling in the police was based on—what shall we call it?—the Mendelian law of breeding as applied to the Stamms?"

Again Leland smiled cynically.

"No, not exactly—though it may have been a factor in rousing my suspicious curiosity."

"And the other factors?"

"There has been considerable drinking here in the last twenty-four hours."

"Oh, yes; alcohol—that great releaser of inhibitions... But let's forgo the academic for the time being."

Leland moved to the centre-table and leaned against it.

"The personages of this particular house-party," he said at length, "are not above gaining their ends at any cost."

Vance inclined his head.

"That remark is more promising," he commented. "Suppose you tell us briefly of these people."

"There are few enough of them," Leland began. "Besides Stamm and his sister, there is a Mr. Alex Greeff, a reputed stock-broker, who unquestionably has some designs on the Stamm fortune. Then there is Kirwin Tatum, a dissipated and disreputable young ne'er-do-well, who, as far as I can make out, exists wholly by sponging on his friends. Incidentally, he has made something of an ass of himself over Bernice Stamm..."

"And Greeff—what are his sentiments toward Miss Stamm?"

"I cannot say. He poses as the family's financial adviser, and I know that Stamm has invested rather heavily at his suggestion. But whether or not he wishes to marry the Stamm fortune is problematical."

"Thanks no end... And now for the other members of the party."

"Mrs. McAdam—they call her Teeny—is the usual type of widow, talkative, gay, and inclined to overindulgence. Her past is unknown. She is shrewd and worldly, and has a practical eye on Stamm—always making a great fuss over him, but obviously with some ulterior motive. Young Tatum whispered to me confidentially, in a moment of drunken laxity, that Montague and this McAdam woman once lived together."

Vance clicked his tongue in mock disapproval.

"I begin to sense the potentialities of the situation. Most allurin'... Any one else to complicate this delightful social *mélange*?"

"Yes, a Miss Steele. Ruby is her first name. She is an intense creature, of indeterminate age, who dresses fantastically and is always playing a part of some kind. She paints pictures and sings and talks of her 'art.' I believe she was once on the stage... And that completes the roster—except for Montague and myself. Another woman was invited, so Stamm told me, but she sent in her regrets at the last minute."

"Ah! Now that's most interestin'. Did Mr. Stamm mention her name?"

"No, but you might ask him when the doctor gets him in shape."

"What of Montague?" Vance asked. "A bit of gossip regarding his proclivities and background might prove illuminatin'."

Leland hesitated. He knocked the ashes out of his pipe and refilled it. When he had got it going again he answered with a show of reluctance:

"Montague was what you might call a professional handsome-man. He was an actor by profession, but he never seemed to get very far—although he was featured in one or two motion pictures in Hollywood. He always lived well, at one of the fashionable and expensive hotels. He attended first nights and was a frequenter of the east-side night-clubs. He had a decidedly pleasant manner and was, I understand, most attractive to women..." Leland paused, packed his pipe, and added: "I really know very little about the man."

"I recognize the type." Vance regarded his cigarette. "However, I shouldn't say the gathering was altogether unusual, or that the elements involved were necess'rily indicative of deliberate tragedy."

"No," Leland admitted. "But it impressed me as noteworthy that practically every one present at the party tonight might have had an excellent motive for putting Montague out of the way."

Vance lifted his eyebrows interrogatively.

"Yes?" he urged.

"Well, to begin with, Stamm himself, as I have said, might have been violently opposed to Montague's marrying his sister. He is very fond of her, and he certainly has intelligence enough to realize that the match would have been a sorry misalliance.—Young Tatum is certainly in a state of mind to murder any rival for Miss Stamm's affections. Greeff is a man who would stop at nothing, and Montague's marrying into the Stamm family might easily have wrecked his financial ambition to control the fortune. Or, perhaps he actually hoped to marry Bernice himself.—Then again, there was unquestionably something between Teeny McAdam and Montague—I noticed it quite plainly after Tatum had told me of their former relationship. She may have resented his deflection to another woman. Nor is she the kind that would tolerate being thrown over. Furthermore, if she really has any matrimonial designs on Stamm, she may have been afraid that Montague would spoil her prospects by telling Stamm of her past."

"And what about the tense *bohémienne*, Miss Steele?"

A hard look came into Leland's face as he hesitated. Then he said, with a certain sinister resolution:

"I trust her least of them all. There was some definite friction between her and Montague. She was constantly making unpleasant remarks about him—in fact, she ridiculed him openly, and rarely addressed an ordinarily civil word to him. When Montague suggested the swim in the pool she walked with him to the *cabañas*, talking earnestly. I could not make out what was said, but I got a decided impression that she was berating him for something. When we came out in our bathing suits and Montague was about to take the first dive, she walked up to him with a leer and said, in a tone which I could not help overhearing, 'I hope you never come up.' And when Montague failed to appear her remark struck me as significant... Perhaps now you can realize—"

"Quite—oh, quite," Vance murmured. "I can see all the possibilities you put forth. A sweet little conclave—eh, what?" He looked up sharply. "And what about yourself, Mr. Leland? Were you, by any chance, interested in Montague's demise?"

"Perhaps more than any of the others," Leland answered with grim frankness. "I disliked the man intensely, and I considered it an outrage that he was to marry Bernice. I not only told her so, but I also expressed my opinion to her brother."

"And why," pursued Vance dulcetly, "should you take the matter so much to heart?"

Leland shifted his position on the edge of the table and took his pipe slowly from his mouth.

"Miss Stamm is a very fine and unusual young woman." He spoke with slow deliberation, as if carefully choosing his words. "I admire her greatly. I have known her since she was a child, and during the past few years we have become very good friends. I simply did not think that Montague was good enough for her." He paused and was about to continue, but changed his mind.

Vance had been watching the man closely.

"You're quite lucid, don't y' know, Mr. Leland," he murmured, nodding slowly and looking vaguely at the ceiling. "Yes—quite so. I apprehend that you had an excellent motive for doing away with the dashing Mr. Montague…"

At this moment there came an unexpected interruption. The portières of the drawing-room had been left parted, and suddenly we heard rapid footsteps on the stairs. We turned toward the door, and a moment later a tall, spectacular woman thrust herself excitedly into the room.

She was perhaps thirty-five years old, with an unusually pallid face and crimson lips. Her dark hair was parted in the middle and smoothed back over her ears into a knot at the back of her neck. She wore a long black chiffon gown which seemed to have been cut in one piece and moulded to her figure. The only touches of color in her costume were supplied by her jade jewelry. She wore long pendant jade earrings, a triple jade bead necklace, jade bracelets, several jade rings, and a large carved jade brooch.

As she entered the room her eyes were fixed blazingly on Leland, and she took a few steps toward him. There was a tiger-like menace in her attitude. Then she cast a quick glance at the rest of us, but immediately brought her gaze back to Leland, who stood regarding her with quizzical imperturbability. Slowly she raised her arm and pointed at him, at the same time leaning toward him and narrowing her eyes.

"There's the man!" she cried passionately, in a deep resonant voice.

Vance had risen lazily to his feet and reached for his monocle. Adjusting it, he regarded the woman mildly but critically.

"Thanks awfully," he drawled. "We have met Mr. Leland informally. But we haven't yet had the pleasure—"

"My name is Steele," she cut in almost viciously. "Ruby Steele. And I could hear some of the things that were being said about me by this man. They are all lies. He is only trying to shield himself—to focus suspicion on others."

She turned her fiery eyes from Vance back to Leland and again lifted an accusing finger.

"He's the man that's responsible for Sanford Montague's death. It was he who planned and accomplished it. He hated Monty, for he himself is in love with Bernice Stamm. And he told Monty to keep away from Bernice, or he would kill him. Monty told me that himself. Ever since I came to this house yesterday morning, I have had a clutching feeling here"—she pressed her hands dramatically against her bosom—"that some terrible thing was going to happen—that this man would carry out his threat." She made a theatrical gesture of tragedy, interlocking her fingers and carrying them to her forehead. "And he has done it!… Oh, he is sly! He is shrewd—"

"Just how, may I ask," put in Vance, in a cool, unemotional voice, "did Mr. Leland accomplish this feat?"

The woman swung toward him disdainfully.

"The technique of crime," she replied throatily, and with exaggerated hauteur, "is not within my province. You should be able to find out how he did it. You're policemen, aren't you? It was this man who telephoned to you. He's sly, I tell you! He thought that if anything suspicious were discovered when poor Monty's body was found, you'd eliminate him as the murderer because he had telephoned to you."

"Very interestin'," nodded Vance, with a touch of irony. "So you formally accuse Mr. Leland of deliberately planning Mr. Montague's death?"

"I do!" the woman declared sententiously, extending her arms in a studied gesture of emphasis. "And I know I'm right, though it's true I do not know how he did it. But he has strange powers. He's an Indian—did you know that?—an Indian! He can tell when people have passed a certain tree, by looking at the bark. He can track people over the whole of Inwood by broken twigs and crushed leaves. He can tell by the moss on stones how long it has been since they were moved or walked over. He can tell by looking at the ashes of fires how long the flames have been out. He can tell by smelling a garment or a hat, to whom it belongs. And he can read strange signs and tell by the scent of the wind when the rain is coming. He can do all manner of things of which white men know nothing. He knows all the secrets of these hills, for his people have lived in them for generations. He's an Indian—a subtle, scheming Indian!" As she spoke her voice rose excitedly and an impressive histrionic eloquence informed her speech.

"But, my dear young lady," Vance protested pleasantly, "the qualities and characteristics which you ascribe to Mr. Leland are not what one would call unusual, except in a comparative sense. His knowledge of woodcraft and his sensitivity to odors are really not a convincing basis for a criminal accusation. Thousands of boy scouts would constantly be in jeopardy if that were the case."

The woman's eyes became sullen, and she compressed her lips into a line of anger. After a moment she extended her hands, palms upward, in a gesture of resignation, and gave a mirthless laugh.

"Be stupid, if you want to," she remarked with forced and hollow lightness. "But some day you'll come to me and tell me how right I was."

"It will be jolly good fun, anyway," smiled Vance. *"Forsan et haec olim meminisse juvabit*, as Vergil put it... In the meantime, I must be most impolite and ask that you be good enough to wait in your room until such time as we shall wish to question you further. We have several little matters to attend to."

Without a word she turned and swept majestically from the room.

CHAPTER THREE

The Splash in the Pool
(Sunday, August 12; 1.15 a.m.)

DURING RUBY STEELE'S diatribe Leland had stood smoking placidly, watching the woman with stoical dignity. He did not seem in the least disturbed by her accusation, and when she had left the room, he shrugged mildly and gave Vance a weary smile.

"Do you wonder," he asked, with a touch of irony, "why I telephoned the police and insisted that they come?"

Vance studied him listlessly.

"You anticipated being accused of having manœuvred Montague's disappearance—eh, what?"

"Not exactly. But I knew there would be all manner of rumors and whisperings, and I thought it best to have the matter over with at once, and to give the authorities the best possible chance of clarifying the situation and fixing the blame. However, I did not expect any such scene as we have just gone through. Needless to tell you, all Miss Steele has just said is a hysterical fabrication. She told but one truth—and that was only half a truth. My mother was an Algonkian Indian—the Princess White Star, a proud and noble woman, who was separated from her people when a child and reared in a southern convent. My father was an architect, the scion of an old New York family, many years my mother's senior. They are both dead."

"You were born here?" asked Vance.

"Yes, I was born in Inwood, on the site of the old Indian village, Shorakapkok; but the house has long since gone. I live here because I love the place. It has many happy associations of my childhood, before I was sent to Europe to be educated."

"I suspected your Indian blood the moment I saw you," Vance remarked, with non-committal aloofness. Then he stretched his legs and took a deep inhalation on his cigarette. "But suppose you tell us, Mr. Leland, just what preceded the tragedy tonight. I believe you mentioned the fact that Montague himself suggested the swim."

"That is true." Leland moved to a straight chair by the table and sat down. "We had dinner about half-past seven. There had been numerous cocktails beforehand, and during dinner Stamm brought out some heavy wines. After the coffee there was brandy and port, and I think every one drank too much. As you know, it was raining and we could not go outdoors. Later we went to the library, and there was more drinking—this time Scotch highballs. There was a little music of a rowdy nature. Young Tatum played the piano and Miss Steele sang. But that did not last long—the drinking had begun to take effect, and every one was uneasy and restless."

"And Stamm?"

"Stamm especially indulged. I have rarely seen him drink so much, though he has managed for years to punish liquor pretty systematically. He was taking Scotch straight, and after he had downed at least half a bottle I remonstrated with him. But he was in no condition to listen to reason. He became sullen and quiet, and by ten o'clock he was ignoring every one and dozing off. His sister, too, tried to bring him back to his senses, but without any success."

"At just what time did you go for your swim?"

"I do not know exactly, but it was shortly after ten. It stopped raining about that time, and Montague and Bernice stepped out on the terrace. They came back almost immediately, and it was then that Montague announced that the rain had ceased and suggested that we all take a swim. Every one was willing—every one, that is, but Stamm. He was in no condition to go anywhere or do anything. Bernice and Montague urged him to join us, thinking perhaps that the water would sober him. But he was ugly and ordered Trainor to bring him another bottle of Scotch..."

"Trainor?"

"That is the butler's name... Stamm was sodden and helpless, so I told the others to leave him alone, and we all went down to the *cabañas*. I myself pushed the switch in the rear hallway, that turns on the lights on the stairs down to the pool and also the flood-lights at the pool. Montague was the first to appear in his bathing suit, but the rest of us were ready a minute or so later... Then came the tragedy—"

"I say, just a moment, Mr. Leland," Vance interrupted, leaning over and breaking the ashes of his cigarette in the fireplace. "Was Montague the first in the water?"

"Yes. He was waiting at the spring-board—posing, I might say—when the rest of us came out of the *cabañas*. He rather fancied himself and his figure, and I imagine there was a certain amount of vanity in his habit of always hurrying to the pool and taking the first plunge when he knew all eyes would be on him."

"And then?"

"He took a high swan dive, beautifully timed and extremely graceful—I'll say that much for the chap. We naturally waited for him to come up before following suit. We waited an interminable time—it was probably not more than a minute, but it seemed much longer. And then Mrs. McAdam gave a scream, and we all went quickly, with one accord, to the very edge of the pool and strained our eyes across the water in every direction. By this time we knew something had happened. No man could stay under water voluntarily as long as that. Miss Stamm clutched my arm, but I threw her off and, running to the end of the spring-board, dived in as near as possible at the point where Montague had disappeared."

Leland compressed his lips, and his gaze shifted.

"I swam downward," he continued, "till I came to the bottom of the pool, and searched round as best I could. I came up for air and went down again, and again I came up. A man was in the water just beside me, and I thought for a moment it was Montague. But it was only Tatum, who had joined me in the water. He too had dived in, in an effort to find Montague. Greeff also, in a bungling kind of way—he is not a very good swimmer—helped us look for the poor fellow… But it was no go. We spent at least twenty minutes in the effort. Then we gave it up…"

"Exactly how did you feel about the situation?" Vance asked, without looking up. "Did you have any suspicions then?"

Leland hesitated and pursed his lips, as if trying to recall his exact emotions. Finally he replied:

"I cannot say just how I did feel about it. I was rather overwhelmed. But still there was something—I do not know just what—in the back of my mind. My instinct at that moment was to get to a telephone and report the affair to the police. I did not like the turn of events—they struck me as too unusual… Perhaps," he added, lifting his eyes to the ceiling with a faraway look, "I remembered—unconsciously—too many tales about the old Dragon Pool. My mother told me many strange stories when I was a child—"

"Yes, yes. Quite a romantic and legend'ry spot," Vance murmured, with a tinge of sarcasm in his words. "But I'd much rather know just what the women were doing and how they affected you when you joined them after your heroic search for Montague."

"The women?" There was a mild note of surprise in Leland's voice, and he looked penetratingly at Vance. "Oh, I see—you wish to know how they acted after the tragedy... Well, Miss Stamm was crouched down on the top of the wall at the edge of the water, with her hands pressed to her face, sobbing convulsively. I do not think she even noticed me—or any one else, for that matter. I got the impression that she was more frightened than anything else.—Miss Steele was standing close beside Bernice, with her head thrown back, her arms outstretched in a precise gesture of tragic supplication..."

"It sounds rather as if she were rehearsing for the rôle of Iphigeneia at Aulis... And what about Mrs. McAdam?"

"Funny thing about her," Leland ruminated, frowning at his pipe. "She was the one who screamed when Montague failed to come to the surface; but when I got out of the water, she was standing back from the bank, under one of the flood-lights, as cold and calm as if nothing had happened. She was looking out across the pool in a most detached fashion, as if there was no one else present. And she was half smiling, in a hard, ruthless sort of way. 'We could not find him,' I muttered, as I came up to her: I do not know why I should have addressed her rather than the others. And without moving her eyes from the opposite side of the pool, she said, to no one in particular: 'So that's that.'"

Vance appeared unimpressed.

"So you came to the house here and telephoned?"

"Immediately. I told the others they had better get dressed and return to the house at once, and after I had telephoned I went back to my *cabaña* and got into my clothes."

"Who notified the doctor about Stamm's condition?"

"I did," the other replied. "I did not enter the library when I first came here to telephone, but when I had got into my clothes I went at once to Stamm, hoping his mind would have cleared sufficiently for him to realize the terrible thing that had happened. But he was unconscious, and the bottle on the tabouret by the davenport was empty. I did my best to arouse him, but did not succeed."

Leland paused, frowned with uncertainty, and then continued:

"I had never before seen Stamm in a state of complete insensibility through overindulgence in liquor, although I had seen him pretty far gone on several occasions. The state of the man shocked me. He was scarcely breathing, and his color was ghastly. Bernice came into the room at that moment and, on seeing her brother sprawled out on the davenport, exclaimed, 'He's dead, too. Oh, my God!' Then she fainted before I could reach her. I intrusted her to Mrs. McAdam—who showed an admirable competency in handling the situation—and went immediately to the telephone to summon Doctor Holliday. He has been the Stamm family physician for many years and lives in 207th Street, near here. Luckily he was at home and hurried over."

Just then a door slammed noisily somewhere at the rear of the house, and heavy footsteps crossed the front hall and approached the drawing-room. Detective Hennessey appeared at the door, his mouth partly open and his eyes protruding with excitement.

He greeted Markham perfunctorily and turned quickly to the Sergeant.

"Something's happened down there at the pool," he announced, jerking his thumb over his shoulder. "I was standing by the spring-board like you told me to do, smoking a cigar, when I heard a funny rumbling noise up at the top of the rock cliff opposite. And pretty soon there was a hell of a splash in the pool—sounded like a ton of bricks had been dumped off the cliff into the water... I waited a coupla minutes, to see if anything else'd happen, and then I thought I'd better come up and tell you."

"Did you see anything?" demanded Heath aggressively.

"Nary a thing, Sergeant." Hennessey spoke with emphasis. "It's dark over there by the rocks, and I didn't go round over the filter ledge, because you told me to keep off that low stretch at the other end."

"I told him to keep off," the Sergeant explained to Markham, "because I wanted to go over that ground again for footprints in the daylight tomorrow." Then he turned back to Hennessey. "Well, what do you think the noise was?" he asked with the gruffness of exasperation.

"I'm not thinkin'," Hennessey retorted. "I'm simply tellin' you all I know."

Leland rose and took a step toward the Sergeant.

"If you will pardon me, I think I can offer a reasonable explanation of what this man heard in the pool. Several large pieces of rock, at the top of the cliff, are loosened where the strata overlap, and I have always had a fear that one of them might come crashing down into the pool. Only this morning Mr. Stamm and I went up to the top of the bluff and inspected those rocks. In fact, we even attempted to pry one of them loose, but could not do so. It is quite possible that the heavy rain tonight may have dislodged the earth that was holding it."

Vance nodded.

"At least that explanation is a pleasin' bit of rationality," he observed lightly.

"Maybe so, Mr. Vance," Heath conceded reluctantly. Hennessey's tale had disturbed him. "But what I want to know is why it should happen on this particular night."

"As Mr. Leland has told us, he and Mr. Stamm attempted to pry the rock loose today—or should I say yesterday? Perhaps they did loosen it, and that would account for its having shifted and fallen after the rain."

Heath chewed viciously on his cigar for a moment. Then he waved Hennessey out of the room.

"Go back and take up your post," he ordered. "If anything else happens down at the pool, hop up here and report *pronto*."

Hennessey disappeared—reluctantly, I thought.

Markham had sat through the entire proceedings with an air of tolerant boredom. He had taken only a mild interest in Vance's questioning, and when Hennessey had left us, he got to his feet.

"Just what is the point in all this discussion, Vance?" he asked irritably. "The situation is normal enough. Admittedly it has certain morbid angles, but all of this esoteric stuff seems to me the result of nerves. Every one's on edge, and I think the best thing for us to do is to go home and let the Sergeant handle the matter in the routine way. How could there be anything premeditated in connection with Montague's possible death when he himself suggested going swimming and then dived off the spring-board and disappeared while every one was looking on?"

"My dear Markham," protested Vance, "you're far too logical. It's your legal training, of course. But the world is not run by logic. I infinitely prefer to be emotional. Think of the masterpieces of poetry that would have been lost to humanity if their creators had been pure logicians—the Odyssey, for instance, the *Ballade des dames du temps jadis*, the *Divina Commedia*, Laus Veneris, the Ode on a Grecian Urn—"

"But what do you propose to do now?" Markham cut in, annoyed.

"I propose," answered Vance, with an exasperating smile, "to inquire of the doctor concerning the condition of our host."

"What could Stamm have to do with it?" protested Markham. "He seems less concerned in the affair than any of the other people here."

Heath, impatient, had risen and started for the door.

"I'll get the doc," he rumbled. And he went out into the dim hallway.

A few minutes later he returned, followed by an elderly man with a closely cropped gray Vandyke. He was clad in a black baggy suit with a high, old-fashioned collar several sizes too large for him. He was slightly stout and moved awkwardly; but there was something in his manner that inspired confidence.

Vance rose to greet him, and after a brief explanation of our presence in the house, he said:

"Mr. Leland has just told us of Mr. Stamm's unfortunate condition tonight, and we'd like to know how he's coming along."

"He's following the normal course," the doctor replied, and hesitated. Presently he went on: "Since Mr. Leland informed you of Mr. Stamm's condition I won't be violating professional ethics in discussing the case with you. Mr. Stamm was unconscious when I arrived. His pulse was slow and sluggish, and his breathing shallow. When I learned of the amount of whisky he had taken since dinner I immediately gave him a stiff dose of apomorphine—a tenth of a grain. It emptied his stomach at once, and after the reaction he went back to sleep normally. He had consumed an astonishing amount of liquor—it was one of the worst cases of acute alcoholism I have ever known. He is just waking up now, and I was about to telephone for a nurse when this gentleman"—indicating Heath—"told me you wished to see me."

Vance nodded understandingly.

"Will it be possible for us to talk to Mr. Stamm at this time?"

"A little later, perhaps. He is coming round all right, and, once I get him up-stairs to bed, you may see him... But you understand, of course," the doctor added, "he will be pretty weak and played out."

Vance murmured his thanks.

"Will you let us know when it is convenient to have us talk to him?"

The doctor inclined his head in assent.

"Certainly," he said, and turned to go.

"And in the meantime," Vance said to Markham, "I think it might be well to have a brief chat with Miss Stamm... Sergeant, will you produce the young lady for us?"

"Just a moment." The doctor turned in the doorway. "I would ask you, sir, not to disturb Miss Stamm just now. When I came here I found her in a very high-strung, hysterical condition over what had happened. So I gave her a stiff dose of bromides and told her to go to bed. She's in no condition to be questioned about the tragedy. Tomorrow, perhaps."

"It really doesn't matter," Vance returned. "Tomorrow will do just as well."

The doctor went lumberingly into the hall, and a moment later we could hear him dialing a number on the telephone.

CHAPTER FOUR

An Interruption
(Sunday, August 12; 1.35 a.m.)

MARKHAM HEAVED A deep, annoyed sigh, and focused his eyes on Vance in exasperation.

"Aren't you satisfied yet?" he demanded impatiently. "I suggest we get along home."

"Oh, my dear Markham!" Vance protested whimsically, lighting a fresh *Régie*. "I should never forgive myself if I went without at least making the acquaintance of Mrs. McAdam. My word! Really now, wouldn't you like to meet her?"

Markham snorted with angry resignation and settled back in his chair.

Vance turned to Heath.

"Shepherd the butler in, Sergeant."

Heath went out with alacrity, returning immediately with the butler in tow. He was a short, pudgy man in his late fifties, with a smug, round face. His eyes were small and shrewd; his nose flat and concave, and the corners of his mouth were pinched into a downward arc. He wore a blond toupee which neither fitted him nor disguised the fact that he was bald. His uniform needed pressing, and his linen was far from immaculate; but he had an unmistakable air of pompous superiority.

"I understand your name is Trainor," said Vance.

"Yes, sir."

"Well, Trainor, there seems to be considerable doubt as to just what happened here tonight. That's why the District Attorney and I have come up." Vance's eyes were fixed on the man with appraising interest.

"If I may be permitted to say so, sir," Trainor submitted in a mincing falsetto, "I think your being here is an excellent idea. One never can tell what is behind these mysterious episodes."

Vance lifted his eyebrows.

"So you think the episode mysterious?... Can you tell us something that might be helpful?"

"Oh, no, sir." The man elevated his chin haughtily. "I haven't the slightest suggestion to make—thanking you, sir, for the honor of asking me."

Vance let the matter drop, and said:

"Doctor Holliday has just told us that Mr. Stamm had a close call tonight, and I understand from Mr. Leland that Mr. Stamm ordered another bottle of whisky at the time the other members of the party went down to the pool."

"Yes, sir. I brought him a fresh quart of his favorite Scotch whisky—Buchanan's Liqueur...although I will say, sir, in extenuation, so to speak, that I took the liberty of protesting with Mr. Stamm, inasmuch as he had already been drinking rather heavily all day. But he became almost abusive, I might say; and I remarked to myself, 'Every man to his own poison'—or words to that effect. It was not my place, you can understand, to refuse to obey the master's orders."

"Of course—of course, Trainor. We certainly do not hold you responsible for Mr. Stamm's condition," Vance assured him pleasantly.

"Thank you, sir. I might say, however, that Mr. Stamm has been quite unhappy about something these past few weeks.

He's been worrying a great deal. He even forgot to feed the fish last Thursday."

"My word! Something really upsettin' must have been preying on his mind... And did you see to it, Trainor, that the fish did not go hungry Thursday?"

"Oh, yes, sir. I am very fond of the fish, sir. And I'm something of an authority on the subject—if I do say so myself. In fact, I disagree with the master quite frequently on the care of some of his rarer varieties. Without his knowing it I have made chemical tests of the water, for acidity and alkalinity— if you know what I mean, sir. And I took it upon myself to increase the alkalinity of the water in the tanks in which the *Scatophagus argus* are kept. Since then, sir, the master has had much better luck with them."

"I myself am partial to brackish water for the *Scatophagus*," Vance commented, with an amused smile. "But we will let that drop for the moment... Suppose you tell Mrs. McAdam that we desire to see her, here in the drawing-room."

The butler bowed and went out, and a few minutes later ushered a short, plump woman into the room.

Teeny McAdam's age was perhaps forty, but from her clothes and her manner it was obvious that she was making a desperate effort to give the impression of youth. There was, however, a hardness about her which she could not disguise. She seemed perfectly calm as she sat down in the chair which Vance held for her.

Vance explained briefly who we were and why we were there, and I was interested in the fact that she showed no surprise.

"It's always well," Vance explained further, "to look into tragedies of this kind, where there is a feeling of doubt in the mind of any one present. And there seems to be considerable doubt in the minds of several witnesses of Mr. Montague's disappearance."

For answer the woman merely gave an arctic smile and waited.

"Are there any doubts in your mind, Mrs. McAdam?" Vance asked quietly.

"Doubts? What kind of doubts? Really, I don't know what you mean." She spoke in a cold, stereotyped voice. "Monty is unquestionably dead. Had it been any one else who disappeared, one might suspect that a practical joke had been played on us. But Monty was never a practical joker. In fact, any sense of humor was painfully lacking in him. He was far too conceited for humor."

"You have known him a long time, I take it."

"Far too long," the woman replied, with what I thought was a touch of venom.

"You screamed, I am told, when he failed to rise to the surface."

"A maidenly impulse," she remarked lightly. "At my age I should, of course, be more reserved."

Vance contemplated his cigarette a moment.

"You weren't, by any chance, expecting the young gentleman's demise at the time?"

The woman shrugged, and a hard light came into her eyes.

"No, not expecting it," she returned bitterly, "but always hoping for it—as were many others."

"Most interestin'," Vance murmured. "But what were you looking for so intently across the pool, after Montague's failure to come up?"

Her eyes narrowed, and her expression belied the careless gesture she made.

"I really do not recall my intentness at that time," she answered. "I was probably scanning the surface of the pool. That was natural, was it not?"

"Quite—oh, quite. One does instinctively scan the water when a diver has failed to reappear—doesn't one? But I was given the impression your attitude was not indicative of this natural impulse. In fact, I was led to believe that you were looking *across* the water, to the rock cliffs opposite."

The woman shifted her gaze to Leland, and a slow contemptuous smile spread over her face.

"I quite understand," she sneered. "This half-breed has been trying to divert suspicion from himself." She swung quickly back to Vance and spoke between clenched teeth. "My suggestion to you, sir, is that Mr. Leland can tell you far more of the tragedy than any one else here."

Vance nodded carelessly.

"He has already told me many fascinatin' things." Then he leaned forward with a half smile that did not extend to his eyes. "By the by," he added, "it may interest you to know that a few minutes ago there was a terrific splash in the pool, near the point, I should say, where you were looking."

A sudden change came over Teeny McAdam. Her body seemed to go taut, and her hands tightened over the arms of her chair. Her face paled perceptibly, and she took a slow deep breath, as if to steady herself.

"You are sure?" she muttered, in a strained voice, her eyes fixed on Vance. "You are sure?"

"Quite sure… But why should that fact startle you?"

"There are strange stories about that pool—" she began, but Vance interrupted.

"Oh, very strange. But you're not, I trust, superstitious?"

She gave a one-sided smile, and her body relaxed.

"Oh, no, I am far too old for that." She was speaking again in her former cold, reserved tone. "But for a moment I got jumpy. This house and its surroundings are not conducive to calm nerves… So there was a splash in the pool? I can't imagine what it might have been. Maybe it was one of Stamm's flying fish," she suggested, with an attempt at humor. Then her face hardened, and she gave Vance a defiant look. "Is there anything else you wish to ask me?"

It was obvious that she had no intention of telling us anything concerning what she may have feared or suspected, and Vance rose listlessly to his feet.

"No, madam," he responded. "I have quite exhausted my possibilities as an interrogator… But I shall have to ask you to remain in your room for the present."

Teeny McAdam rose also, with an exaggerated sigh of relief.

"Oh, I expected that. It's so messy and inconvenient when any one dies... But would it be against the rules and regulations if the tubby Trainor brought me a drink?"

"Certainly not." Vance bowed gallantly "I will be delighted to send you anything you desire—if the cellar affords it."

"You are more than kind," she returned sarcastically. "I'm sure Trainor can scratch me up a stinger."

She thanked Vance facetiously, and left the room.

Vance sent for the butler again.

"Trainor," he said, when the man entered, "Mrs. McAdam wants a stinger—and you'd better use two jiggers each of brandy and *crème de menthe*."

"I understand, sir."

As Trainor went from the room, Doctor Holliday appeared at the door.

"I have Mr. Stamm in bed," he told Vance, "and the nurse is on her way. If you care to speak to him now it will be all right."

The master bedroom was on the second floor, just at the head of the main stairs, and when we entered, ushered in by Doctor Holliday, Stamm stared at us with resentful bewilderment.

I could see, even as he lay in bed, that he was an unusually tall man. His face was lined and cadaverous. His piercing eyes were ringed with shadows, and his cheeks were hollow. He was slightly bald, but his eyebrows were heavy and almost black. Despite his pallor and his obviously weakened condition, it was evident he was a man of great endurance and physical vitality. He was the type of man that fitted conventionally into the stories of his romantic exploits in the South Seas.

"These are the gentlemen that wished to see you," the doctor told him, by way of introduction.

Stamm looked from one to the other of us, turning his head weakly.

"Well, who are they, and what do they want?" His voice was low and peevish.

Vance explained who we were, and added:

"There has been a tragedy here on your estate tonight, Mr. Stamm; and we are here to investigate it."

"A tragedy? What do you mean by a tragedy?" Stamm's sharp eyes did not leave Vance's face.

"One of your guests has, I fear, been drowned."

Stamm suddenly became animated. His hands moved nervously over the silk spread, and he raised his head from the pillow, his eyes glaring.

"Some one drowned!" he exclaimed. "Where? And who?... I hope it was Greeff—he's been pestering the life out of me for weeks."

Vance shook his head.

"No, it was not Greeff—it was young Montague. He dived into the pool and didn't come up."

"Oh, Montague." Stamm sank back on his pillow. "That vain ass!... How is Bernice?"

"She's sleeping," the doctor informed him consolingly. "She was naturally upset, but she will be all right in the morning."

Stamm seemed relieved, and after a moment he moved his head wearily toward Vance.

"I suppose you want to ask questions."

Vance regarded the man on the bed critically and, I thought, suspiciously. I admit that I myself got a distinct impression that Stamm was playing a part, and that the remarks he had made were fundamentally insincere. But I could not say specifically what had caused this impression. Presently Vance said:

"We understand that one of the guests you invited to your week-end party did not put in an appearance."

"Well, what of it?" complained Stamm. "Is there anything so unusual about that?"

"No, not unusual," Vance admitted, "but a bit interestin'. What was the lady's name?"

Stamm hesitated and shifted his eyes.

"Ellen Bruett," he said finally.

"Could you tell us something about her?"

"Very little," the man answered ungraciously. "I haven't seen her for a great many years. I met her on a boat going to Europe, and I ran across her again in Paris. I know nothing of her personally, except that she's a pleasant sort, and extremely attractive. Last week I was surprised to receive a telephone call from her. She said she had just returned from the Orient and intimated that she would like to renew our acquaintance. I needed another woman for the party; so I asked her to join us. Friday morning she phoned me again to say she was leaving unexpectedly for South America... That's the extent of what I know about her."

"Did you," asked Vance, "by any chance, mention to her the names of the other guests you had invited?"

"I told her that Ruby Steele and Montague were coming. They had both been on the stage, and I thought she might know the names."

"And did she?" Vance raised his cigarette deliberately to his lips.

"As I recall, she said she had met Montague once in Berlin."

Vance walked to the window and back.

"Curious coincidence," he murmured.

Stamm's eyes followed him.

"What's curious about it?" he demanded sourly.

Vance shrugged and halted at the foot of the bed. "I haven't the groggiest notion—have you?"

Stamm raised himself from the pillow and glared.

"What do you mean by that question?"

"I mean simply this, Mr. Stamm:"—Vance's tone was mild—"every one we have talked to so far seems to have a peculiar *arrière-pensée* with regard to Montague's death, and there have been intimations of foul play—"

"What about Montague's body?" Stamm broke in. "Haven't you found it yet? That ought to tell the story. He probably bashed his skull while doing a fancy dive to impress the ladies."

"No, his body has not yet been found. It was too late to get a boat and grappling hooks to the pool tonight…"

"You don't have to do that," Stamm informed him trucu-lently. "There are two big gates in the stream just above the filter, and they can be closed. And there's a turnstile lock in the dam. That lets the water drain from the pool. I drain it every year or so, to clean it out."

"Ah! That's worth knowing—eh, Sergeant?" Then to Stamm: "Are the gates and lock difficult to manipulate?"

"Four or five men can do the job in an hour."

"We'll attend to all that in the morning then." Vance looked at the other thoughtfully. "And, by the by, one of Sergeant Heath's men just reported that there was quite a noisy splash in the pool a little while ago—somewhere near the opposite side."

"A part of that damned rock has fallen," Stamm remarked. "It's been loose for a long time." Then he moved uneasily, and asked: "What difference does it make?"

"Mrs. McAdam seemed rather upset about it."

"Hysteria," snorted Stamm. "Leland has probably been telling her stories about the pool… But what are you driving at, anyway?"

Vance smiled faintly.

"I'm sure I don't know. But the fact that a man disap-peared in the Dragon Pool tonight seems to have impressed several people in a most peculiar fashion. None of them seem wholly convinced that it was an accidental death."

"Tommy-rot!"

Stamm drew himself up until he rested on his elbows, and thrust his head forward. A wild light came into his glaring eyes, and his face twitched spasmodically.

"Can't a man get drowned without having a lot of policemen all over the place?" His voice was loud and shrill. "Montague—bah! The world's better off without him. I wouldn't give him tank space with my Guppies—and I feed them to the Scalares."

Stamm became more and more excited, and his voice grew shriller. "Montague jumped into the pool, did he? And he didn't come up? Is that any reason to annoy me when I'm ill?..."

At this moment there came a startling and blood-chilling interruption. The door into the hall had been left open, and there suddenly came to us, from the floor above, a woman's maniacal and terrifying scream.

CHAPTER FIVE

The Water-Monster
(Sunday, August 12; 2 a.m.)

THERE WAS A second of tense startled silence. Then
Heath swung round and rushed toward the door, his hand slipping into his outer coat pocket where he carried his gun. As he
reached the threshold Leland stepped quickly up to him and
placed a restraining hand on his shoulder.

"Do not bother," he said quietly. "It is all right."

"The hell it is!" Heath shot back, throwing off the other's
hand and stepping into the hallway.

Doors had begun to open along the hallway, and there
were several smothered exclamations.

"Get back in your rooms!" bawled Heath. "And stay in
'em." He planted himself aggressively outside the door, glowering down the corridor.

Evidently some of the guests, frightened by the scream,
had come out to see what the trouble was. But confronted with
the menacing attitude of the Sergeant and cowed by his angry
command, they returned to their quarters, and we could hear

the doors close again. The Sergeant, confused and indecisive, turned threateningly to Leland who was standing near the door with a calm but troubled look on his face.

"Where'd that scream come from?" he demanded. "And what does it mean?"

Before Leland could answer Stamm raised himself to a semi-recumbent position and glowered at Vance.

"For the love of God," he complained irritably, "will you gentlemen get out of here! You've done enough damage already... Get out, I tell you! Get out!" Then he turned to Doctor Holliday. "Please go up to mother, doctor, and give her something. She's having another attack—what with all this upheaval round the house."

Doctor Holliday left the room, and we could hear him mounting the stairs.

Vance had been unimpressed by the whole episode. He stood smoking casually, his eyes resting dreamily on the man in bed.

"Deuced sorry to have upset your household, Mr. Stamm," he murmured. "Every one's nerves are raw, don't y' know. Hope you'll be better in the morning... We'll toddle down-stairs—eh, what, Markham?"

Leland looked at him gratefully and nodded.

"I am sure that would be best," he said, leading the way.

We went out of the room and descended the stairs. Heath, however, remained in the hall for a moment glaring up toward the third floor.

"Come, Sergeant," Vance called to him. "You're over-wrought."

Heath finally took his hand from his coat pocket and followed us reluctantly.

Again in the drawing-room, Vance settled into a chair and, looking at Leland inquiringly, waited for an explanation.

Leland took out his pipe again and slowly packed it.

"That was Stamm's mother, Matilda Stamm," he said when he had got his pipe going. "She occupies the third floor of the house. She is a little unbalanced…" He made a slight but significant gesture toward his forehead. "Not dangerous, you understand, but erratic—given occasionally to hallucinations. She has queer attacks now and then, and talks incoherently."

"Sounds like mild paranoia," Vance murmured. "Some hidden fear, perhaps."

"That is it, I imagine," Leland returned. "A psychiatrist they had for her years ago suggested a private sanitarium, but Stamm would not hear of it. Instead he turned the third floor over to her, and there is some one with her all the time. She is in excellent physical health and is perfectly rational most of the time. But she is not permitted to go out. However, she is well taken care of, and the third floor has a large balcony and a conservatory for her diversion. She spends most of her time cultivating rare plants."

"How often do her attacks come?"

"Two or three times a year, I understand, though she is always full of queer ideas about people and things. Nothing to worry about, though."

"And the nature of these attacks?"

"They vary. Sometimes she talks and argues with imaginary people. At other times she becomes hysterical and babbles of events that occurred when she was a girl. Then, again, she will suddenly take violent dislikes to people, for no apparent reason, and proceed to berate and threaten them."

Vance nodded.

"Typical," he mused. Then, after several deep inhalations on his *Régie*, he asked in an offhand manner: "On which side of the house are Mrs. Stamm's balcony and conservat'ry?"

Leland's eyes moved quickly toward Vance, and he lifted his head.

"On the northeast corner," he answered with a slightly rising inflection, as if his answer were purposely incomplete.

"Ah!" Vance took his cigarette slowly from his mouth. "Overlooking the pool, eh?"

Leland nodded. Then, after a brief hesitation, he said:

"The pool has a curious hold on her fancy. It is the source of many of her hallucinations. She sits for hours gazing at it abstractedly, and the German woman who looks after her—a capable companion-nurse named Schwarz—tells me that she never goes to bed without first standing in rapt attention for several minutes at the window facing the pool."

"Very interestin'... By the by, Mr. Leland, do you know when the pool was constructed?"

Leland frowned thoughtfully.

"I cannot say exactly. I know it was built by Stamm's grand-father—that is to say, he built the dam to broaden the water of the stream. But I doubt if he had anything in mind except a scenic improvement. It was Stamm's father—Joshua Stamm—who put in the retaining wall on this side of the pool, to keep the water from straying too far up the hill toward the house. And it was Stamm himself who installed the filter and the gates, when he first began to use the pool for swimming. The water was not particularly free from rubbish, and he wanted some way of filtering the stream that fed it, and also of closing off the inflow, so that the pool could be cleaned out occasionally."

"How did the pool get its name?" asked Vance casually.

Leland gave a slight shrug.

"Heaven only knows. From some old Indian tradition, probably. The Indians hereabouts originally called it by various terms—*Amangaming, Amangemokdom Wikit,* and sometimes *Amangemokdomipek*—but as a rule the shorter word, *Amangaming,* was used, which means, in the Lenape dialect of the Algonkians, the 'place of the water-monster.'*

---

*   *I made a note of these unusual words, and years later, when Vance and I were in California, to see the Munthe Collection of Chinese art, I brought up the subject with Doctor M. R. Harrington, the author of "Religion and Ceremonies of the Lenapes," and now Curator of the Southwest Museum in Los Angeles. He explained that* Amangemok-doming *meant "Dragon-place";* Amangemokdom Wikit, *"Dragon his-house"; and* Amangemokdomipek, *"Dragon-pond." He also explained that the word* amangam, *though sometimes translated "big fish," seems to have meant "water-monster" as well; and that it*

When I was a child my mother always referred to the pool by that name, although at that time it was pretty generally known as the Dragon Pool, which is a fairly accurate transliteration of its original name. Many tales and superstitions grew up around it. The water-dragon—*Amangemokdom** or, sometimes, *Amangegach*—was used as a bogy with which to frighten recalcitrant children..."

Markham got to his feet impatiently and looked at his watch.

"This is hardly the hour," he complained, "for a discussion of mythology."

"Tut, tut, old dear," Vance chided him pleasantly. "I say, these ethnological data are most fascinatin'. For the first time tonight we seem to be getting a little forrader. I'm beginning to understand why nearly every one in the house is filled with doubts and misgivings."

He smiled ingratiatingly and turned his attention again to Leland.

"By the by," he went on, "is Mrs. Stamm given to such distressin' screams during her cloudy moments?"

Again Leland hesitated, but finally answered: "Occasionally—yes."

"And do these screams usually have some bearing on her hallucinations regarding the pool?"

Leland inclined his head.

"Yes—always." Then he added: "But she is never coherent as to the exact cause of her perturbation. I have been present when Stamm has tried to get an explanation from her, but

---

would yield the shorter compound Amangaming. *This evidently was the word preferred by the Lenapes in Inwood.*

*   *In the Walum Olum the word* amangam *is translated as "monster" and Brinton in his notes derives it from* amangi, *"great or terrifying," and* names, *"fish with reference to some mythical water-monster." In the Brinton and Anthony dictionary, however,* amangamek, *the plural form, is translated simply as "large fishes." The Indians regarded such a creature, not as a mere animal, but as a* manitto, *or being endowed with supernatural as well as physical power.*

she has never been lucid on the subject. It is as if she feared something in the future which her momentarily excited mind could not visualize. An inflamed and confused projection of the imagination, I should say—without any definite mental embodiment..."

At this moment the curtains parted, and Doctor Holliday's troubled face looked into the room.

"I am glad you gentlemen are still here," he said. "Mrs. Stamm is in an unusual frame of mind, and insists on seeing you. She is having one of her periodical attacks—nothing serious, I assure you. But she seems very much excited, and she refused to let me give her something to quiet her... I really don't feel that I should mention these facts to you, but in the circumstances—"

"I have explained Mrs. Stamm's condition to these gentlemen," Leland put in quietly.

The doctor appeared relieved.

"That being the case," he went on, "I can tell you quite frankly that I am a little worried. And, as I say, she insists that she see the police—as she calls you—at once." He paused as if uncertain. "Perhaps it might be best—if you do not mind. Since she has this idea, a talk with you might bring about the desired reaction... But I warn you that she is a bit hallucinated, and I trust that you will treat her accordingly..."

Vance had risen.

"We quite understand, doctor," he said assuringly, adding significantly: "It might be better for all of us if we talked with her."

We retraced our way up the dimly lighted stairs, and at the second-story hallway turned upward to Mrs. Stamm's quarters.

On the third floor the doctor led the way down a wide passage, toward the rear of the house, to an open door through which a rectangular shaft of yellow light poured into the gloom of the hall. The room into which we were ushered was large and crowded with early Victorian furniture. A dark green shabby carpet covered the floor, and on the walls was faded green paper. The overstuffed satin-covered chairs had once been white and chartreuse green, but were now gray and dingy. An enormous canopied bed stood at the right of the door, draped in pink damask; and similar damask, with little of its color left, formed the long overdrapes at the window. The Nottingham-lace curtains beneath were wrinkled and soiled. Opposite the bed was a fireplace, on the hearth of which lay a collection of polished conch shells; and beside it stood a high spool what-not overladen with all manner of hideous trifles of the period. Several large faded oil paintings were suspended about the walls on wide satin ribbons which were tied in bows at the moulding.

As we entered, a tall, capable-looking gray-haired woman, in a Hoover apron, stepped aside to make way for us.

"You had better remain, Mrs. Schwarz," the doctor suggested as we passed her.

On the far side of the room, near the window, stood Mrs. Stamm; and the sight of her sent a strange chill through me. She was leaning with both hands on the back of a chair, her head thrust forward in an attitude of fearful expectancy. Even in the brilliant light of the room her eyes seemed to contain a fiery quality. She was a small, slender woman, but she gave forth an irresistible impression of great strength and vitality, as if every sinew in her body were like whipcord; and her large-boned hands, as they grasped the back of the chair, were more like a man's than a woman's. (The idea occurred to me that she could easily have lifted the chair and swung it about.) Her nose was Roman and pinched; and her mouth was a long slit distorted into a sardonic smile. Her hair was gray, streaked with black, and was tucked back over prominent ears. She wore a faded red silk kimono which trailed the floor, showing only the toes of her knitted slippers.

Doctor Holliday made a brief, nervous presentation which Mrs. Stamm did not even acknowledge. She stood gazing at us with that twisted smile, as if gloating over something that only she herself knew. Then, after several moments' scrutiny, the smile faded from her mouth, and a look of terrifying hardness came into her face. Her lips parted, and the blazing light in her eyes grew brighter.

"The dragon did it!" were her first words to us. "I tell you the dragon did it! There's nothing more you can do about it!"

"What dragon, Mrs. Stamm?" asked Vance quietly.

"What dragon, indeed!" She gave a scornful hollow laugh. "The dragon that lives down there in the pool below my window." She pointed vaguely with her hand. "Why do you think it's called the Dragon Pool? I'll tell you why. Because it's the home of the dragon—the old water-dragon that guards the lives and the fortunes of the Stamms. When any danger threatens my family the dragon arises in his wrath."

"And what makes you think"—Vance's voice was mild and sympathetic—"that the dragon exercised his tutelary powers tonight?"

"Oh, I know, I know!" A shrewd fanatical light came into her eyes, and again that hideous smile appeared on her lips. "I sit here alone in this room, year in and year out; yet I know all that is going on. They try to keep things from me, but they can't. I know all that has happened the last two days—I am aware of all the intrigues that are gathering about my house. And when I heard strange voices a while ago, I came to the top of the stairs and listened. I heard what my poor son said. Sanford Montague dived into the pool—and he didn't come up! He couldn't come up—he will never come up! The dragon killed him—caught him beneath the water and held him there and killed him."

"But Mr. Montague was not an enemy," Vance suggested mildly. "Why should the protective deity of your family kill him?"

"Mr. Montague *was* an enemy," the woman declared, pushing the chair aside and stepping forward. "He had fascinated my little girl and planned to marry her. But he wasn't worthy of her. He was always lying to her, and when her back was turned he was having affairs with other women. Oh, I've witnessed much these last two days!"

"I see what you mean," nodded Vance. "But is it not possible that, after all, the dragon is only a myth?"

"A myth?" The woman spoke with the calmness of conviction. "No, he's no myth. I've seen him too often. I saw him as a child. And when I was a young girl I talked with many people who had seen him. The old Indians in the village saw him too. They used to tell me about him when I would go to their huts. And in the long summer twilights I would sit on the top of the cliff and watch for him to come out of the pool, for water-dragons always come out after sundown. And sometimes, when the shadows were deep over the hills and the mists came drifting down the river, he would rise from the water and fly away—yonder—to the north. And then I would sit up all night at my window, when my governess thought I was asleep, and wait for his return; for I knew he was a friend and would protect me; and I was afraid to go to sleep until he had come back to our pool. But sometimes, when I waited for him on the cliff, he wouldn't come out of the pool at all, but would just ripple the water a little to let me know he was there. And those were the nights when I could sleep, for I didn't have to sit up and wait for his return."

Mrs. Stamm's voice, as she related these strange imaginary things, was poetic in its intensity. She stood before us, her arms hanging calmly at her sides, her eyes, which now seemed to have become misty, gazing past us over our heads.

"That's all very interestin'," Vance murmured politely; but I noticed that he kept a steady, appraising gaze on the woman from beneath partly lowered eyelids. "However, could not all that you have told us be accounted for by the romantic imaginings of a child? After all, don't y' know, the existence of dragons scarcely fits in with the conceptions of modern science."

"Modern science—bah!" She turned scornful eyes on Vance and spoke with almost vitriolic bitterness. "Science—science, indeed! A pleasant word to cover man's ignorance. What does any man know of the laws of birth and growth and life and death? What does any man know of what goes on under the water? And the greater part of the world is water—unfathomable depths of water. My son collects a few specimens of fish from the mouths of rivers and from shallow streams—but has he ever plumbed the depths of the vast oceans? Can he say that no monsters dwell in those depths? And even the few fish he has caught are mysteries to him. Neither he nor any other fish collector knows anything about them... Don't talk to me of science, young man. I know what these old eyes have seen!"

"All that you say is quite true," Vance concurred, in a low voice. "But even admitting that some giant flying fish inhabits this pool from time to time, are you not attributing to him too great an intelligence—too great an insight into the affairs of your household?"

"How," she retorted contemptuously, "can any one gauge the intelligence of creatures of whom one knows nothing? Man flatters himself by assuming that no creature can have a greater intelligence than his own."

Vance smiled faintly.

"You are no lover of humanity, I perceive."

"I hate humanity," the woman declared bitterly. "This would be a cleaner, better world if mankind had been omitted from the scheme of things."

"Yes, yes, of course." Vance's tone suddenly changed, and he spoke with a certain decisive positivity. "But may I ask—the hour is getting rather late, y' know—just why you insisted on seeing us?"

The woman stiffened and leaned forward. The intense hysterical look came back into her eyes, and her hands flexed at her sides.

"You're the police—aren't you?—and you're here trying to find out things... I wanted to tell you how Mr. Montague lost his life. Listen to me! He was killed by the dragon—do you understand that? He was killed by the dragon! No one in this house had anything to do with his death—no one!... That's what I wanted to tell you." Her voice rose as she spoke, and there was a terrific passion in her words.

Vance's steady gaze did not leave her.

"But why, Mrs. Stamm," he asked, "do you assume that we think some one here had a hand in Montague's death?"

"You wouldn't be here if you didn't think so," she retorted angrily, with an artful gleam in her eyes.

"Was what you heard your son say, just before you screamed," Vance asked, "the first inkling you had of the tragedy?"

"Yes!" The word was an ejaculation. But she added more calmly: "I have known for days that tragedy was hanging over this house."

"Then why did you scream, Mrs. Stamm?"

"I was startled—and terrified, perhaps—when I realized what the dragon had done."

"But how could you possibly have known," argued Vance, "that it was the dragon who was responsible for Montague's disappearance under the water?"

Again the woman's mouth twisted into a sardonic smile.

"Because of what I had heard and seen earlier tonight."

"Ah!"

"Oh, yes! About an hour ago I was standing by the window here, looking down at the pool—for some reason I was unable to sleep and had gotten out of bed. Suddenly I saw a great shape against the sky, and I heard the familiar flutter of wings coming nearer...nearer... And then I saw the dragon sweep over the tree-tops and down before the face of the cliff opposite. And I saw him dive into the pool with a great splash, and I saw the white spray rise from the water where he had disappeared... And then all was silence again. The dragon had returned to his home."

Vance walked to the window and looked out.

"It's pretty dark," he commented. "I'm dashed if I can see the cliff from here—or even the water."

"But *I* can see—*I* can see," the woman protested shrilly, turning on Vance and shaking her finger at him. "I can see many things that other people can't see. And I tell you I saw the dragon return—"

"Return?" repeated Vance, studying the woman calmly. "Return from where?"

She gave a shrewd smile.

"I won't tell you that—I won't give away the dragon's secret... But I will tell you this," she went on: "he had taken the body away to hide it."

"Mr. Montague's body?"

"Of course. He never leaves the bodies of his victims in the pool."

"Then there have been other victims?" Vance inquired.

"Many victims." The woman spoke in a strained sepulchral voice. "And he always hides their bodies."

"It might upset your theory a bit, Mrs. Stamm," Vance pointed out to her, "if we should find Mr. Montague's body in the pool."

She chuckled in a way that sent a shiver through me.

"Find his body? Find his body in the pool? You can't find it. It's not there!"

Vance regarded her a moment in silence. Then he bowed.

"Thank you, Mrs. Stamm, for your information and help. I trust the episode has not disturbed you too much and that you will rest tonight."

He turned and walked toward the door, and the rest of us followed him. In the hall Doctor Holliday stopped.

"I'm staying up here for a while," he told Vance. "I think I can get her to sleep now... But, for Heaven's sake, don't take anything she said tonight seriously. She often has these little periods of hallucinosis. It's really nothing to worry about."

"I quite understand," Vance returned, shaking hands with him.

CHAPTER SIX

A Contretemps
(Sunday, August 12; 2.20 a.m.)

WE DESCENDED TO the main hallway, and Vance led the way back to the drawing-room.

"Well, are you through now?" Markham asked him irritably.

"Not quite."

I had rarely seen Vance so serious or so reluctant to postpone an investigation. I knew that he had been deeply interested in Mrs. Stamm's hysterical recital; but I could not understand, at the time, his reason for prolonging an interview that seemed to me both futile and tragic. As he stood before the fireplace his mind seemed far away, and there was a puzzled corrugation on his forehead. He watched the curling smoke from his cigarette for several moments. Suddenly, with a slight toss of the head, he brought himself back to his surroundings and turned to Leland who was leaning against the centre-table.

"What did Mrs. Stamm mean," he asked, "when she referred to other victims whose bodies the dragon had hidden?"

Leland moved uneasily and looked down at his pipe.

"There was a modicum of truth in that remark," he returned. "There have been two authentic deaths in the pool that I know of. But Mrs. Stamm was probably referring also to the wild stories which the old crones tell of mysterious disappearances in the pool in the old days."

"Sounds something like the old-timers' tales of Kehoe's Hole in Newark*... What were the two authentic cases you speak of?"

"One happened about seven years ago, shortly after Stamm and I returned from our expedition to Cocos Island. Two suspicious characters were scouting the neighborhood—probably with a view to burglary—and one of them fell off the cliff on the far side of the pool, and was evidently drowned. Two schoolgirls from this vicinity saw him fall, and later the police picked up his companion who eventually, under questioning, verified the other's disappearance."

"Disappearance?"

Leland nodded grimly.

"His body was never found."

There was the suggestion of a skeptical smile on Vance's mouth as he asked: "How do you account for that?"

"There is only one sensible way of accounting for it," answered Leland, with a slightly aggressive accent, as if

---

*   *Kehoe's Hole, of which the lake in West Side Park, Newark, is the last vestige, has had a most unusual history. The once great swamp was also called, at different times, Magnolia Swamp and Turtle Ditch, and an enterprising newspaper reporter has dubbed the present lake Suicide Lake. The old swamp had the distinction of being considered bottomless; and many strange tales are told, by the old-timers and pseudo-archivists in the neighborhood, of mysterious drownings in its waters, and of the remarkable disappearances of the bodies despite every effort to find them. One story tells of the disappearance beneath its surface of a team of horses and a wagon. These amazing tales—extending over a period of forty years or more—may be accounted for by the fact that there were once quicksands in parts of the swamp. But tradition still has it that the bottom of the present lake has not been fathomed and that once a body sinks beneath its surface, it is never found.*

endeavoring to convince himself with his own words. "The stream gets swollen at times, and there is quite a flow of water over the dam—sufficient to carry a floating body over, if it happened to be caught by the current at a certain angle. This fellow's body was probably washed over the dam and carried down to the Hudson River."

"A bit far-fetched, but none the less tenable... And the other case?"

"Some boys trespassed here one afternoon and went swimming. One of them, as I recall, dived from a ledge of the cliff into the shallow water, and did not come up. As soon as the authorities were notified—by an unidentified telephone call, incidentally—the pool was drained, but there was no trace of the body. Later, however, after the newspapers had made a two-days' sensation of the affair, the boy's body was found in the Indian Cave on the other side of the Clove. He had fractured his skull."

"And do you, by any chance, have an explanation for that episode also?" Vance asked, with a tinge of curtness.

Leland shot him a quick glance.

"I should say the boy struck his head in diving, and the other boys in the party became frightened and, not wanting to leave the body in the pool, lest they become involved, carried it down to the cave and hid it. It was probably one of them that telephoned to the police."

"Oh, quite. Very simple, don't y' know." Vance looked into space meditatively. "Yet both cases have ample esoteric implications to have taken root in Mrs. Stamm's weakened mind."

"Undoubtedly," Leland agreed.

A short silence ensued. Vance walked slowly across the room and back, his hands in his outer coat pockets, his head forward on his chest, his cigarette drooping from his lips. I knew what this attitude signified:—some stimulus had suddenly roused a train of thought in his mind. He again took up his position before the mantel and crushed out his cigarette on the hearth. He slowly turned his head toward Leland.

"You mentioned your expedition to Cocos Island," he said lazily. "Was it the lure of the *Mary Dear* treasure?"

"Oh, yes. The other famous caches are all too vague. Captain Thompson's treasure, however, is undeniably real and unquestionably the largest."

"Did you use the Keating map?"*

"Not altogether." Leland seemed as puzzled as the rest of us by Vance's line of questioning. "It is hardly authentic now, and I imagine several purely romantic directions entered into it—such as the stone turnstile to the cave. Stamm ran across an old map in his travels, which antedated, by many years, the original British survey of Cocos Island of 1838. So similar was it to this chart that he believed it to be genuine. We followed the directions on this map, checking them with the navigators' chart in the Hydrographic Office of the United States Navy Department."

"Did this map of Stamm's," pursued Vance, "indicate the treasure as hidden in one of the island caves?"

"The details were a bit hazy on that point. And that was what so impressed Stamm and, I must confess, myself also. You see, this old map differed in one vital respect from the United States Navy navigators' chart, in that it indicated land where the United States chart shows Wafer Bay; and it was on this section of land that the hiding-place of the treasure was indicated."

A flicker came into Vance's eyes, but when he spoke his tone was casual and but mildly animated.

"By Jove! I see the point. Most interestin'. There's no doubt that landslides and tropical rains have altered the topography

---

* *What is purported to be the Keating map, or a copy of it, has been almost generally used by treasure seekers on Cocos Island. It is supposed to have been made by Captain Thompson himself, who left it to a friend named Keating. Keating, with a Captain Bogue, outfitted an expedition to the island. There was mutiny on board the boat, and Bogue died on the island; but Keating miraculously escaped. At his death his widow turned the map over to Nicholas Fitzgerald, who, in turn, willed it to Commodore Curzon-Howe of the British navy.*

of Cocos Island, and many of the old landmarks have doubtless disappeared. I presume Mr. Stamm assumed that the land where the treasure was originally hidden now lies under the waters of the bay which is indicated on the more recent charts."

"Exactly. Even the French survey of 1889 did not show as large a bay as the American survey made in 1891; and it was Stamm's theory that the treasure lay beneath the waters of Wafer Bay, which is rather shallow at that spot."

"A difficult undertaking," Vance commented. "How long were you at the island?"

"The better part of three months." Leland smiled ruefully. "It took Stamm that length of time to realize that he did not possess the proper equipment. The shoals in the bay are treacherous, and there are curious holes at the bottom of the water, owing, no doubt, to geological conditions; and our diving equipment would have been scorned by any good pearl-fisher. What we needed, of course, was a specially constructed diving-bell, something like Mr. Beebe's bathysphere. Even that would have been just a beginning, for we were helpless without powerful submarine dredges. The one we took along was wholly inadequate..."

Markham, who had been noticeably chafing under Vance's discussion of hidden treasure, now rose and strode forward, his cigar held tightly between his teeth.

"Where is all this getting us, Vance? If you are contemplating a trip to Cocos Island, I'm sure Mr. Leland would be willing to make a future appointment with you to discuss the details. And as for all the other investigations you have made here tonight: I can't see that anything has been brought to light that hasn't an entirely normal and logical explanation."

Heath, who had been following all the proceedings closely, now projected himself into the conversation.

"I'm not so sure about things around here being normal, sir." Though deferential, his tone was vigorous. "I'm for going ahead with this case. Some mighty queer things have happened tonight, and I don't like 'em."

Vance smiled appreciatively at the Sergeant.

"Stout fella!" He glanced toward Markham. "Another half-hour and we'll stagger home."

Markham gave in ungraciously.

"What more do you want to do here tonight?"

Vance lighted another cigarette.

"I could bear to commune with Greeff... Suppose you tell the butler to fetch him, Sergeant."

A few minutes later Alex Greeff was ushered into the drawing-room by Trainor. He was a large, powerfully built man, with a ruddy bulldog type of face—wide-spaced eyes, a short, thick nose, heavy lips, and a strong, square chin. He was slightly bald, and there were cushions of gray hair over his small, close-set ears. He was wearing a conventional dinner suit, but there were certain touches of vulgar elegance in his attire. The satin lapels of his coat were highly peaked. There were two diamond studs in his shirt-bosom. Across his satin waistcoat was draped a platinum chain set with large pearls. His tie, instead of being solid black, had white pin-stripes running through it; and his wing collar seemed too high for his stocky neck.

He took a few steps toward us with his hands in his pockets, planted himself firmly, and glowered at us angrily.

"I understand one of you gentlemen is the District Attorney—" he began aggressively.

"Oh, quite." Vance indicated Markham with a careless movement of the hand.

Greeff now centred his bellicose attention on Markham.

"Well, perhaps *you* can tell me, sir," he growled, "why I am being held a virtual prisoner in this house. This man"—indicating Heath—"ordered me to remain in my room until further notice, and refused to let me go home. What is the meaning of such high-handed tactics?"

"A tragedy has taken place here tonight, Mr. Greeff—" Markham began, but he was interrupted by the other.

"Suppose an accident *has* happened, is that any reason why I should be held a prisoner without due process of law?"

"There are certain phases of the case," Markham told him, "that we are looking into, and it was to facilitate the investigation that Sergeant Heath requested all the witnesses to remain here until we could question them."

"Well, go ahead and question me." Greeff seemed a little mollified, and his tone had lost some of its belligerency.

Vance moved forward.

"Sit down and have a smoke, Mr. Greeff," he suggested pleasantly. "We sha'n't keep you long."

Greeff hesitated, looked at Vance suspiciously; then shrugged, and drew up a chair. Vance waited until the man had fitted a cigarette into a long jewelled holder, and then asked:

"Did you notice—or sense—anything peculiar about Montague's disappearance in the pool tonight?"

"Peculiar?" Greeff looked up slowly, and his eyes narrowed to shrewd slits. "So that's the angle, is it? Well, I'm not saying there wasn't something peculiar about it, now that you mention it; but I'm damned if I can tell you what it was."

"That seems to be the general impression," Vance returned; "but I was hoping you might be more lucid on the point than the others have been."

"What's there to be lucid about?" Greeff seemed to be avoiding the issue. "I suppose it's reasonable enough when a chap like Montague—who's always been riding for a fall—gets what's coming to him. But somehow, when it happens so neatly and at the right time, we're apt to think it's peculiar."

"Yes, yes, of course. But it wasn't the logical eventualities I was referring to." Vance's voice held a tinge of annoyance. "I was referring to the fact that the conditions in the house here during the last two days constituted a perfect atmosphere for a type of tragedy quite removed from the merely accidental."

"You're right about the atmosphere." Greeff spoke harshly. "There was murder in the air—if that's what you mean. And if Montague had passed out by any other means except drowning, I'd say his death warranted a pretty thorough investigation. But he wasn't poisoned; he wasn't accidentally shot; he didn't get vertigo and fall out of a window; and he didn't tumble down-stairs and break his neck. He simply dived off a spring-board, with every one looking on."

"That's what makes it so difficult, don't y' know… I under-stand that you and Mr. Leland and young Tatum dived in after the johnny."

"It was the least we could do," Greeff came back pugna-ciously; "though I'm frank to admit it was more or less a gesture on my part, as I can't swim much, and if I had run into him he'd probably have dragged me down with him. Still, you hate to see any fellow, however rotten, pass out of this world in front of your eyes without making some attempt to save him."

"Quite noble of you, I'm sure," Vance murmured indiffer-ently. "By the by, I understand Montague was engaged to Miss Stamm."

Greeff nodded and drew on his cigarette.

"I never knew why it was, except that good women always fall for that type of man," he commented, with a philosophic air. "But I think she would have broken the engagement sooner or later."

"Would you mind my asking what your own feelings toward Miss Stamm are?"

Greeff opened his eyes in surprise, then laughed noisily.

"I see what you're getting at. But you can't make me out the villain of the piece. I like Bernice—everybody who knows her likes her. But as for my being sentimental about her: I'm too old and wise for that. My feeling for her has always been a fatherly one. She often comes to me for advice when Stamm's too deep in his cups. And I give her good advice—yes, by Gad! I told her only yesterday that she was making a fool of herself to think of marrying Montague."

"How did she take this advice, Mr. Greeff?"

"The way all women take advice—haughtily and contemp-tuously. No woman ever wants advice. Even when they ask for it, they're merely looking for agreement with what they've already decided to do."

Vance changed the subject.

"Just what do you think happened to Montague tonight?"

Greeff spread his hands vaguely.

"Bumped his head on the bottom—or got a cramp. What else could have happened to him?"

"I haven't the vaguest notion," Vance admitted blandly. "But the episode is teeming with possibilities. I was hopin', don't y' know, that you might help to lead us out of our darkness." He spoke lightly, but his eyes were fixed with cold steadiness on the man opposite.

Greeff returned the gaze for several moments in silence, and his ruddy face tightened into a mask.

"I understand perfectly," he enunciated at length, in a chill, even tone. "But my advice to you, my friend, is to forget it. Montague had it coming to him, and he got it. It was an accident that fitted in with everybody's wishes. You can play with the idea till doomsday, but you'll end up with the fact I'm telling you now: *Montague was accidentally drowned.*"

Vance smiled cynically.

"My word! Are you intimatin' that Montague's death is that liter'ry pet of the armchair criminologists—the perfect crime?"

Greeff moved forward in his chair and set his jaw.

"I'm not intimating anything, my friend. I'm merely telling you."

"Really, y' know, we're dashed grateful." Vance crushed out his cigarette. "Anyway, I think we'll do a bit of pryin' around..."

At this moment there came an interruption. We heard what sounded like a scuffle on the stairs, and there came to us the angry, shrill tones of Stamm's voice:

"Let go of my arm. I know what I'm doing."

And then Stamm jerked the drawing-room portières aside and glared at us. Behind him, fuming and remonstrative, stood Doctor Holliday. Stamm was clad in his pajamas, and his hair was dishevelled. It was obvious that he had just risen from bed. He fixed his watery eyes on Greeff with angry apprehension.

"What are you telling these policemen?" he demanded, bracing himself against the door jamb.

"My dear Rudolf," Greeff protested ingratiatingly, rising from his chair. "I'm telling them nothing. What is there to tell?"

"I don't trust you," Stamm retorted. "You're trying to make trouble. You're always trying to make trouble here. You've tried to turn Bernice against me, and now, I'll warrant, you're trying to turn these policemen against me." His eyes glared, and he had begun to tremble. "I know what you're after—money! But you're not going to get it. You think that if you talk enough you can blackmail me..." His voice sank almost to a whisper, and his words become incoherent.

Doctor Holliday took him gently by the arm and tried to lead him from the room, but Stamm, with an exhausting effort, threw him off and moved unsteadily forward.

Greeff had stood calmly during this tirade, looking at his accuser with an expression of commiseration and pity.

"You're making a great mistake, old friend," he said in a quiet voice. "You're not yourself tonight. Tomorrow you'll realize the injustice of your words, just as you'll realize that I would never betray you."

"Oh, you wouldn't, eh?" Much of the anger had gone out of Stamm's attitude, but he still seemed to be dominated by the idea of Greeff's persecution. "I suppose you haven't been telling these people"—he jerked his head toward us—"what I said about Montague—"

Greeff raised his hand in protest and was about to reply, but Stamm went on hurriedly:

"Well, suppose I did say it! I had more right to say it than any one else. And as far as that goes, you've said worse things. You hated him more than I did." Stamm cackled unpleasantly. "And I know why. You haven't pulled the wool over my eyes about your feelings for Bernice." He raised his arm and wagged a quivering finger at Greeff. "If anybody murdered Montague, it was you!"

Exhausted by his effort, he sank into a chair and began to shake as if with palsy.

Vance stepped quickly to the stricken man.

"I think a grave mistake has been made here tonight, Mr. Stamm," he said in a kindly but determined voice. "Mr. Greeff has reported nothing to us that you have said. No remark he has made to us could possibly be construed as disloyalty to you. I'm afraid you're a bit overwrought."

Stamm looked up blearily, and Greeff went to his side, placing a hand on his shoulder.

"Come, old friend," he said, "you need rest."

Stamm hesitated. A weary sob shook his body and he permitted Greeff and Doctor Holliday to lift him from the chair and lead him to the door.

"That will be all tonight, Mr. Greeff," Vance said. "But we will have to ask you to remain here till tomorrow."

Greeff turned his head and nodded over his shoulder.

"Oh, that's all right." And he and the doctor piloted Stamm across the hallway toward the stairs.

A moment later the front door-bell rang. Trainor admitted the nurse for whom Doctor Holliday had telephoned and led her immediately up-stairs.

Vance turned from the door, where he had been standing, and came back into the room, halting before Leland who had remained passive throughout the strange scene between Stamm and Greeff.

"Have you, by any chance," he asked, "any comments to make on the little *contretemps* we have just witnessed?"

Leland frowned and inspected the bowl of his pipe.

"No-o," he replied, after a pause, "except that it is obvious Stamm is frightfully on edge and in a state of shock after his excessive drinking tonight… And it might be, of course," he supplemented, "that in the back of his mind there has been a suspicion of Greeff in connection with financial matters, which came to the surface in his weakened condition."

"That sounds reasonable," Vance mused. "But why should Stamm mention the word murder?"

"He is probably excited and suspicious because of the presence of you gentlemen here," Leland suggested. "Not having been a witness to the tragedy, he is ignorant of all the details."

Vance did not reply. Instead he walked to the mantelpiece and inspected a carved gold clock which stood there. He ran his fingers over the incised scroll-work for a moment, and then turned slowly. His face was serious, and his eyes were looking past us.

"I think that will be all for tonight," he said in a flat, faraway tone. "Thank you for your help, Mr. Leland. But we must ask you too to remain here till tomorrow. We will be here again in the morning."

Leland bowed and, without a word, went softly from the room.

When he had gone, Markham rose.

"So you're coming here again in the morning?"

"Yes, old dear." Vance's manner had suddenly changed. "And so are you, don't y' know. You owe it to your constituency. It's a most absorbin' case. And I'd wager one of my Cézanne water-colors that when Montague's body is found, the Medical Examiner's report will be anything but what you expect."

Markham's eyelids fluttered, and he looked searchingly at Vance.

"You think you have learned something that would point to an explanation other than accidental death?"

"Oh, I've learned an amazin' amount," was all that Vance would vouchsafe. And Markham knew him well enough not to push the matter further at that time.

CHAPTER SEVEN

The Bottom of the Pool
(Sunday, August 12; 9.30 a.m.)

AT HALF-PAST NINE the following day Vance drove to
Markham's quarters to take him back to the old Stamm estate
in Inwood. On the way home the night before, Markham had
protested mildly against continuing the case before the Medical
Examiner had made his report; but his arguments were of no
avail. So determined was Vance to return to the house next day,
that Markham was impressed. His long association with Vance
had taught him that Vance never made such demands without
good reason.

Vance possessed what is commonly called an intuitive
mind, but it was, in fact, a coldly logical one, and his decisions,
which often seemed intuitive, were in reality based on his
profound knowledge of the intricacies and subtleties of human
nature. In the early stages of any investigation he was always
reluctant to tell Markham all that he suspected: he preferred to
wait until he had the facts in hand. Markham, understanding
this trait in him, abided by his unexplained decisions; and

these decisions had rarely, to my knowledge, proved incorrect, founded, as they were, on definite indications which had not been apparent to the rest of us. It was because of Markham's past experiences with Vance that he had grudgingly, but none the less definitely, agreed to accompany him to the scene of the tragedy the following morning.

Before we left the Stamm house the night before, there had been a brief consultation with Heath, and a course of action had been mapped out under Vance's direction. Every one in the house was to remain indoors; but no other restrictions were to be placed upon their actions. Vance had insisted that no one be allowed to walk through the grounds of the estate until he himself had made an examination of them; and he was particularly insistent that every means of access to the pool be kept entirely free of people until he had completed his inspection. He was most interested, he said, in the small patch of low ground north of the filter, where Heath and Hennessey had already looked for footprints.

Doctor Holliday was to be permitted to come and go as he chose, but Vance suggested that the nurse whom the doctor had called in be confined to the house, like the others, until such time as she was given permission to depart. Trainor was ordered to instruct the other servants—of whom there were only two, a cook and a maid—that they were to remain indoors until further notice.

Vance also suggested that the Sergeant place several of his men around the house at vantage points where they could see that all orders were carried out by the guests and members of the household. The Sergeant was to arrange for a small corps of men to report at the estate early the following morning to close the gates above the filter and open the lock in the dam, in order that the pool might be drained.

"And you'd better see that they come down the stream from the East Road, Sergeant," Vance advised, "so there won't be any new footprints round the pool."

Heath was placed in complete charge of the case by Markham, who promised to get the official verification of the assignment from Commanding Officer Moran of the Detective Bureau.

Heath decided to remain at the house that night. I had never seen him in so eager a frame of mind. He admitted frankly that he could see no logic in the situation; but, with a stubbornness which verged on fanaticism, he maintained that he knew something was vitally wrong.

I was also somewhat astonished at Vance's intense interest in the case. Heretofore he had taken Markham's criminal investigations with a certain nonchalance. But there was no indifference in his attitude in the present instance. That Montague's disappearance held a fascination for him was evident. This was owing, no doubt, to the fact that he had seen, or sensed, certain elements in the affair not apparent to the rest of us. That his attitude was justified is a matter of public record, for the sinister horror of Montague's death became a national sensation; and Markham, with that generosity so characteristic of him, was the first to admit that, if it had not been for Vance's persistence that first night, one of the shrewdest and most resourceful murderers of modern times would have escaped justice.

Although it was long past three in the morning when we arrived home, Vance seemed loath to go to bed. He sat down at the piano and played that melancholy yet sublime and passionate third movement from Beethoven's Sonata, Opus 106; and I knew that not only was he troubled, but that some deep unresolved intellectual problem had taken possession of his mind. When he had come to the final major chord he swung round on the piano bench.

"Why don't you go to bed, Van?" he asked somewhat abstractedly. "We have a long, hard day ahead of us. I've a bit of reading to do before I turn in." He poured himself some brandy and soda and, taking the glass with him, went into the library.

For some reason I was too nervous to try to sleep. I picked up a copy of "Marius the Epicurean," which was lying on the centre-table, and sat down at the open window. Over an hour later, on my way to my room, I looked in at the library door, and there sat Vance, his head in his hands, absorbed in a large quarto volume which lay on the table before him. A score of books, some of them open, were piled haphazardly about him, and on the stand at his side was a sheaf of yellowed maps.

He had heard me at the door, for he said: "Fetch the Napoléon and soda, will you, Van? There's a good fellow."

As I placed the bottles in front of him I looked over his shoulder. The book he was reading was an old illuminated copy of "Malleus Maleficarum." At one side, opened, lay Elliot Smith's "The Evolution of the Dragon" and Remy's "Demonolatry." At his other side was a volume of Howey's work on ophiolatry.

"Mythology is a fascinatin' subject, Van," he remarked. "And many thanks for the cognac." He buried himself in his reading again; and I went to bed.

Vance was up before I was the next morning. I found him in the living-room, dressed in a tan silk poplin suit, sipping his matutinal Turkish coffee and smoking a *Régie*.

"You'd better ring for Currie," he greeted me, "and order your plebeian breakfast. We're picking up the reluctant District Attorney in half an hour."

We had to wait nearly twenty minutes in Vance's car before Markham joined us. He was in execrable mood, and his greeting to us, as he stepped into the tonneau, was barely amiable.

"The more I think of this affair, Vance," he complained, "the more I'm convinced that you're wasting your time and mine."

"What else have you to do today?" Vance asked dulcetly.

"Sleep, for one thing—after your having kept me up most of the night. I was slumbering quite peacefully when the hall boy rang my phone and told me that you were waiting for me."

"Sad...sad." Vance wagged his head in mock commiseration. "By Jove, I do hope you sha'n't be disappointed."

Markham grunted and lapsed into silence; and little more
was said during our ride to the Stamm estate. As we drove up
the circular roadway and came to a halt in the parking-space in
front of the house, Heath, who had evidently been waiting for
us, came down the stairs to meet us. He seemed disgruntled
and ill at ease, and I noticed also that there was a skepticism
and insecurity in his manner, as if he distrusted his suspicions
of the night before.

"Things are moving," he reported half-heartedly; "but
nothing's happened yet. Everything is going smoothly indoors,
and the whole outfit is acting like human beings for a change.
They all had breakfast together, like a lot of turtle-doves."

"That's interestin'," Vance remarked. "What about
Stamm?"

"He's up and about. Looks a little green around the gills;
but he's already taken two or three eye-openers."

"Has Miss Stamm put in an appearance this morning?"

"Yes." Heath looked puzzled. "But there's something
queer about that dame. She was having hysterics last night and
fainting in every open space; but this morning she's bright and
snappy, and—if you ask me—she seems relieved that her boy-
friend is out of the way."

"On whom did she lavish her attentions this morning,
Sergeant?" Vance asked.

"How should I know?" returned Heath, in an injured
tone. "They didn't ask me to eat at the table with 'em—I was
lucky to get any groceries at all... But I noticed that after
breakfast she and Leland went into the drawing-room alone
and had a long palaver."

"Really now." Vance meditated a moment, regarding his
cigarette critically. "Very illuminatin'."

"Well, well," snorted Markham, giving Vance a disdainful
look. "I suppose you regard that fact as an indication that your
plot is thickening?"

Vance looked up facetiously.

"Thickening? My dear Markham! The plot is positively congealin', not to say stiffenin'." He sobered and turned back to Heath. "Any news from Mrs. Stamm?"

"She's all right today. The doctor was here a little while ago. He looked over the situation and said there was no more need of his services at the present. Said he'd be back this afternoon, though... And speaking of doctors, I telephoned to Doc Doremus* and asked him to hop out here. I figured it was Sunday and I might not be able to catch him later; and we'll have Montague's body in a little while."

"Your men have got the pool gates closed then?"

"Sure. But it was a tough job. One of the gates had got water-logged. Anyway, they're all set now. Luckily the stream was pretty low and there wasn't much of a flow of water. The dam lock was corroded, too, but we hammered it open. It'll take about another hour for the pool to drain, according to Stamm... By the way, he wanted to go down and supervise the operations, but I told him we could get along without him."

"It was just as well," nodded Vance. "Have your men put a screen of some kind over the lock in the dam? The body might go through, don't y' know."

"I thought of that too," Heath returned with a little self-satisfaction. "But it's all right. There was a coarse wire mesh already over the lock."

"Any visitors at the house this morning?" Vance asked next.

"Nobody, sir. They wouldn't have got in anyway. Burke and Hennessey and Snitkin are back on the job this morning— I had another bunch of fellows here last night guarding the place. Snitkin is at the east gate, and Burke's here in the vestibule. Hennessey's down at the pool seeing that nobody approaches from that direction." Heath looked at Vance with

---

* _Doctor Emanuel Doremus, Chief Medical Examiner._

an uneasy, questioning eye. "What do you want to do first, sir? Maybe you want to interview Miss Stamm and this young Tatum. There's something wrong about both of 'em, if you ask me."

"No," drawled Vance. "I don't think we'll chivy the members of the household just yet. I'd like to meander round the grounds first. But suppose you ask Mr. Stamm to join us, Sergeant."

Heath hesitated a second; then went into the house. A few moments later he returned accompanied by Rudolf Stamm.

Stamm was dressed in gray tweed plus fours and a gray silk sleeveless sport shirt open at the throat. He wore no coat and was bareheaded. His face was pale and drawn, and there were hollows under his eyes, but his gait was steady as he came down the steps toward us.

He greeted us pleasantly and, I thought, a bit diffidently.

"Good morning, gentlemen. Sorry I was so crotchety last night. Forgive me. I was under the weather—and unstrung…"

"That's quite all right," Vance assured him. "We understand perfectly—a dashed tryin' situation… We're thinking of looking over the estate a bit, especially down by the pool, and we thought you'd be good enough to pilot us around."

"Delighted." Stamm led the way down a path on the north side of the house. "It's a unique place I've got here. Nothing quite like it in New York—or in any other city, for that matter."

We followed him past the head of the steps that led down to the pool, and on toward the rear of the house. We came presently to a slight embankment at the foot of which ran a narrow concrete road.

"This is the East Road," Stamm explained. "My father built it many years ago. It runs down the hill through those trees and joins one of the old roadways just outside the boundary of the estate."

"And where does the old roadway lead?" asked Vance.

"Nowhere in particular. It passes along the Bird Refuge toward the south end of the Clove, and there it divides. One branch goes to the Shell Bed and the Indian Cave to the north, and joins the road which circles the headland and connects with the River Road. The other branch runs down by the Green Hill and turns into Payson Avenue north of the Military Ovens. But we rarely use the road—it's not in good condition."

We walked down the embankment. To our right, and to the southeast of the house, stood a large garage, with a cement turning-space in front of it.

"An inconvenient place for the garage," Stamm remarked. "But it was the best we could do. If we'd placed it in front of the house it would have spoiled the vista. However, I extended the cement road to the front of the house on the south side there."

"And this East Road runs past the pool?" Vance was glancing down the wooded hill toward the little valley.

"That's right," Stamm nodded, "though the road doesn't go within fifty yards of it."

"Suppose we waddle down," suggested Vance. "And then we can return to the house by way of the pool steps—eh, what?"

Stamm seemed pleased and not a little proud to show us the way. We walked down the sloping hill, across the short concrete bridge over the creek which fed the pool, and, circling a little to the left, got a clear view of the high stone cliff which formed the north boundary of the pool. A few feet ahead of us was a narrow cement walk—perhaps eighteen inches wide—which led off at right angles to the road in the direction of the pool.

Stamm turned into the walk, and we followed him. On either side of us were dense trees and underbrush, and it was not until we had come to the low opening at the northeast corner of the pool, between the cliff and the filter, that we were able to take our bearings accurately. From this point we could look diagonally across the pool to the Stamm mansion which stood on the top of the hill opposite.

The water-level of the pool was noticeably lower. In fact, half of the bottom—the shallow half nearest the cliff—was already exposed, and there remained only a channel of water, perhaps twenty feet wide, on the opposite side, nearest the house. And even this water was sinking perceptibly as it ran through the lock at the bottom of the dam.

The gates above the filter, immediately on our left, were tightly closed, thus acting as an upper dam and creating a miniature pond to the east of the pool. Fortunately, at this time of year the flow of the stream was less abundant than usual, and there was no danger that the water would reach the top of the gates or overflow its banks for several hours. Only a negligible amount of water trickled through the crack between the gates.

As yet the dead man had not come into view, and Heath, scanning the surface of the pool perplexedly, remarked that Montague must have met his death in the deep channel on the other side.

Directly ahead of us, within a few feet of the cliff, the apex of a large conical piece of jagged rock was partly imbedded in the muddy soil, like a huge inverted stalagmite. Stamm pointed at it.

"There's that damned rock I told you about," he said. "That's where you got your splash last night. I've been afraid for weeks it would fall into the pool. Luckily it didn't hit anybody, although I warned every one not to get too close to the cliff if they went swimming... Now I suppose it will have to be dragged out. A mean job."

His eyes roamed over the pool. Only a narrow channel of water now remained along the concrete wall on the far side. And there was still no indication of the dead man.

"I guess Montague must have bumped his head just off the end of the spring-board," Stamm commented sourly. "Damn shame it had to happen. People are always getting drowned here. The pool is unlucky as the devil."

"What devil?" asked Vance, without glancing up. "The *Piasa*?"*

Stamm shot Vance a quick look and made a disdainful noise which was half a laugh.

"I see that you, too, have been listening to those crazy yarns. Good Lord! the old wives will soon have *me* believing there's a man-eating dragon in this pool... By the way, where did you get that term *Piasa*? The word the Indians round here use for the dragon is *Amangemokdom*. I haven't heard the word *Piasa* for many years, and then it was used by an old Indian chief from out West who was visiting here. Quite an impressive old fellow. And I shall always remember his hair-raising description of the *Piasa*."

"*Piasa* and *Amangemokdom* mean practically the same thing—a dragon-monster," Vance returned in a low voice, his eyes still focused on the gradually receding water on the floor of the pool. "Different dialects, don't y' know. *Amangemokdom* was used by the Lenapes,† but the Algonkian Indians along the Mississippi called their devil-dragon the *Piasa*."

The water remaining in the channel seemed to be running out more swiftly now, and Stamm started to walk across the small flat area of sod at the edge of the pool, in order, I

---

* *In a pamphlet published in Morris, Illinois, in 1887, written by the Honorable P. A. Armstrong and entitled "The Piasa, or the Devil Among the Indians," there is an old engraving showing the Piasa as a monster with a dragon's head, antlers like a deer, the scales of a great fish, claws, and large wings, and with a long tail, like that of a sea-serpent, coiled about its body. The petroglyphs, or pictographs, carved on rock, of this devil-dragon were first found by Father Marquette in the valley of the Mississippi about 1665; and his description of the Piasa, given in Armstrong's pamphlet, reads thus: "They are as large as a calf, with head and horns like a goat, their eyes are red, beard like a tiger's, and a face like a man's. Their tails are so long that they pass over their bodies and between their legs, ending like a fish's tail."*

† *Lenape is the generic name for the Algonkian tribes in Pennsylvania, New Jersey, and vicinity; and it was one of these tribes that inhabited Inwood.*

presume, to get a better view; but Vance caught him quickly by the arm.

"Sorry and all that," he said a bit peremptorily; "but we may have to go over this patch of ground for footprints..."

Stamm looked at him with questioning surprise, and Vance added:

"Silly idea, I know. But it occurred to us that Montague might have swum across the pool to this opening and walked away."

Stamm's jaw dropped.

"Why, in God's name, should he do that?"

"I'm sure I don't know," Vance replied lightly. "He probably didn't. But if there's no body in the pool it will be most embarrassin'. And we'll have to account for his disappearance, don't y' know."

"Tommy-rot!" Stamm seemed thoroughly disgusted. "The body'll be here all right. You can't make a voodoo mystery out of a simple drowning."

"By the by," inquired Vance, "what sort of soil is on the bottom of this pool?"

"Hard and sandy," Stamm said, still rankled by Vance's former remark. "At one time I thought of putting in a cement bottom, but decided it wouldn't be any better than what was already there. And it keeps pretty clean, too. That accumulation of muddy silt you see is only an inch or so deep. When the water gets out of the pool you can walk over the whole bottom in a pair of rubbers without soiling your shoes."

The water in the pool was now but a stream scarcely three feet wide, and I knew it would be only a matter of minutes before the entire surface of the basin would be visible. The five of us—Vance, Markham, Heath, Stamm and myself—stood in a line at the end of the cement walk, looking out intently over the draining pool. The water at the upper end of the channel had disappeared, and, as the rest of the constantly narrowing stream flowed through the lock, the bottom of the channel gradually came into view.

We watched this receding line as it moved downward toward the dam, foot by foot. It reached the *cabañas*, and passed them. It approached the spring-board, and I felt a curious tension in my nerves... It reached the spring-board— then passed it, and moved down along the cement wall to the lock. A strange tingling sensation came over me, and, though I seemed to be held fascinated, I managed to drag my eyes away from the rapidly diminishing water and look at the four men beside me.

Stamm's mouth was open, and his eyes were fixed as if in hypnosis. Markham was frowning in deep perplexity. Heath's face was set and rigid. Vance was smoking placidly, his eyebrows slightly raised in a cynical arc; and there was the suggestion of a grim smile on his ascetic mouth.

I turned my gaze back to the lock in the dam... All the water had now gone through it...

At that moment there rang out across the hot sultry air, a hysterical shriek followed by high-pitched gloating laughter. We all looked up, startled; and there, on the third-floor balcony of the old mansion, stood the wizened figure of Matilda Stamm, her arms outstretched and waving toward the pool.

For a moment the significance of this distracting and blood-chilling interlude escaped me. But then, suddenly, I realized the meaning of it. From where we stood we could see every square foot of the empty basin of the pool.

And there was no sign of a body!

CHAPTER EIGHT

Mysterious Footprints
(*Sunday, August 12; 11.30 a.m.*)

So EXTRAORDINARY AND unexpected was the result of the draining of the Dragon Pool, that none of us spoke for several moments.

I glanced at Markham. He was scowling deeply, and I detected in his expression a look of fear and bafflement, such as one might have in the presence of things unknown. Heath, as was usual whenever he was seriously puzzled, was chewing viciously on his cigar, and staring belligerently. Stamm, whose bulging eyes were focused on the lock in the dam through which the water had disappeared, was leaning rigidly forward, as if transfixed by a startling phenomenon.

Vance seemed the calmest of us all. His eyebrows were slightly elevated, and there was a mildly cynical expression in his cold gray eyes. Moreover, his lips held the suggestion of a smile of satisfaction, although it was evident from the tensity of his attitude that he had not been entirely prepared for the absence of Montague's body.

Stamm was the first to speak.

"I'll be damned!" he muttered. "It's incredible—it's not possible!" He fumbled nervously in the pocket of his sport shirt and drew out a small black South American cigarette which he lit with some difficulty.

Vance shrugged almost imperceptibly.

"My word!" he murmured. He, too, reached in his pocket for a cigarette. "Now the search for footprints will be more fascinatin' than ever, Sergeant."

Heath made a wry face.

"Maybe yes and maybe no… What about that rock that fell in the pool over there? Maybe our guy's under it."

Vance shook his head.

"No, Sergeant. The apex of that piece of rock, as it lies buried in the pool, is, I should say, barely eighteen inches in diameter. It couldn't possibly hide a man's body."

Stamm took his black cigarette from his mouth and turned in Vance's direction.

"You're right about that," he commented. "It's not a particularly pleasant subject for conversation, but the fact of the matter is, the bottom of the pool is too hard to have a body driven into it by a rock." He looked back toward the dam. "We'll have to find another explanation for Montague's disappearance."

Heath was both annoyed and uneasy.

"All right," he mumbled. Then he turned to Vance. "But there wasn't any footprints here last night—at least Snitkin and I couldn't find 'em."

"Suppose we take another peep," Vance suggested. "And it might be just as well to hail Snitkin, so that we can go about the task systematically."

Without a word Heath turned and trotted back down the cement path toward the roadway. We could hear him whistling to Snitkin who was on guard at the gate, a hundred feet or so down the East Road.

Markham moved nervously a few paces back and forth.

"Have you any suggestion, Mr. Stamm," he asked, "as to what might have become of Montague?"

Stamm, with a perplexed frown, again scrutinized the basin of the pool. He shook his head slowly.

"I can't imagine," he replied, after a moment, "—unless, of course, he deliberately walked out of the pool on this side."

Vance gave Markham a whimsical smile.

"There's always the dragon as a possibility," he remarked cheerfully.

Stamm wheeled about. His face was red with anger, and his lips trembled as he spoke.

"For the love of Heaven, don't bring that up again!" he pleaded. "Things are bad enough as they are, without dragging in that superstitious hocus-pocus. There simply must be a rational explanation for everything."

"Yes, yes, to be sure," sighed Vance. "Rationality above all else."

At this moment I happened to look up at the third-floor balcony of the house, and I saw Mrs. Schwarz and Doctor Holliday step up to Mrs. Stamm and lead her gently back into the house.

A few seconds later Heath and Snitkin joined us.

The search for footprints along the level area between us and the high-water mark of the pool took considerable time. Beginning close to the filter on the left, Vance, Snitkin and Heath worked systematically across the level space to the perpendicular edge of the cliff that formed the north wall of the pool, on our right. The area was perhaps fifteen feet square. The section lying nearest to the pool was of encrusted earth, and the strip nearest to where Markham, Stamm and I were standing, at the end of the cement path, was covered with short, irregular lawn.

When, at length, Vance turned at the edge of the cliff and walked back toward us, there was a puzzled look on his face.

"There's no sign of a footprint," he remarked. "Montague certainly didn't walk out of the pool at this point."

Heath came up, solemn and troubled.

"I didn't think we'd find anything," he grumbled. "Snitkin and I made a pretty thorough search last night, with our flashlights."

Markham was studying the edge of the cliff.

"Is there any way Montague might have crawled up on one of those ledges and hopped over to the walk here?" he asked of no one in particular.

Vance shook his head unhappily.

"Montague might have been an athlete, but he was no inyala."

Stamm stood as if in hypnotized reflection.

"If he didn't get out of the pool at this end," he said, "I don't see how the devil he got out at all."

"But he did get out, don't y' know," Vance returned. "Suppose we do a bit of pryin' around."

He led the way toward the filter and mounted its broad coping. We followed him in single file, hardly knowing what to expect. When he was half-way across the filter he paused and looked down at the water-line of the pool. It was fully six feet below the coping of the filter and eight feet below the top of the gates. The filter was of small galvanized wire mesh, backed by a thin coating of perforated porous material which looked like very fine cement. It was obvious that no man could have climbed up the side of the filter to the coping without the aid of an accomplice.

Vance, satisfied, continued across the filter to the *cabañas* on the far side of the pool. A cement retaining wall about four feet above the water-level of the pool ran from the end of the filter to the dam.

"It's a sure thing Montague didn't climb over this wall," Heath observed. "Those flood-lights play all along it, and some one would certainly have seen him."

"Quite right," agreed Stamm. "He didn't escape from the pool on this side."

We walked down to the dam, and Vance made a complete inspection of it, testing the strength of the wire mesh over the lock and making sure there was no other opening. Then he went down to the stream bed below the dam, where all the water had now flowed off, and wandered for a while over the jagged, algæ-covered rocks.

"There's no use looking for his body down there," Stamm called to him at length. "There hasn't been enough flow here for the last month to wash as much as a dead cat over the dam."

"Oh, quite," Vance returned abstractedly, climbing back up the bank to where we stood. "I really wasn't looking for the corpse, d' ye see. Even if there had been a strong flow over the dam, Montague wouldn't have been carried over with it. It would take at least twenty-four hours for his body to come to the surface if he had been drowned."

"Well, just what were you looking for?" Markham demanded testily.

"I'm sure I don't know, old dear," Vance replied. "Just sightseein'—and hopin'... Suppose we return to the other side of the pool. That little square of ground over there, without any footprints, is dashed interestin'."

We retraced our steps, along the retaining wall and over the coping of the filter, to the small tract of low ground beyond.

"What do you expect to find here, Vance?" Markham asked, with a show of irritation. "This whole section has already been gone over for footprints."

Vance was serious and reflective.

"And still, don't y' know, there should be footprints here," he returned with a vague gesture of hopelessness. "The man didn't fly out of the pool..." Suddenly he paused. His eyes were fixed dreamily on the small patch of bare grass at our feet, and a moment later he moved forward several paces and knelt down. After scrutinizing the earth at this point for a few seconds he rose and turned back to us.

"I thought that slight indentation might bear closer inspection," he explained. "But it's only a right-angle impression which couldn't possibly be a footprint."

Heath snorted.

"I saw that last night. But it don't mean anything, Mr. Vance. Looks as if somebody set a box or a heavy suit-case there. But that might have been weeks or months ago. Anyway, it's at least twelve feet from the edge of the pool. So even if it had been a footprint, it wouldn't help us any."

Stamm threw his cigarette away and thrust his hands deep in his pockets. There was a baffled look on his pale face.

"This situation has me dumbfounded," he said; "and to tell you the truth, gentlemen, I don't like it. It means more scandal for me, and I've had my share of scandal with this damned swimming pool."

Vance was looking upward along the cliff before us.

"I say, Mr. Stamm, would it have been possible, do you think, for Montague to have scaled those rocks? There are several ledges visible even from here."

Stamm shook his head with finality.

"No. He couldn't have gone up there on the ledges. They aren't connected and they're too far apart. I got stranded on one of them when I was a kid—couldn't go back and couldn't go on—and it took the pater half a day to get me down."

"Could Montague have used a rope?"

"Well...yes. It might have been done that way. He was a good athlete, and could have gone up hand over hand. But, damn it, I don't see the point..."

Markham interrupted him.

"There may be something in that, Vance. Going up over the cliff is about the only way he could have got out of the pool. And you remember, of course, Leland's telling us how Mrs. McAdam was staring across the pool toward the cliff after Montague had disappeared. And later, when she heard about the splash, she was pretty much upset. Maybe she had some inkling of Montague's scheme—whatever it was."

Vance pursed his lips.

"Sounds a bit far-fetched," he observed. "But, after all, the johnny *has* disappeared, hasn't he?... Anyway, we can verify the theory." He turned to Stamm. "How does one get to the top of the cliff from here?"

"That's easy," Stamm told him. "We can go down to the East Road, and turn up the slope from the Clove. You see, the cliff is highest here, and the plateau slopes quickly away through the Clove and the Indian Life Reservation, till it hits the water-level at Spuyten Duyvil. Ten minutes' walk'll get us there—if you think it worth while going up."

"It might be well. We could easily see if there are any footprints along the top of the cliff."

Stamm led the way back to the East Road, and we walked north toward the gate of the estate. A hundred yards or so beyond the gate we turned off to the west, along a wide footpath which circled northward and swung sharply toward the foot of the Clove. Then the climb up the steep slope to the cliff began. A few minutes later we were standing on the rocks, looking down into the empty basin of the pool, which was about a hundred feet below us. The old Stamm residence, on the hill opposite, was almost level with us.

One topographical feature of the spot that facilitated matters in looking for footprints was the sheer drop of rocks on either side of a very narrow plateau of earth; and it was only down this plateau—perhaps ten feet across—that any one, even had he scaled the cliff from the pool, could have retreated down the hill to the main road.

But, although a thorough inspection of the surrounding terrain was made by Vance and Heath and Snitkin, there were no evidences whatever of any footprints, or disturbances, on the surface of the earth that would indicate that anybody had been there since the heavy rains of the night before. Even to my untrained eye this fact was only too plain.

Markham was disappointed.

"It's obvious," he admitted hopelessly, "that this method of exit from the pool is eliminated."

"Yes, I fear so." Vance took out a cigarette and lighted it with studious deliberation. "If Montague left the pool by way of this cliff he must have flown over."

Stamm swung round, his face pale.

"What do you mean by that, sir? Are you going back to that silly story of the dragon?"

Vance raised his eyebrows.

"Really now, my figure of speech bore no such intimation. But I see what you mean. The *Piasa*, or *Amangemokdom*, did have wings, didn't he?"

Stamm glowered at him, and then gave a grim, mirthless laugh.

"These dragon stories are getting on my nerves," he apologized. "I'm fidgety today, anyway."

He fumbled for another cigarette and stepped toward the edge of the cliff.

"There's that rock I was telling you about." He pointed to a low boulder just at the apex of the cliff. "It was the top of it that fell into the pool last night." He inspected the sides of the boulder for a moment, running his hand under the slight crevasse on a line with the plateau. "I was afraid it would break off at this point, where the strata overlap. This is where Leland and I tried to pry it loose yesterday. We didn't think the top would fall off. But the rest seems pretty solid now, in spite of the rains."

"Very interestin'." Vance was already making his way down the slope toward the Clove and the East Road.

When we had reached the narrow cement footpath that led from the road to the pool, Vance, to my surprise, turned into it again. That little section of low ground between the filter and the cliff seemed to fascinate him. He was silent and meditative as he stood at the end of the walk, looking out again over the empty basin of the pool.

Just behind us, and a little to the right of the walk, I had noticed a small stone structure, perhaps ten feet square and barely five feet high, almost completely covered with English ivy. I had paid scant attention to it and had forgot its existence altogether until Vance suddenly addressed Stamm.

"What is that low stone structure yonder that looks like a vault?"

"Just that," Stamm replied. "It's the old family vault. My grandfather had the idea he wanted to be buried here on the estate, so he had it built to house his remains and those of the other members of the family. But my father refused to be buried in it—he preferred cremation and a public mausoleum—and it has not been opened during my lifetime. However, my mother insists that she be placed in it when she dies." Stamm hesitated and looked troubled. "But I don't know what to do about it. All this property will some day be taken over by the city—these old estates can't go on forever, with conditions what they are today. Not like Europe, you know."

"The curse of our commercial civilization," murmured Vance. "Is there any one besides your grandfather buried in the vault?"

"Oh, yes." Stamm seemed uninterested. "My grandmother is in one of the crypts. And a couple of aunts are there, I believe, and my grandfather's youngest brother—they died before I was born. It's all duly recorded in the family Bible, though I've never taken the trouble to verify the data. The fact is, I'd probably have to dynamite the iron door if I wanted to get in. I've never known where the key to the vault is."

"Perhaps your mother knows where the key is," Vance remarked casually.

Stamm shot him a quick look.

"Funny you should say that. Mother told me years ago she had hidden the key, so that no one could ever desecrate the vault. She has queer ideas like that at times, all connected with the traditions of the family and the superstitions of the neighborhood."

"Anything to do with the dragon?"

"Yes, damn it!" Stamm clicked his teeth. "Some silly idea that the dragon guards the spirits of our dead and that she's assisting him in caring for the dusty remains of the Stamms. You know how such notions possess the minds of the old." (He spoke with irritation, but there was an undercurrent of apology in his voice.) "As for the key, if she ever really did hide it, she's probably forgotten by now where it is."

Vance nodded sympathetically.

"It really doesn't matter," he said. "By the by, was the vault ever mentioned, or discussed, before any of your guests?"

Stamm thought a moment.

"No," he concluded. "I doubt if any of them even knows it's on the estate. Excepting Leland, of course. You see, the vault's hidden from the house by the trees here, and no one ever comes over to this side of the pool."

Vance stood looking up contemplatingly at the old Stamm house; and while I was conjecturing as to what was going on in his mind he turned slowly.

"Really, y' know," he said to Stamm, "I could bear to have a peep at that vault. It sounds rather romantic." He moved off the path through the trees, and Stamm followed him with an air of resigned boredom.

"Isn't there a path to the vault?" Vance asked.

"Oh, yes, there's one leading up from the East Road, but it's probably entirely overgrown with weeds."

Vance crossed the ten or twelve feet between the path and the vault and stood looking at the squat stone structure for several moments. Its tiled roof was slightly peaked, to allow for drainage, but the ivy had long since climbed up to the low cornice. The stone of its walls was the same as that of the Stamm house. On the west elevation was a nail-studded door of hammered iron which, despite its rust and appearance of antiquity, still gave forth an impression of solid impregnability. Leading down to the door were three stone steps, overgrown with moss. As Stamm explained to us, the vault had been built partly underground, so that at its highest point it was only about five feet above the level of the ground.

Beside the vault, on the side nearest the walk, lay a pile of heavy boards, warped and weather-stained. Vance, after walking round the vault and inspecting it, halted beside the pile of boards.

"What might the lumber be for?" he asked.

Just some timber left over from the water-gates above the filter," Stamm told him.

Vance had already turned away and started back toward the cement walk.

"Amazin'," he commented when Stamm had come up to him. "It's difficult to realize that one is actually within the city limits of Manhattan."

Markham, up to this point, had refrained from any comment, though it was evident to me that he was annoyed at Vance's apparent digressions. Now, however, he spoke with an irritation which reflected his impatience.

"Obviously there's nothing more we can do here, Vance. Even though there are no footprints, the irresistible inference is that Montague got out of the pool some way—which will probably be explained later, when he's ready to show up... I think we'd better be getting along."

The very intensity of his tone made me feel that he was arguing against his inner convictions—that, indeed, he was far from satisfied with the turn of events. None the less, there was a leaven of common sense in his attitude, and I myself could see little else to do but to follow his suggestion.

Vance, however, hesitated.

"I admit, Markham, that your conclusion is highly rational," he demurred; "but there's something deuced irrational about Montague's disappearance. And, if you don't mind, I think I'll nose about the basin of the pool a bit." Then, turning to Stamm: "How long will the pool remain empty before the stream above the gates overflows?"

Stamm went to the filter and looked over into the rising water above.

"I should say another half-hour or so," he reported. "The pool has now been empty for a good hour and a half, and two hours is about the limit. If the gates aren't opened by that time, the stream overflows its banks and runs all over the lower end of the estate and down on the property beyond the East Road."

"Half an hour will give me ample time," Vance returned… "I say, Sergeant, suppose we fetch those boards from the vault and stretch them out there in the silt. I'd like to snoop at the basin between this point and the place where Montague went in."

Heath, eager for anything that might lead to some explanation of the incredible situation that confronted us, beckoned Snitkin with a jerk of the head, and the two of them hastened off to the vault. Within ten minutes the boards had been placed end to end, leading from the low land where we stood to the centre of the pool. This had been accomplished by laying one board down first, and then using that as a walk on which to carry the next one which was placed beyond the first board, and so on, until the boards had all been used up. These boards, which were a foot wide and two inches thick, thus formed a dry wooden passage along the floor of the pool, as the muddy silt was not deep enough at any point to overrun the timber.

During the operation Markham had stood resignedly, his head enveloped in a cloud of cigar smoke.

"This is just another waste of time," he complained, as Vance turned up the cuffs of his trousers and stepped down the first gently sloping plank. "What, in Heaven's name, do you expect to find out there? You can see the entire bottom of the pool from here."

Vance gave him a puckish look over the shoulder.

"To be scrupulously truthful, Markham, I don't expect to find anything. But this pool fascinates me. I really couldn't endure to hobble away without visiting the very seat, so to speak, of the mystery… Come, the Sergeant's bridge is quite dry—or, as you lawyers would say in a legal brief, anhydrous."

Reluctantly Markham followed him.

"I'm glad you admit you don't expect to find anything," he mumbled sarcastically. "For a moment I thought you might be looking for the dragon himself."

"No," smiled Vance. "The *Piasa*, according to all the traditions, was never able to make himself invisible, although some of the dragons of Oriental mythology were able to change themselves into beautiful women at will."

Stamm, who was walking just in front of me down the planks, halted and brushed his hand across his forehead.

"I wish you gentlemen would drop these damnable allusions to a dragon," he objected, in a tone of mingled anger and fear. "My nerves won't stand any more of it this morning."

"Sorry," murmured Vance. "Really, y' know, we had no intention of upsettin' you."

He had now come to the end of the last board, a little beyond the centre of the pool, and stood looking about him, shading his eyes with his hand. The rest of us stood in a row beside him. The sun poured down on us unmercifully, and there was not a breath of air to relieve the depressing stagnation of the heat. I was looking past Stamm and Markham at Vance, as his gaze roved over the muddy basin, and I wondered what strange whim had driven him to so seemingly futile an escapade. Despite my respect for Vance's perspicacity and instinctive reasoning, I began to feel very much as I knew Markham felt; and I went so far as to picture a farcical termination to the whole adventure...

As I speculated I saw Vance suddenly kneel down on the end of the plank and lean forward in the direction of the spring-board.

"Oh, my aunt!" I heard him exclaim. "My precious doddering aunt!"

And then he did an astonishing thing. He stepped off the board into the muddy silt and, carefully adjusting his monocle, leaned over to inspect something he had discovered.

"What have you found, Vance?" called Markham impatiently.

Vance held up his hand with a peremptory gesture.

"Just a minute," he returned, with a note of suppressed excitement. "Don't step out here."

He then walked further away, while we waited in tense

silence. After a moment he turned slowly about, toward the cliff, and came back, following a line roughly parallel with the improvised boardwalk on which we stood. All the time his eyes were fixed on the basin of the pool, and, instinctively, we kept pace with him along the boards as he walked nearer and nearer to the small plot of low ground at the end of the cliff. When he had come within a few feet of the sloping bank he halted.

"Sergeant," he ordered, "throw the end of that board over here."

Heath obeyed with alacrity.

When the board was in place, Vance beckoned to us to step out on it. We filed along the narrow piece of timber in a state of anticipatory excitement; there could be no doubt, from the strained look on Vance's face and the unnatural tone of his voice, that he had made a startling discovery. But none of us could visualize, even at that moment, how grisly and uncanny, how apparently removed from all the sane realities of life, that discovery was to prove.

Vance leaned over and pointed to a section of the muddy basin of the pool.

"That's what I've found, Markham! And the tracks lead from beyond the centre of the pool, near the spring-board, all the way back to this low embankment. Moreover, they're confused, and they go in opposite directions. And they circle round in the centre of the pool."

At first the thing at which Vance pointed was almost indistinguishable, owing to the general roughness of the silt; but as we looked down in the direction of his indicating finger, the horror of it gradually became plain.

There before us, in the shallow mud, was the unmistakable imprint of what seemed to be a great hoof, fully fourteen inches long, and corrugated as with scales. And there were other imprints like it, to the left and to the right, in an irregular line. But more horrible even than those impressions were numerous demarcations, alongside the hoof-prints, of what appeared to be the three-taloned claw of some fabulous monster.

CHAPTER NINE

A New Discovery
(Sunday, August 12; 12.30 p.m.)

So APPALLING AND stupefying was the sight of those hideous hoof-prints, that it was several seconds before the actual realization of their significance was borne in upon us. Heath and Snitkin stood like petrified men, their eyes fixed upon them; and Markham, despite his customary capacity to absorb the unusual, gazed down in speechless bewilderment, his hands opening and shutting nervously as if he had received a physical shock and was unable to control his reflex twitching. My own feeling was one of horror and unbelief. I strove desperately to throw off the sense of hideous unreality which was creeping over me and making every nerve in my body tingle.

But the man most affected was Stamm. I had never seen any one so near a state of complete collapse from sheer terror. His face, already pale from the excesses of the night before, turned an ugly ashen yellow, and his taut body swayed slightly. Then his head jerked back as if he had been struck by an unseen hand, and he drew in a long, rasping breath. Blood suddenly suffused his cheeks, turning them almost crimson; and there was a spasmodic twitching of the muscles about his mouth and throat. His eyes bulged like those of a man afflicted with exophthalmic goitre.

It was Vance's cool, unemotional voice that brought us out of our trance of horror and helped to steady us.

"Really now," he drawled, "these imprints are most fascinatin'. They have possibilities—eh, what?... But suppose we return to dry land. My boots are a beastly mess."

We filed back slowly along the diverted board, and Heath and Snitkin replaced it as it had been set down originally, so that we could walk back to the shore without following Vance's example of stepping off into the mud.

When we were again on the little patch of low ground Stamm plucked at Vance's sleeve nervously.

"What—do you make of it?" he stammered. His voice sounded strangely flat and far away, like the unmodulated voice of a deaf man.

"Nothing—yet," Vance answered carelessly. Then, addressing Heath: "Sergeant, I'd like some copies of those footmarks—just as a matter of record. The gates will have to be opened pretty soon, but I think there'll be time enough."

The Sergeant had partly regained his self-control.

"You bet I'll get the drawings." He addressed Snitkin officiously. "Copy those footprints in your notebook, and measure 'em. And make it snappy. When you're through, get the boards back out of the pool and pile 'em up. Then have the men open the gates and close the lock in the dam. Report to me when you're finished."

Vance smiled at the Sergeant's businesslike seriousness.

"That being capably settled," he said, "I think we'll toddle along back to the house. There's nothing more we can do here... The short route this time, what?"

We proceeded across the coping of the filter toward the *cabañas* opposite. The water in the stream above the pool had risen considerably and was within a foot of the top of the closed gates. As I looked back I saw Snitkin kneeling on two of the boards, with his notebook spread before him, diligently transcribing those astounding markings Vance had found on the basin of the pool. There was no better man in the New York Police Department for such a task, and I recalled that Snitkin had been especially chosen by the Sergeant to make the measurements of the mysterious footprints in the snow outside the old Greene mansion in East 53rd Street.*

As we passed the *cabañas* on our way to the steps leading up to the house, Vance halted abruptly.

"I say, Sergeant, have you rescued the departed Montague's garments from his *cabaña*? If not, we might take them along with us. They may hold secrets…a suicide note, or a threatening letter from a lady, or some other jolly clue such as the newspapers adore." Despite his jocular tone I knew that he was troubled and was reaching out in every direction for some light on the incredible situation.

Heath grunted assent and began searching through the several *cabañas*. Presently he emerged with Montague's attire over one arm; and we proceeded to the house.

As we reached the top of the steps, Doctor Emanuel Doremus, the Medical Examiner, drove up to the front of the house. Seeing us, he stepped jauntily across the lawn to where we stood. He was a short, dapper man, breezy and petulant in manner, who suggested the stock-broker rather than the shrewd physician that he was. He was dressed in a pale gray sport suit, and his straw hat was set at a rakish angle. He greeted us with a familiar wave of the hand, planted himself with his feet wide apart, thrust his hands in his pockets, and fixed a baleful eye on the Sergeant.

"A fine time," he complained waspishly, "to drag me out into the country. Don't you think I ever need any rest—even on Sunday?… Well, where's the body? Let's get the business

---

*   *The Greene Murder Case*

over with, so I can get back in time for lunch." He teetered a moment on his toes while Heath cleared his throat and looked embarrassed.

"The fact is, doc,"—Heath spoke apologetically—"there ain't no body…"

Doremus squinted, settled down on his heels, and studied the Sergeant maliciously.

"What's that!" he snapped. "No corpse?" He pushed his hat further back on his head and glowered. "Whose clothes are those you're holding?"

"They belong to the guy that I wanted you to report on," Heath returned sheepishly. "But we can't find the guy himself."

"Where was he when you phoned me?" Doremus demanded irritably. "I suppose the corpse said 'toodle-oo' to you and walked off… Say, what is this—a practical joke?"

Markham stepped diplomatically into the breach.

"We're sorry for the trouble we've caused you, doctor. But the explanation is simple. The Sergeant had every reason to believe that a man had been drowned, under suspicious circumstances, in the swimming pool down the hill. But when the pool was drained there was no body in it, and we're all a bit mystified."

Doctor Doremus nodded curtly in acknowledgment of Markham's explanation, and turned back to the unhappy Sergeant.

"I don't head the Bureau of Missing Persons," he grumbled. "I happen to be the Chief Medical Examiner…"

"I thought—" Heath began, but the doctor interrupted him.

"Good Gad!" He glared at the Sergeant in mock astonishment. "You 'thought'! Where did the members of the Homicide Bureau get the idea that they could think?… Sunday! The day of rest. Hot, too! And I'm dragged out of my easy chair into this God-forsaken part of the country, because you had a thought… I don't want thoughts—I want bodies. And when there aren't any bodies I want to be let alone."

The Sergeant was piqued, but his many experiences with the peppery Medical Examiner had taught him not to take the other too seriously; and he finally grinned good-naturedly.

"When I have a corpse for you," he retorted, "you complain about it. Now when I haven't got one and there's nothing for you to do, you complain anyway... Honest, doc, I'm sorry I got you up here, but if you'd been in my place—"

"Heaven forbid!" Doremus fixed a commiserating look on the Sergeant and shook his head dolefully. "A homicide sleuth without a corpse!"

Markham was, I thought, a little annoyed at the Medical Examiner's frivolous manner.

"This is a serious situation, doctor," he said. "The man's body should logically have been in the pool, and the case is enough to upset any one's nerves."

Doremus sighed exaggeratedly, and extended his hands, palms upward.

"But, after all, Mr. Markham, I can't perform an autopsy on a theory. I'm a doctor—not a philosopher."

Vance exhaled a long ribbon of smoke.

"You can still have your luncheon on time, don't y' know. Really, doctor, you should be deuced grateful to the Sergeant for not detaining you."

"Huh! I suppose you're right, though." Doremus grinned and wiped his brow with a blue silk handkerchief. "Well, I'll be running along."

"If we find the body—" Heath began.

"Oh, don't consider my feelings," the doctor returned. "I don't care if you never find another body. But, if you do, for Gad's sake, don't make it at mealtime." He waved a cheery farewell, which included all of us, and hurried back across the lawn to his car.

"The Sergeant having been duly chastened for his precipitancy," smiled Vance, "suppose we proceed on our way."

Stamm opened the side door for us with his key, and we entered the dingy hallway that led from the main stairs to the rear of the house. Even in the daytime, the depressing musty atmosphere of a bygone age enveloped us, and the sunlight that filtered into the hall from the main entrance appeared dead and dusty, as if it too had been vitiated by the stagnation of accumulated decay.

As we approached the library we heard the low murmur of several voices within, and it was evident that most of the household had gathered in that room. There was a sudden lull in the conversation, and Leland came out into the hallway to greet us.

Despite his inherent calm, he appeared drawn and restless. After the brief greetings, he asked in a voice that struck me as somewhat strained:

"Have you discovered anything new?"

"Oh, a number of things," Vance answered cheerfully. "But Montague himself has eluded us in the most amazin' fashion."

Leland shot Vance a swift, quizzical look.

"He was not in the pool?"

"Oh, not at all," said Vance blandly. "He was entirely absent, don't y' know. Mystifyin', what?"

Leland frowned, studied Vance a moment, and then glanced quickly at the rest of us. He started to say something but refrained.

"By the by," Vance continued, "we're going up to Montague's room for a bit of sartorial inspection. Would you care to limp along?"

Leland seemed confused for a moment; then he caught sight of the wearing apparel the Sergeant was carrying.

"By George!" he exclaimed. "I had quite forgotten the poor chap's clothes. I should have brought them to the house last night... You think they may contain something that will explain his disappearance?"

Vance shrugged, and proceeded to the front entrance hall.

"One never knows, does one?" he murmured.

Stamm summoned Trainor, who was standing near the main door, and told him to fetch a pair of slippers for Vance to wear while his shoes were being cleaned. As soon as the butler had made the exchange we went up-stairs.

The bedroom that had been assigned to Montague was far down on the north side of the second-story hallway, directly under, as I figured it, the bedroom of Mrs. Stamm. It was not as large a room as hers, but it had a similar window overlooking the Dragon Pool. The room was comfortably furnished, but it possessed none of the air of having been lived in, and I surmised that it was used merely as an overflow guest-chamber.

On a low table by the chest of drawers was a black sealskin travelling bag, its cover thrown back against the wall. It was fitted with silver toilet articles, and appeared to contain only the usual items of male attire. Over the foot of the colonial bed hung a suit of mauve silk pajamas, and on a chair nearby had been thrown a purple surah silk dressing-gown.

Heath placed the clothes he had found in the *cabaña* on the centre-table and began a systematic search of the pockets.

Vance walked leisurely to the open window and looked out across the pool. Four men were busily engaged in the operation of opening the stream gates, and Snitkin, his drawings evidently completed, was dragging the last board up the bank toward the vault. Vance stood for several moments gazing out, smoking thoughtfully, his eyes moving from the filter to the dam and then to the cliff opposite.

"Really, y' know," he remarked to Stamm, "that fallen piece of rock should be removed before the water is let in."

Stamm, for some reason, seemed disconcerted by the suggestion.

"There wouldn't be time," he answered. "And, anyway, the water's shallow at that point. I'll get the rock out in a day or so."

Vance appeared hardly to have heard him and turned back to the room, walking slowly toward the centre-table where the Sergeant had made a small heap of the contents of Montague's dinner clothes.

Heath turned one more pocket inside out, and then spread his hands in Vance's direction.

"That's the total," he said, with patent disappointment. "And there's nothing here that will tell us anything."

Vance glanced cynically at the various objects on the table—a platinum watch and chain, a small pocket-knife, a gold cigarette-case and lighter, a fountain-pen, several keys, two hand-kerchiefs, and a small amount of silver and paper money. Then he walked to the suit-case and made an inspection of its contents.

"There's nothing helpful here either, Sergeant," he said at length.

He glanced about him, examined the top of the dressing-table, opened the two drawers, looked under the pillows on the bed, and finally felt in the pockets of the pajamas and the dressing-gown.

"Everything's quite conventional and in order," he sighed, dropping into a chair by the window. "I fear we'll have to look elsewhere for clues."

Stamm had gone to the clothes-closet and opened the door; and Leland, as if animated by the spirit of the search, had followed him. Stamm reached up and turned on the light in the closet.

Leland, looking over the other's shoulder, nodded approvingly.

"Of course," he murmured, without any great show of enthusiasm. "His day suit."

Vance rose quickly.

"'Pon my soul, Mr. Leland, I'd quite forgot it... I say, Sergeant, fetch the johnny's other togs, will you?"

Heath hastened to the closet and brought Montague's sport suit to the centre-table. An examination of its pockets failed to reveal anything of importance until a leather wallet was removed from the inside coat pocket. Within the wallet were three letters, two in envelopes and one merely folded, without a covering. The two in envelopes were a circular from a tailor and a request for a loan.

The letter without an envelope, however, proved to be one of the most valuable clues in the dragon murder. Vance glanced through it, with a puzzled expression, and then, without a word, showed it to the rest of us. It was a brief note, in characteristically feminine chirography, on pale blue scented notepaper. It was without an address, but it was dated August 9th (which was Thursday, the day before the house-party began) and read:

> Dearest Monty—
> I will be waiting in a car, just outside the gate on the East Road, at ten o'clock.
> Ever thine,
> ELLEN.

Stamm was the last to read the note. His face went pale, and his hand trembled as he gave it back to Vance.

Vance barely glanced at him: he was gazing with a slight frown at the signature.

"Ellen…Ellen," he mused. "Wasn't that the name, Mr. Stamm, of the woman who said she wasn't able to join your house-party because she was sailing for South America?"

"Yes—that's it." Stamm's tone was husky. "Ellen Bruett. And she admitted she knew Montague… I don't get it at all. Why should she be waiting for him with a car? And even if Montague was in love with her, why should he join her in such an outlandish fashion?"

"It strikes me," Leland put in grimly, "that Montague wanted to disappear in order to join this woman. The man was a moral coward, and he did not have the courage to come out and tell Bernice he wanted to break his engagement with her because he was in love with another woman. Moreover, he was an actor and would concoct just such a dramatic episode to avoid his obligations. The fellow was always spectacular in his conduct. Personally, I am not surprised at the outcome."

Vance regarded him with a faint smile.

"But, Mr. Leland, really, don't y' know, there isn't any outcome just yet…"

"But surely," protested Leland, with mild emphasis, "that note explains the situation."

"It explains many things," Vance conceded. "But it doesn't explain how Montague could have emerged from the pool to keep his rendezvous without leaving the slightest sign of footprints."

Leland studied Vance speculatively, reaching in his pocket for his pipe.

"Are you sure," he asked, "that there are no footprints whatever?"

"Oh, there are footprints," Vance returned quietly. "But they couldn't have been made by Montague. Furthermore, they are not on the plot of ground at the edge of the pool which leads out to the East Road... The footprints, Mr. Leland, are in the mud on the bottom of the pool."

"On the bottom of the pool?" Leland drew in a quick breath, and I noticed that he spilled some of the tobacco as he filled his pipe. "What kind of footprints are they?"

Vance listlessly shifted his gaze to the ceiling.

"That's difficult to say. They looked rather like marks which might have been made by some gigantic prehistoric beast."

"The dragon!" The exclamation burst almost explosively from Leland's lips. Then the man uttered a low nervous laugh and lighted his pipe with unsteady fingers. "I cannot admit, however," he added lamely, "that Montague's disappearance belongs in the realm of mythology."

"I'm sure it does not," Vance murmured carelessly. "But, after all, d' ye see, one must account for those amazin' imprints in the pool."

"I should like to have seen those imprints," Leland returned dourly. "But I suppose it is too late now." He went to the window and looked out. "The water is already flowing through the gates..."

Just then came the sound of heavy footsteps in the hall, and Snitkin appeared at the door, with several pieces of paper in his hand.

"Here are the copies, Sergeant." The detective spoke in a strained tone: it was evident that our morning's adventure on the basin of the pool had had a disquieting effect on him. "I've got the men working on the gates, and the lock in the dam is about closed. What's the orders now?"

"Go back and boss the job," Heath told him, taking the sketches. "And when it's done send the boys home and take up your post at the road gate."

Snitkin saluted and went away without a word.

Vance walked over to Heath and, taking out his monocle, studied the drawings.

"My word!" he commented admiringly. "They're really clever, don't y' know. The chap is a natural draughtsman... I say, Mr. Leland, here are copies of the footprints we found in the pool."

Leland moved—somewhat hesitantly, I thought—to the Sergeant's side and looked at the drawings. I watched him closely during his examination of the sketches, but I was unable to detect the slightest change of expression on his face.

At length he looked up, and his calm eyes slowly turned to Vance.

"Quite remarkable," he said, and added in a colorless voice: "I cannot imagine what could have made such peculiar imprints in the pool."

CHAPTER TEN

The Missing Man
(Sunday, August 12; 1 p.m.)

IT WAS NOW one o'clock. Stamm insisted on ordering lunch for us, and Trainor served it in the drawing-room. Stamm himself and Leland ate with the others in the dining-room. We were no sooner alone than Markham turned a troubled gaze on Vance.

"What do you make of it all?" he asked. "I can't understand those marks on the bottom of the pool. They're—they're frightful."

Vance shook his head despairingly: there could be no doubt that he too was troubled.

"I don't like it—I don't at all like it." There was discouragement in his tone. "There's something dashed sinister about this case—something that seems to reach out beyond the ordin'ry every-day experiences of man."

"If it were not for all this curious dragon lore surrounding the Stamm estate," said Markham, "we'd probably have dismissed those large imprints with the simple explanation that the water draining over the mud had tended to enlarge or distort ordinary footmarks."

Vance smiled wearily.

"Yes, quite so. But we'd have been unscientific. Some of the footprints were pointed in the direction of the flow of the water, while others were at right-angles to it; yet their character was not changed at any point. Moreover, the receding water flowed very gently, and the shallow mud on the bottom of the pool is rather tenacious,—even the scale-like formations on the imprints were not washed away... But even if one could account reasonably for the larger impressions, what about those astonishing claw-like imprints—?"

Suddenly Vance leapt to his feet and, going swiftly to the door, drew one of the portières aside. Before him stood Trainor, his pudgy face a ghastly white, his eyes staring like those of a man in a trance. In one hand he held Vance's shoes.

Vance regarded him ironically and said nothing; and the man, with a quiver that ran over his entire body, made an effort to draw himself together.

"I'm—I'm sorry, sir," he stammered. "I—I heard you talking and—didn't wish to disturb you...so I waited. I have your boots, sir."

"That's quite all right, Trainor." Vance returned to his chair. "I was merely curious as to who was hoverin' outside the portières... Thanks for the boots."

The butler came forward obsequiously, knelt down and, removing the slippers from Vance's feet, replaced them with the oxfords. His hands trembled perceptibly as he tied the laces.

When he left the room with the tray of luncheon dishes Heath glared after him belligerently.

"Now, what was that baby snooping around for?" he snarled. "There's something on his mind."

"Oh, doubtless." Vance smiled moodily. "I'd say it was the dragon."

"See here, Vance,"—Markham spoke with acerbity—"let's drop this poppycock about a dragon." There was a certain desperation in his tone. "How do you account for that note in Montague's pocket—and what does it mean?"

"My word, Markham, I'm no Chaldean." Vance leaned back in his chair and lighted another *Régie*. "Even if the whole affair was a spectacular plot in which the histrionic Montague was to make his exit in the approved dramatic manner, I still can't imagine how he joined his inamorata without leaving some evidence as to his means of departure from the pool. It's mystifyin' no end."

"Hell!" The forthright Sergeant cut into the discussion. "The bird got away somehow, didn't he, Mr. Vance? And if we can't find the evidence, he out-foxed us."

"Tut, tut, Sergeant. You're far too modest. I'll admit the explanation should be simple, but I've a feelin' that it's going to prove dashed complex."

"Nevertheless," Markham argued, "that note from the Bruett woman and Montague's disappearance complement each other perfectly."

"Granted," nodded Vance. "Too perfectly, in fact. But the imprints in the pool and the absence of any kind of footprints on the opposite bank, are two conflictin' elements."

He got to his feet and walked the length of the room and back.

"Then there's the car in which the mysterious lady waited... I say, Markham, I think a brief chat with Miss Stamm might prove illuminatin'... Fetch the quakin' butler, will you, Sergeant?"

Heath went swiftly from the room, and when Trainor came in Vance requested him to ask Miss Stamm to come to the drawing-room. A few minutes later she appeared.

Bernice Stamm was not exactly a beautiful girl, but she was unquestionably attractive, and I was amazed at her air of serenity, after the reports of her hysterical condition the night before. She had on a sleeveless white crêpe-de-Chine tennis dress. Her legs were bare, but she wore orange-colored woollen socks, rolled at the ankles, and white buckskin sandals. Though not exactly an athletic type, she gave one the same impression of strength and vitality as did her brother.

Vance offered her a chair. But she declined it courteously, saying that she preferred to stand.

"Perhaps you'll have a cigarette," he suggested, proffering her his case.

She accepted one with a slight bow, and he held his lighter for her. Her manner seemed strangely detached, as if both her thoughts and her emotions were far away from her immediate surroundings; and I remembered the Sergeant's criticism of her to the effect that she had not seemed as much concerned about the tragedy itself as about something indirectly connected with it. Perhaps Vance received the same impression, for his first question was:

"Exactly how do you feel, Miss Stamm, about the tragedy that took place here last night?"

"I hardly know what to say," she answered, with apparent frankness. "Of course, I was tremendously upset. I think we all were."

Vance studied her searchingly a moment.

"But surely your reaction must have been deeper than that. You were engaged to Mr. Montague, I understand."

She nodded wistfully.

"Yes—but that was a great mistake. I realize it now... If it had not been a mistake," she added, "I'm sure I would feel much more deeply about the tragedy than I do."

"You think this tragedy was accidental?" Vance asked with sudden bluntness.

"Of course it was!" The girl turned on him with blazing eyes. "It couldn't have been anything else. I know what you mean—I've heard all the silly chatter round this house—but it's quite impossible to attribute Monty's death to anything but an accident."

"You don't put any stock, then, in these tales of a dragon in the pool?"

She laughed with genuine amusement.

"No, I don't believe in fairy-tales. Do you?"

"I still believe in tales of Prince Charming," Vance returned lightly; "though I've always rather suspected the chap. He was much too good to be true."

The girl let her eyes rest on Vance calmly for several moments. Then she said:

"I haven't the slightest idea what you mean."

"It really doesn't matter," he returned. "But it's a bit disconcertin' not to have found the body of the gentleman who dived into the pool last night."

"You mean—"

"Yes—quite. Mr. Montague has disappeared completely."

She gave him a startled look.

"But—at lunch—my brother—he didn't tell me... You're quite sure that Monty has disappeared?"

"Oh, yes. We drained the pool, don't y' know." Vance paused and regarded the girl mildly. "All we found were some fantastic footprints."

Her eyes widened and the pupils dilated.

"What kind of footprints?" she asked, in a tense, hushed voice.

"I've never seen any like them before," Vance returned. "If I believed in mythical submarine monsters, I might conclude that some such creature had made them."

Bernice Stamm was standing near the portières, and involuntarily she reached out and clutched one of them with her hand, as if to steady herself. But her sudden loss of composure was only momentary. She forced a smile and, walking further into the room, leaned against the mantelpiece.

"I am afraid"—she spoke with obvious effort—"I'm too practical to be frightened by any seeming evidences of the dragon's presence here."

"I'm sure you are, Miss Stamm," Vance replied pleasantly. "And since you are so practical, perhaps this missive will interest you." He took from his pocket the blue, scented note that had been found in Montague's day suit, and handed it to her.

The girl read it without change of expression, but when she gave it back to Vance I noticed that she sighed deeply, as if the implication of its contents had brought her peace of mind.

"That note is far more reasonable than the footprints you speak of," she remarked.

"The note in itself is reasonable enough," Vance admitted. "But there are correlative factors which make it appear most unreasonable. For one thing, there's the car in which the ever-thine Ellen was to have waited. Surely, in the night-time silence of Inwood, the sound of an automobile could have been heard at a distance of a few hundred yards."

"It was—it was!" she exclaimed. "I heard it!" The color rushed back to her cheeks, and her eyes glistened. "I didn't realize it until this minute. When Mr. Leland and the others were in the pool searching for Monty—ten minutes or so after he had dived in—I heard a car starting and the hum of the motor picking up as when the gears are being shifted—you know the sort of noise I mean. *And it was down on the East Road...*"

"The car was going away from the estate?"

"Yes—yes! It was going away—toward Spuyten Duyvil... It all comes back to me now. I was kneeling there, at the edge of the pool, frightened and dazed. And the sound of this car drifted in on me, mixed with the sound of splashing in the water. But I didn't think about the car at the time—it seemed so unimportant...the suspense of those few minutes—I think you understand what I am trying to say. I completely forgot such a trivial thing as the sound of a car, until that note brought it back to me." The girl spoke with the intensity of unassailable veracity.

"I understand exactly," Vance assured her consolingly. "And your remembering the sound of the car has helped us no end."

He had been standing by the centre-table during the interview, and he now came forward toward the girl and held out his hand in an attitude of friendly sympathy. With a spontaneous gesture of gratitude, she put her hand in his; and he led her to the door.

"We sha'n't bother you any more now," he said gently. "But will you be good enough to ask Mr. Leland to come here?"

She nodded and walked away toward the library.

"Do you think she was telling the truth about hearing an automobile?" Markham asked.

"Oh, undoubtedly." Vance moved back to the centre-table and smoked for a moment in silence: there was a puzzled look on his face. "Curious thing about that girl. I doubt if she thinks Montague escaped in a car—but she unquestionably did hear a car. I wonder...she may be trying to shield some one... A nice gel, Markham."

"You think perhaps she knows or suspects something?"

"I doubt if she *knows* anything." Vance turned and sought a nearby chair. "But, my word! she certainly has suspicions..."

At this moment Leland entered the drawing-room. He was smoking his pipe, and, though he tried to appear cheerful, his expression belied his manner.

"Miss Stamm told me you wished to see me," he said, taking his stand before the fireplace. "I hope you have said nothing to upset her."

Vance watched him intently for a moment.

"Miss Stamm," he said, "did not seem particularly upset by the fact that Montague has departed this *milieu*."

"Perhaps she has come to realize—" Leland began, and then stopped abruptly, busying himself with repacking his pipe. "Did you show her the note?"

"Yes, of course." Vance kept his eyes on the other.

"That note reminds me of something," Leland went on. "The automobile, you know. I have been thinking about that ever since I saw the note, trying to recall my impressions last night, after Montague had disappeared under the water. And I remember quite distinctly now that I did hear a motor-car on the East Road when I came to the surface of the pool, after having looked for the chap. Naturally, I thought nothing of it at the time—I was too intent on the task in hand; that is probably why it went out of my mind until that note recalled it."

"Miss Stamm also remembers hearing a car," Vance informed him. "By the by, how long would you say it was, after Montague's mysterious dive, that you heard the car on the East Road?"

Leland thought a moment.

"Perhaps ten minutes," he said finally, but he added: "However, it is rather difficult to gauge the passage of time in a situation of that kind."

"Quite so," Vance murmured. "But you are certain it was not merely two or three minutes?"

"It could not possibly have been as soon as that," Leland answered with a slight show of emphasis. "You see, we all waited a couple of minutes for the chap to show up after his dive, and I had already gone into the water and made a fairly thorough search for him before I was aware of the sound of the car."

"That being the case," submitted Vance, "it is far from conclusive to connect the sound of the car with the absent Ellen; for it would not have taken Montague more than a minute or so to reach his waiting Juliet at the gate. Certainly he wouldn't have tarried en route; nor would he have lingered for a loving tête-à-tête in the parked car."

"I see what you mean." Leland inclined his head and looked troubled. "Still, he might have decided there was no need for haste and gotten into some togs before driving off."

"Quite so," Vance admitted carelessly. "There are various possibilities, don't y' know..."

The conversation was interrupted by Doctor Holliday and Stamm descending the stairs. They crossed the hall and came into the drawing-room.

"I'm sorry to trouble you again, gentlemen." The doctor, his face clouded, addressed us apologetically. "When I first came here this morning, I found Mrs. Stamm markedly improved, and I expected she would soon be her normal self again. But when I returned, a little later, she had relapsed. The events of last night seem to have upset her strangely, and she is now in a most unusual mood. She insisted on watching the draining of the pool, and the result threw her into a state of unprecedented excitement. There is, I believe, some fixed idea in her mind, which she will not confide to me or to her son."

Doctor Holliday shifted his position awkwardly and cleared his throat.

"I'm inclined to think," he went on, "in view of the fact that her interview with you last night seemed to relieve somewhat the tension of this pent-up hallucination, it might be helpful if you gentlemen would see her again. She may be willing to talk about this suppressed idea to you. It is worth trying, at any rate—if you don't mind. I suggested the interview to her, and she seemed more than willing—quite anxious for it, in fact."

"We would be very glad to see Mrs. Stamm, doctor," Vance returned. "Shall we go up alone?"

Doctor Holliday hesitated, and then nodded jerkily.

"I think that might be best. It may be that this supposed secret of hers is being withheld, for some irrational reason, only from members of the family and those she knows."

We went immediately to Mrs. Stamm's quarters, leaving Doctor Holliday, with Stamm and Leland, in the drawing-room.

Mrs. Schwarz was waiting for us at the door: evidently the doctor had told her we were coming. Mrs. Stamm was seated near the window, her hands folded in her lap. She appeared quite calm, and there was none of the sardonic tenseness about her that we had encountered the night before; instead, there was a look of almost humorous satisfaction on her wizened face.

"I thought you'd be back," she greeted us, with a low cackle of triumph. "I told you that the dragon had killed him. And I told you that his body would not be found in the pool. But you didn't believe me. You thought it was the ravings of an old woman's cracked mind. But now you know that I told you the truth, and so you've come back to learn more. That's why you're here—isn't it? Your foolish science has failed you."

She chuckled, and something in the sound of that hideous nasal laughter brought back to me the witches' cavern scene in "Macbeth," with the dragon's scale that was added to the cauldron.

"I saw you looking for the young man's footprints on the bank opposite and on the cliffs," she continued, in a gloating tone. "But the dragon rises to the surface of the water and flies away with his victims. I've seen him too often!... And I stood here, at the window, when the water was running out of the pool, and saw you waiting...waiting, and watching for the thing that was not there. And then I saw you walk out across the boards, as if you could not believe your eyes. Didn't I tell you last night that there would be no body in the pool? Yet you thought that you could find something." She unfolded her hands and placed them on the arms of the chair, her fingers flexing and unflexing like great talons.

"But we did find something, Mrs. Stamm," Vance said gently. "We found strange imprints in the mud."

She smiled at him, like an older person humoring a child.

"I could have told you that too," she said. "They were the imprints of the dragon's claws. Didn't you recognize them?" (The matter-of-fact simplicity of this astounding statement sent a chill up my spine.)

"But where," asked Vance, "did the dragon take the body of this man he killed?"

A sly look came into the woman's eyes.

"I knew you would ask me that question," she answered, with a satisfied, tight-lipped smile. "But I shall never tell you! That's the dragon's secret—the dragon's and mine!"

"Has the dragon a home other than the pool?"

"Oh, yes. But this is his real home. That's why it is called the Dragon Pool. Sometimes, though, he flies away to the Hudson and hides in its waters. At other times he lies beneath the surface of Spuyten Duyvil. And on cold nights he flies down the valley and seeks shelter in the Indian caves. But he doesn't put his victims in any of those places. He has a different hiding-place for them. It is older than history—older even than man. It is a cavern made for him when the world was young…" Her voice trailed out, and a fanatical look came into her eyes—a look such as I imagine shone in the eyes of the old religious martyrs when they were led to the rack.

"That's all most interestin'," Vance remarked. "But I am afraid it is not very helpful to us in our present dilemma. You are sure you could not be persuaded to tell us where the dragon took young Montague's body?"

"Never!" The woman sat up rigidly in her chair and glared straight ahead.

Vance regarded her sympathetically for a moment; then terminated the distressing interview.

When we had again descended to the drawing-room he explained briefly to Doctor Holliday the result of his conversation, and the doctor and Stamm took leave of us and went up-stairs.

Vance smoked in moody silence for a while.

"Queer about her prognostications," he mused. "I wonder…" He moved restively in his chair, and then, glancing up, questioned Leland regarding the superstition connected with the dragon's various abodes.

But Leland, though obviously frank in his answers, was unable to throw any light on Mrs. Stamm's fanciful remarks.

"The old tales of the dragon," he said, "contained references to his visits to neighboring waters, such as the Hudson and Spuyten Duyvil, and even Hell Gate. And I remember hearing, when I was a child, that he occasionally was seen in the Indian caves. But he was generally supposed to make his home in the pool here."

"There was one thing Mrs. Stamm said," Vance persisted, "that struck me as unusually fantastic. In speaking of the place where the dragon hides his victims she mentioned that it was older than both history and man, and that it was shaped for him when the world was young. Have you any idea what she could have meant by that?"

Leland frowned thoughtfully for a moment. Then his face lighted up, and he took his pipe from his mouth.

"The pot-holes, of course!" he exclaimed. "Her description fits them perfectly. The glacial pot-holes, you know—there are several of them at the foot of the rocks near the Clove. They were fashioned in the ice age—the result of glacial gyrations, I believe—but they are really nothing but small cylindrical cavities in the rocks..."*

"Yes, yes, I know what pot-holes are," Vance interrupted, with a note of suppressed excitement. "But I didn't know there were any in Inwood. How far are they from here?"

"Ten minutes' walk, I should say, toward the Clove."

"Near the East Road?"

"Just to the west of it."

"A car would be quicker, then." Vance walked hurriedly into the hall. "Come, Markham, I think we'll take a bit of a ride... Will you be our guide, Mr. Leland?" He was already headed for the front door. We followed, wondering at this new whim that had suddenly animated him.

"What wild-goose chase is this, Vance?" Markham protested, as we went through the vestibule and down the front steps.

"I don't know, old dear," Vance admitted readily. "But I have a cravin' just now to see those pot-holes."

He stepped into his car and we climbed in after him, as if led irresistibly by the tenseness of his decision. A moment later we were circling the house on the south and turning into the East Road. At the boundary of the estate Snitkin opened the

---

*   The glacial pot-holes in Inwood Hill Park were recently discovered. They are excellent geological specimens of deeply bored, striated cavities formed in the glacial period by the grinding action of the lower gravel surface of the massive continental ice sheet that covered the northeastern part of North America between 30,000 and 50,000 years ago. One of these sub-glacial holes is about three and a half feet in diameter and five feet deep. Another is over four feet across; and still another is eight feet in diameter.

gate for us; and we drove rapidly past the Bird Refuge and on toward the Clove.

We had gone perhaps five hundred yards, when Leland gave the signal to stop. Vance drew up at the side of the road and stepped down. We were about fifty feet from the base of a precipitous rocky ridge which was an extension of the cliff that formed the north boundary of the Dragon Pool.

"And now for a bit of geological reconnoitring." Though he spoke lightly, there was, beneath his words, a sombre intentness.

"There are several large glacial pot-holes here," Leland offered, leading the way toward the cliff. "There's an oak tree growing in one of them; and one of the others is not as clearly marked as the rest. But there's one excellent deep-cut example of glacial activity—there, just ahead."

We had now come to the foot of the cliff. Before us, as if chiselled in the steep rock, was a great irregular, oval scar, perhaps twenty feet long and spreading outward toward the bottom to a width of about four feet—it was as if some falling meteor had dropped perpendicularly and cut its pathway along the rock and down into the earth. Across the bottom of this upright tunnel was the projection of the frontal rock, about five feet high, which formed a sort of wall across the lower section of the pot-hole, making of it a miniature well.*

"That is the most interesting of the pot-holes," Leland explained. "You can see the three successive borings which indicate, no doubt, the advance and retreat of the ice during the long glacial period. The striæ and polish have been well preserved, too."

Vance threw away his cigarette and approached it.

Markham was standing behind him.

---

*   *There is a slab of Archæan-age granite with glacial markings from Vinalhaven, Maine, in front of the American Museum of Natural History, showing the formation of a glacial pot-hole. The cylindrical boring in it, however, is much smaller than those in Inwood.*

"What, in the name of Heaven, do you expect to find here, Vance?" he asked irritably. "Surely, you're not taking Mrs. Stamm's maunderings seriously."

Vance, by this time, had climbed on the low wall and was looking over into the depths of the pot-hole.

"It might interest you, nevertheless, to see the interior of this pot-hole, Markham," he said, without turning his eyes from the depths beyond.

There was an unwonted note of awe in his voice, and we quickly came to the edge of the narrow stone wall and looked over into the ancient rock cavity.

And there we saw the huddled, mangled body of a man in a bathing suit. On the left side of his head was a great ragged gash; and the blood that had run down over his shoulder was black and clotted. The jersey of his suit had been torn down over the chest, and three long gaping wounds on his body marked the line of the tear. His feet were drawn up under him in a hideous distorted posture; and his arms lay limply across his torso, as if detached from his body. The first impression I got was that he had been dropped into the pot-hole from a great height.

"That is poor Montague," said Leland simply.

CHAPTER ELEVEN

A Sinister Prophecy
(Sunday, August 12; 2.30 p.m.)

DESPITE THE HORROR of the sight that confronted us in the pot-hole, the discovery of Montague's mangled body did not come altogether as a shock. Although Markham had shown evidences, throughout the investigation, of discounting Heath's strong contentions that there had been foul play, he was, nevertheless, prepared for the finding of the body. My impression was that he had battled against the idea as a result of his mental attitude toward the absence of any logical indications pointing to murder. Vance, I knew, had harbored grave suspicions of the situation from the very first; and I myself, in spite of my skepticism, realized, upon my first glimpse of Montague's body, that there had long been, in the back of my mind, definite doubts as to the seemingly fortuitous facts behind Montague's disappearance. The Sergeant, of course, had, from the beginning, been thoroughly convinced that there was a sinister background to the superficially commonplace disappearance of the man.

There was a grim look on Leland's face as he stared down into the pot-hole, but there was no astonishment in his expression; and he gave me the impression of having anticipated the result of our short ride. After identifying the body as that of Montague he slid down from the wall and stood looking thoughtfully at the cliffs at the left. His eyes were clouded, and his jaw was set rigidly as he reached in his pocket for his pipe.

"The dragon theory seems to be working out consistently," he commented, as if thinking aloud.

"Oh, quite," murmured Vance. "Too consistently, I should say. Fancy finding the johnny here. It's a bit rococo, don't y' know."

We had stepped away from the wall of the pot-hole and turned back toward the parked car.

Markham paused to relight his cigar.

"It's an astonishing situation," he muttered between puffs. "How, in the name of Heaven, could he have got into that pot-hole?"

"Anyhow," observed Heath, with a kind of vicious satisfaction, "we found what we've been looking for, and we've got something that we can work on... If you don't mind, Mr. Vance, I wish you'd drive me up to the gate, so as I can get Snitkin on guard down here before we return to the house."

Vance nodded and climbed into his place behind the wheel. He was in a peculiarly abstracted frame of mind; and I knew there was something about the finding of Montague's body that bothered him. From his manner throughout the investigation I realized that he had been expecting some definite proof that a crime had been committed. But I knew now that the present state of affairs did not entirely square with his preconceived idea of the case.

We drove to the gate and brought Snitkin back to the pot-hole, where Heath gave him orders to remain on guard and to let no one approach that side of the cliff from the road. Then we drove back to the Stamm house. As we got out of the car Vance suggested that nothing be said for a while regarding the finding of Montague's body, as there were one or two things he wished to do before apprising the household of the gruesome discovery we had just made.

We entered the house by the front door, and Heath strode immediately to the telephone.

"I've got to get Doc Doremus—" He checked himself suddenly and turned toward Markham with a sheepish smile. "Do you mind calling the doc for me, Chief?" he asked. "I guess he's sort of sore at me. Anyhow, he'll believe *you* if you tell him we've got the body for him now."

"Phone him yourself, Sergeant," Markham returned in an exasperated tone. He was in a bad frame of mind; but the Sergeant's hesitancy and appealing look softened him, and he smiled back good-naturedly. "I'll attend to it," he said. And he went to the telephone to notify the Medical Examiner of the finding of Montague's body.

"He's coming right out," he informed us as he replaced the receiver.

Stamm had evidently heard us come in, for at this moment he came down the front stairs, accompanied by Doctor Holliday.

"I saw you driving down the East Road a while ago," he said, when he had reached us. "Have you learned anything new?"

Vance was watching the man closely.

"Oh, yes," he replied. "We've unearthed the *corpus delicti*. But we wish the fact kept from the other members of the household, for the time being."

"You mean—you found Montague's body?" the other stammered. (Even in the dim light of the hall I could see his face go pale.) "Where, in God's name, was it?"

"Down the road a bit," Vance returned in a casual voice, taking out a fresh *Régie* and busying himself with the lighting of it. "And not a pretty picture, either. The chap had an ugly wound on his head, and there were three long gashes down the front of his chest—"

"*Three gashes?*" Stamm turned vaguely, like a man with vertigo, and steadied himself against the newel post. "What kind of gashes? Tell me, man! Tell me what you mean!" he demanded in a thick voice.

"If I were superstitious," Vance replied, smoking placidly, "I'd say they might have been made by the talons of a dragon—same like those imprints we saw on the bottom of the pool." (He had dropped into a facetious mood—for what reason I could not understand.)

Stamm was speechless for several moments. He swayed back and forth, glaring at Vance as if at a spectre from which he could not tear his eyes. Then he drew himself up, and the blood rushed back into his face.

"What damned poppycock is this?" he burst out in a half-frenzied tone. "You're trying to upset me." When Vance did not answer, he shifted his frantic gaze to Leland and thrust out his jaw angrily. "You're to blame for this nonsense. What have you been up to? What's the truth about this affair?"

"It is just as Mr. Vance has told you, Rudolf," Leland replied calmly. "Of course, no dragon made the gashes on poor Montague's body—but the gashes are there."

Stamm seemed to quiet down under Leland's cool regard. He gave a mirthless laugh in an effort to throw off the horror that had taken possession of him at Vance's description of Montague's wounds.

"I think I'll have a drink," he said, and swung quickly down the hallway toward the library.

Vance had seemed indifferent to Stamm's reaction, and he now turned to Doctor Holliday.

"I wonder if we might see Mrs. Stamm again for a few moments?" he asked.

The doctor hesitated; then he nodded slowly.

"Yes, I think you might. Your visit to her after lunch seems to have had a salutary effect. But I might suggest that you do not remain with her too long."

We went immediately up-stairs, and Leland and the doctor followed Stamm into the library.

Mrs. Stamm was seated in the same chair in which she had received us earlier in the day, and though she appeared more composed than she had been on our previous visit, she none the less showed considerable surprise at seeing us. She looked up with slightly raised eyebrows, and there was an ineluctable dignity in her mien. A subtle and powerful change had come over her.

"We wish to ask you, Mrs. Stamm," Vance began, "if, by any chance, you heard an automobile on the East Road last night, a little after ten."

She shook her head vaguely.

"No, I heard nothing. I didn't even hear my son's guests go down to the pool. I was dozing in my chair after dinner."

Vance walked to the window and looked out.

"That's unfortunate," he commented; "for the pool can be seen quite plainly from here—and the East Road, too." The woman was silent, but I thought I detected the suggestion of a faint smile on her old face.

Vance turned back from the window and stood before her.

"Mrs. Stamm," he said, with earnest significance, "we believe that we have discovered the place where the dragon hides his victims."

"If you have, sir," she returned, with a calmness that amazed me, "then you surely must know a great deal more than when you were last here."

"That is true," Vance nodded. Then he asked: "Weren't the glacial pot-holes what you had in mind when you spoke of the dragon's hiding-place?"

She smiled with enigmatic shrewdness. "But if, as you say, you have discovered the hiding-place, why do you ask me about it now?"

"Because," Vance said quietly, "the pot-holes were discovered only recently—and, I understand, quite by accident."*

---

*   The fact is that one Patrick Coghlan, a resident of Inwood, found these pot-holes only a few years ago, on one of his rambling walks. They have since been cleared by the Dyckman Institute and made available for public inspection and study.

"But I knew of them when I was a child!" the woman protested. "There was nothing in this whole countryside that I did not know. And I know things about it now that none of you will ever know." She looked up quickly, and a strange apprehensive light came into her eyes. "Have you found the young man's body?" she asked, with new animation.

Vance nodded.

"Yes, we have found it."

"And weren't the marks of the dragon on it?" There was a gleam of satisfaction in her eyes.

"There are marks on the body," said Vance. "And it lies in the large pot-hole at the foot of the cliff, near the Clove."

Her eyes flashed and her breath came faster, as if with suppressed excitement; and a hard, wild look spread over her face.

"Just as I told you, isn't it!" she exclaimed in a strained, high-pitched voice. "He was an enemy of our family—and the dragon killed him, and took him away and hid him!"

"But after all," Vance commented, "the dragon didn't do a very good job of hiding him. We found him, don't y' know."

"If you found him," the woman returned, "it was because the dragon intended you to find him."

Despite her words, a troubled look came into her eyes. Vance inclined his head and made a slight gesture with his hand, which was both an acceptance and a dismissal of her words.

"Might I ask, Mrs. Stamm,"—Vance spoke with casual interest—"why it was that the dragon himself was not found in the pool when it was drained?"

"He flew away this morning at dawn," the woman said. "I saw him when he rose into the air, silhouetted against the first faint light in the eastern sky. He always leaves the pool after he has killed an enemy of the Stamms—he knows the pool will be drained."

"Is your dragon in the pool now?"

She shook her head knowingly.

"He comes back only at dusk when there are deep shadows over the land."

"You think he will return tonight?"

She lifted her head and stared past us inscrutably, a tense, fanatical look on her face.

"He will come back tonight," she said slowly, in a hollow, sing-song tone. "His work is not yet completed." (She was like the rapt priestess of some ancient cult pronouncing a prophecy; and a shiver ran over me at her words.)

Vance, unimpressed, studied the strange creature before him for several seconds.

"When will he complete his work?" he asked.

"All in good time," she returned with a cold, cruel smirk; then added oracularly: "Perhaps tonight."

"Indeed! That's very interestin'." Vance did not take his eyes from her. "And, by the by, Mrs. Stamm," he went on, "in what way is the dragon concerned with the family vault across the pool yonder?"

"The dragon," the woman declared, "is the guardian of our dead as well as our living."

"Your son tells me that you have the key to the vault, and that no one else knows where it is."

She smiled cunningly.

"I have hidden it," she said, "so that no one can desecrate the bodies that lie entombed there."

"But," pursued Vance, "I understand that you wish to be placed in the vault when you die. How, if you have hidden the key, can that wish of yours be carried out?"

"Oh, I have arranged for that. When I die the key will be found—but only then."

Vance asked no further questions, but took his leave of this strange woman. I could not imagine why he had wanted to see her. Nothing seemed to have been gained by the interview: it struck me as both pathetic and futile, and I was relieved when we returned down-stairs and went into the drawing-room.

Markham evidently felt as I did, for the first question he put to Vance, when we were alone, was:

"What was the sense of bothering that poor deluded woman again? Her babbling about the dragon is certainly not going to help us."

"I'm not so sure, old dear." Vance sank into a chair, stretched his legs, and looked up to the ceiling. "I have a feelin' that she may hold the key to the mystery. She is a shrewd woman, despite her hallucinations about a dragon inhabiting the pool. She knows much more than she will tell. And, don't forget, her window overlooks the pool and the East Road. She wasn't in the least upset when I told her we had found Montague in one of the pot-holes. And I received a distinct impression from her that, although she has built up a romantic illusion about the dragon, which has unquestionably unbalanced her mind, she is carrying the illusion much further than her own convictions—as if she wishes to emphasize the superstition of the dragon. It may be she is endeavorin', with some ulterior motive, to throw us off the track and, through a peculiar protective mechanism, to cover up a wholly rational fact upon which she thinks we may have stumbled."

Markham nodded thoughtfully.

"I see what you mean. I got that same impression from her myself during her fantastic recital of the dragon's habits. But the fact remains that she seems to harbor a definite belief in the dragon."

"Oh, quite. And she firmly believes that the dragon lives in the pool and protects the Stamms from all enemies. But another element has entered into her projection of the dragon myth—something quite human and intimate. I wonder..." Vance's voice trailed off and, settling deeper in his chair, he smoked meditatively for several minutes.

Markham moved uneasily.

"Why," he asked, frowning, "did you bring up the subject of the key to the vault?"

"I haven't the faintest notion," Vance admitted frankly, but there was a far-away, pensive look on his face. "Maybe it was because of the proximity of the vault to the low ground, on the other side of the pool, to which the imprints led." He lifted himself up and regarded the ash on his cigarette for a moment. "That mausoleum fascinates me. It's situated at a most strategic point. It's like the apex of a salient, so to speak."

"What salient?" Markham was annoyed. "From all the evidence, no one emerged from the pool along that low stretch of ground; and the body was found far away—chucked into a pot-hole."

Vance sighed.

"I can't combat your logic, Markham. It's unassailable. The vault doesn't fit in at all... Only," he added wistfully, "I do wish it had been built on some other part of the estate. It bothers me no end. It's situated, d' ye see, almost on a direct line between the house here and the gate down the East Road. And along that line is the plot of low ground which is the only means of egress from the pool."

"You're talking nonsense," Markham said hotly. "You'll be babbling next of relativity and the bending of light rays."

"My dear Markham—my very dear Markham!" Vance threw away his cigarette and stood up. "I emerged from the interstellar spaces long ago. I'm toddling about in a realm of mythology, where the laws of physics are abrogated and where unearthly monsters hold sway. I've become quite childlike, don't y' know."

Markham gave Vance a quizzical perturbed look. Whenever Vance took this frivolous attitude in the midst of a serious discussion, it meant only one thing: that his mind was operating along a very definite line of ratiocination—that he had, in fact, found some ray of light in the darkness of the situation and was avoiding the subject until he had penetrated its beams to their source. Markham realized this, and dropped the matter forthwith.

"Do you," he asked, "wish to pursue the investigation now, or wait until the Medical Examiner has made his examination of Montague's body?"

"There are various things I should like to do now," Vance returned. "I want to ask Leland a question or two. I crave verbal intercourse with young Tatum. And I'm positively longin' to inspect Stamm's collection of tropical fish—oh, principally the fish. Silly—eh, what?"

Markham made a wry face and beat a nervous tattoo on the arm of his chair.

"Which shall it be first?" he asked with ungracious resignation.

Vance rose and stretched his legs.

"Leland. The man is full of information and pertinent suggestions."

Heath rose with alacrity and went to fetch him.

Leland looked troubled when he came into the drawing-room.

"Greeff and Tatum almost came to blows a moment ago," he told us. "They accused each other of having something to do with Montague's disappearance. And Tatum intimated strongly that Greeff had not been sincere in his search for Montague in the pool last night. I do not know what he was driving at, but Greeff became livid with anger, and only the combined efforts of Doctor Holliday and myself prevented him from attacking Tatum."

"That's most revealin'," murmured Vance. "By the by, have Stamm and Greeff reconciled their differences?"

Leland shook his head slowly.

"I am afraid not. There has been bad blood between them all day. Stamm meant all the things he said to Greeff last night—he was just in the frame of mind to let down the barriers of his emotions and blurt the truth—or rather, what he believed to be the truth. I do not pretend to understand the relationship. Sometimes I feel that Greeff has a hold of some kind on Stamm, and that Stamm has reason to fear him. However, that is mere speculation."

Vance walked to the window and looked out into the brilliant sunlight.

"Do you happen to know," he asked, without turning, "what Mrs. Stamm's sentiments toward Greeff are?"

Leland started slightly and stared speculatively at Vance's back.

"Mrs. Stamm does not like Greeff," he returned. "I heard her warn Stamm against him less than a month ago."

"You think she regards Greeff as an enemy of the Stamms?"

"Undoubtedly—though the reason for her prejudice is something I do not understand. She knows a great deal, however, that the other members of the household little suspect."

Vance slowly turned from the window and walked back to the fireplace.

"Speaking of Greeff," he said, "how long was he actually in the pool during the search for Montague?"

Leland seemed taken aback by the question.

"Really, I could not say. I dived in first and Greeff and Tatum followed suit... It might have been ten minutes—perhaps longer."

"Did Greeff keep within sight of every one during the entire time?"

A startled look came into Leland's face.

"No, he did not," he returned with great seriousness. "He dived once or twice, as I recall, and then swam across to the shallow water below the cliffs. I remember his calling to me from the darkness there, and telling me he had found nothing. Tatum remembered the episode a while ago—it was doubtless the basis for his accusing Greeff of having a hand in Montague's disappearance." The man paused and then slowly shook his head, as if throwing off an unpleasant conclusion that had forced itself upon him. "But I think Tatum is wrong. Greeff is not a good swimmer, and I imagine he felt safer with his feet on the ground. It was natural for him to go to the shallow water."

"How long after Greeff called to you did he return to this side of the pool?"

Leland hesitated.

"I really do not remember. I was frightfully upset, and the actual chronology of events during that time was confused. I recall only that when I eventually gave up the search and climbed back on the retaining wall, Greeff followed shortly afterwards. Tatum, by the way, was the first out of the water. He had been drinking a lot, and was not in the best condition. He seemed pretty well exhausted."

"But Tatum did not swim across the pool?"

"Oh, no. He and I kept in touch the whole time. I will say this for him—little as I like him: he showed considerable courage and stamina during our search for Montague; and he kept his head."

"I'm looking forward to talking with Tatum. Y' know, I haven't seen him yet. Your description of him rather prejudiced me against him, and I was hopin' to avoid him entirely. But now he has added new zest to the affair... Battling with Greeff, what? Fancy that. Greeff is certainly no *persona grata* in this domicile. No one loves him. Sad...sad..."

Vance sat down again and lighted another cigarette. Leland watched him curiously but said nothing. Vance looked up after a while and asked abruptly:

"What do you know of the key to the vault?"

I expected Leland to show some astonishment at this question, but his stoical expression did not change: he seemed to regard Vance's query as both commonplace and natural.

"I know nothing of it," he said, "except what Stamm told me. It was lost years ago, but Mrs. Stamm claims that she has hidden it. I have not seen it since I was quite a young man."

"Ah! You have seen it, then. And you would know it if you saw it again?"

"Yes, the key is quite unmistakable," Leland returned. "The bow was of curious scroll-work, somewhat Japanese in design. The stem was very long—perhaps six inches—and the bit was shaped like a large 'S.' In the old days the key was always kept hanging on a hook over Joshua Stamm's desk in the den... Mrs. Stamm may or may not know where it is now. But does it really matter?"

"I suppose not," Vance murmured. "And I'm most grateful to you for your help. The Medical Examiner, as you know, is on his way here, and I'd jolly well like to have a few words with Tatum in the interim. Would you mind asking him to come here?"

"I am glad to do anything I can to help." Leland bowed and left the room.

CHAPTER TWELVE

Interrogations
(Sunday, August 12; 3 p.m.)

KIRWIN TATUM WAS a man in his early thirties, slender, wiry and loose-jointed. His face was thin and skeleton-like, and, as he stood at the drawing-room door that Sunday afternoon, staring at us, there was a bloodless, haggard look in his expression, which may have been the result of fright or of the ravages of his recent dissipation. But there was a sullen craftiness in his eyes which was almost vulpine. His blond hair, heavily pomaded, was brushed straight back from a peaked forehead with sloping parietals. From one corner of his feral thin-lipped mouth a cigarette drooped. He was dressed in sport clothes of gay and elaborate design; and a heavy gold chain bracelet hung loosely on his left wrist. He stood in the doorway for several minutes, gazing at us shiftily, his long spatulate fingers moving nervously at his sides. That he was uneasy and afraid was apparent.

Vance regarded him with critical coldness, as he might have inspected some specimen in a laboratory. Then he waved his hand toward a chair beside the table.

"Come in and sit down, Tatum." His tone was at once condescending and peremptory.

The man moved forward with a shambling gait, and threw himself into the chair with affected nonchalance.

"Well, what do you want?" he asked, with a show of spirit, glancing about the room.

"I understand you play the piano," remarked Vance.

Tatum ceased fidgeting and looked up with smouldering anger.

"Say, what is this—a game of some kind?"

Vance nodded gravely.

"Yes—and a dashed serious game. You were a bit unsettled, we have been told, by the disappearance of your rival, Mr. Montague."

"Unsettled?" Tatum nervously relighted his cigarette which had gone out. Vance had thrown him off his guard, and his deliberate and prolonged pause patently indicated that he was endeavoring to readjust his equilibrium. "Well, why not? But I haven't been shedding crocodile tears over Monty, if that's what you mean. He was a rotter, and it's just as well, for everybody, that he is out of the way."

"Do you think he will ever return?" asked Vance casually.

Tatum made an unpleasant noise in his throat, which was probably intended to be a scornful laugh.

"No, he won't show up again—because he can't. You don't think he planned the disappearance himself, do you? He didn't have enough sense—or courage. It meant going out of the limelight; and Monty couldn't live or breathe unless he was in the limelight... *Somebody got him!*"

"Who do you think it was?"

"How should I know?"

"Do you think it was Greeff?"

Tatum's eyes half closed, and a cold, hard look spread over his drawn face.

"It might have been Greeff," the man said between his teeth. "He had ample reason."

"And didn't you yourself have 'ample reason'?" Vance returned quietly.

"Plenty." A ferocious smile came to Tatum's lips, then faded immediately away. "But I'm in the clear. You can't pin anything on me." He leaned forward and fixed Vance with his eyes. "I'd hardly got into my bathing suit when the fellow jumped from the spring-board, and I even went into the pool myself and tried to find him when he failed to come up. I was with the rest of the party all the time. You can ask them."

"We shall, no doubt," Vance murmured. "But if you are so immaculately free from suspicion, how can you suggest that Greeff may have had a hand in Montague's mysterious fading from the scene? He seems to have followed very much the same course you did."

"Oh, yes?" Tatum retorted, with cynical scorn. "The hell he did!..."

"You refer, I take it," said Vance mildly, "to the fact that Greeff swam to the opposite side of the pool into the shallow water."

"Oh, you know that, do you?" Tatum looked up shrewdly. "But do you know what he was doing during the fifteen minutes when no one could see him?"

Vance shook his head.

"I haven't the groggiest notion... Have you?"

"He might have been doing almost anything," Tatum returned, with a sly nod.

"Such as draggin' Montague's body out of the pool?"

"And why not?"

"But the only place where he could have emerged from the water was devoid of any footprints. That fact was checked both last night and this morning."

Tatum frowned. Then he said, with a certain aggressiveness:

"What of it? Greeff's as shrewd as they come. He may have found some way to avoid making footprints."

"It sounds a bit vague, don't y' know. But, even if your theory is correct, what could he have done with the body in so short a time?"

The ashes of Tatum's cigarette broke and fell on his coat: he leaned forward and shook them off.

"Oh, you'll probably find the body somewhere on the other side of the pool," he returned, readjusting himself in the chair.

Vance's gaze rested calculatingly on the man for several minutes.

"Is Greeff the only possibility you have to suggest?" he asked at length.

"No," Tatum answered, with a one-sided smile, "there are plenty of possibilities. But the point is to hook them up with the circumstances. If Leland hadn't been alongside of me the whole time I was in the pool, I wouldn't give him a clean bill of health for a split second. And Stamm had plenty of cause to bump Monty off; but he's out of the running because of all the liquor he'd poured into himself. And the women here, too—the McAdam dame and Ruby Steele—they'd have welcomed an opportunity of getting rid of the handsome Monty. But I don't see how they could have managed it."

"Really, y' know, Tatum," Vance remarked, "you're simply bulging with suspects. How do you happen to have overlooked old Mrs. Stamm?"

Tatum sucked in his breath, and his face took on the expression of a death's-head. His long fingers closed over the arms of his chair.

"She's a devil—that woman!" he muttered huskily. "They say she's crazy. But she sees too much—she knows too much." He stared straight ahead blankly. "*She's capable of anything!*" There was something approaching abject fear in his manner. "I've seen her only twice; but she haunts this whole house like a ghost. You can't get away from her."

Vance had been watching Tatum closely, without appearing to do so.

"Your nerves are a bit on edge, I fear," he commented. Then he took a deep inhalation on his cigarette and, rising, walked to the mantelpiece, where he stood almost directly facing the other. "Incidentally," he said casually, dropping his ash into the fireplace, "Mrs. Stamm's theory is that a dragon in the pool killed Montague and hid his body."

Tatum gave a tremulous, cynical laugh.

"Oh, sure, I've heard that wild story before. Maybe a dodo trampled on him—or a unicorn gored him."

"It might interest you to know, however, that we have found Montague's body—"

Tatum started forward.

"Where?" he interrupted.

"In one of the sub-glacial pot-holes down the East Road... And there were three long claw-marks down his chest, such as this mythical dragon might have made."

Tatum sprang to his feet. His cigarette fell from his lips, and he shook his finger hysterically at Vance.

"Don't try to frighten *me*—don't try to frighten *me*." His voice was high-pitched and shaky. "I know what you're trying to do—you're trying to break down my nerves and get me to admit something. But I won't talk—do you understand?—I won't talk..."

"Come, come, Tatum." Vance spoke mildly but sternly. "Sit down and calm yourself. I'm telling you the exact truth. And I'm only endeavorin' to find some solution to Montague's murder. It merely occurred to me that you might be able to help us."

Tatum, soothed and reassured by Vance's manner, sank back into his chair and lit another cigarette.

"Did you," Vance asked next, "notice anything peculiar about Montague last night before he went to the pool? Did he, for instance, appear to you like a man who might have been drugged?"

"He was drugged with liquor, if that's what you mean," Tatum replied rationally. "Although—I'll say this for Monty— he carried his liquor pretty well. And he hadn't had any more than the rest of us—and much less than Stamm, of course."

"Did you ever hear of a woman named Ellen Bruett?"

Tatum puckered his brow.

"Bruett?... The name sounds familiar... Oh, I know where I've heard it. Stamm told me, when he asked me to come here, that there was an Ellen Bruett coming to the party. I imagine I was to be paired with her. Thank God she didn't come, though." He looked up shrewdly. "What's she got to do with it?"

"She's an acquaintance of Montague's—so Stamm told us," Vance explained carelessly. Then he asked quickly: "When you were in the pool, last night, did you hear an automobile on the East Road?"

Tatum shook his head.

"Maybe I did, but I certainly don't remember it. I was too busy diving round for Monty."

Vance dismissed the subject and put another query to Tatum.

"After Montague's disappearance, did you feel immediately that there had been foul play of some kind?"

"Yes!" Tatum compressed his lips and nodded ominously. "In fact, I had a feeling all day yesterday that something was going to happen. I came pretty near leaving the party in the afternoon—I didn't like the set-up."

"Can you explain what gave you that impression of impending disaster?"

Tatum thought a moment, and his eyes shifted back and forth.

"No, I can't say," he muttered at length. "A little of everything, perhaps. But especially that crazy woman up-stairs..."

"Ah!"

"She'd give any one the heebie-jeebies. Stamm makes a habit, you know, of taking his guests to see her for a few moments when they arrive—to pay their respects, or something of the kind. And I remember when I got here, Friday afternoon, Teeny McAdam and Greeff and Monty were already up-stairs with her. She seemed pleasant enough—smiled at all of us and bid us welcome—but there was a queer look in her eyes as she studied each one of us individually—something calculating and ill-omened, if you know what I'm trying to get at. I had the feeling that she was making up her mind which one of us she disliked the most. Her eyes rested a long time on Monty—and I was glad she didn't look at me the same way. When she dismissed us she said, 'Have a good time'—but she was like a cobra grinning at her victims. It took three shots of whisky to bring me back to normal."

"Did the others feel the same way about it?"

"They didn't say much, but I know they didn't like it. And of course the whole party here has been one continual round of back-biting and underhand animosity."

Vance rose and waved his hand toward the door.

"You may go now, Tatum. But I warn you, we want nothing said yet about the finding of Montague's body. And you're to stay indoors with the rest, until further orders from the District Attorney."

Tatum started to say something, checked himself, and then went out.

When the man had gone Vance moved back and forth between the fireplace and the door several times, smoking, his head down. Slowly he looked up at Markham.

"A shrewd, unscrupulous lad, that... Not a nice person— not at all a nice person. And as ruthless as a rattlesnake. Moreover, he knows—or, at least, he seriously suspects— something connected with Montague's death. You recall that, even before he knew we had found the body, he was quite sure it would be discovered somewhere on the other side of the pool. That wasn't altogether guesswork on his part—his tone was far too casual and assured. And he was pretty certain regarding the time Greeff spent in the shallow water. Of course, he ridiculed the dragon idea—and did it cleverly... His comments on Mrs. Stamm were rather interestin', too. He thinks she knows and sees too much—but, after all, why should he care? Unless, of course, he has something to hide... And he told us he didn't hear any car last night, though others heard it..."

"Yes, yes." Markham made a vague gesture with his hand, as if to dismiss Vance's speculations. "Everything here seems contradictory. But what I'd like to know is: was it possible for Greeff to have manipulated the whole thing from his position at the shallow side of the pool?"

"The answer to that question," returned Vance, "seems to lie in the solution of the problem of how Montague got out of the pool and into the pot-hole... Anyway, I think it would be a bully idea, while we're waiting for Doremus, to have another brief parley with Greeff.—Will you please fetch him, Sergeant?"

Greeff entered the drawing-room a few minutes later, dressed in a conventional light-weight business suit, and wearing a small gardenia in his buttonhole. Despite his rugged healthy complexion, he showed unmistakable signs of strain, and I imagined that he had done considerable drinking since we had interviewed him the night before. Much of his aggressiveness was gone, and his fingers shook slightly as he moved his long cigarette holder to and from his lips.

Vance greeted him perfunctorily and asked him to sit down. When Greeff had chosen a chair, Vance said:

"Both Mr. Leland and Mr. Tatum have told us that when you were in the pool, helping them search for Montague, you swam immediately across to the shallow water below the cliffs."

"Not immediately." There was the suggestion of indignant protestation in Greeff's voice. "I made several efforts to find the chap. But, as I've already told you, I am not a good swimmer, and it occurred to me that perhaps his body had drifted across the pool, since he had dived in that direction; and I thought I might be of more help by looking about over there than by interfering with Leland and Tatum with my clumsy splashing about." He shot a quick look at Vance. "Was there any reason why I shouldn't have done it?"

"No-o," Vance drawled. "We were just interested in checkin' the whereabouts of the various members of the party during that particular period."

Greeff squinted, and the color deepened on his cheeks.

"Then what's the point of the question?" he snapped.

"Merely an attempt to clarify one or two dubious items," Vance returned lightly, and then went on, before the other could speak again: "By the by, when you were in the shallow water at the other side of the pool, did you, by any chance, hear a motor-car along the East Road?"

Greeff stared at Vance for several moments in startled silence. The color left his face, and he rose to his feet with jerky ponderance.

"Yes, by Gad! I did hear one." He stood with hunched shoulders, emphasizing his words with his long cigarette holder which he held in his right hand, like a conductor's baton. "And I thought at the time it was damned queer. But I forgot all about it last night, and didn't think of it again until you mentioned it just now."

"It was about ten minutes after Montague had dived in, wasn't it?"

"Just about."

"Both Mr. Leland and Miss Stamm heard it," Vance remarked. "But they were a trifle vague about it."

"I heard it, all right," Greeff muttered. "And I wondered whose car it was."

"I'd jolly well like to know that myself." Vance contemplated the tip of his cigarette. "Could you tell which way the car was going?"

"Toward Spuyten Duyvil," Greeff answered, without hesitation. "And it started somewhere to the east of the pool. When I got over into the shallow water everything was quiet—too damned quiet to suit me. I didn't like it. I called to Leland, and then made some further efforts to see if Montague's body had drifted over to the shoal at that side of the pool. But it was no go. And as I stood there, with my head and shoulders above the surface of the water, on the point of swimming back, I distinctly heard some one starting the motor of a car—"

"As if the car had been parked in the road?" interrupted Vance.

"Exactly... And then I heard the gears being shifted; and the car went on down the East Road—and I swam back across the pool, wondering who was leaving the estate."

"According to a billet-doux we found in one of Montague's coats, a lady was waiting for him in a car, down near the east gate, at ten o'clock last night."

"So?" Greeff gave an unpleasant laugh. "So that's the way the wind blows, is it?"

"No, no, not altogether. There was some miscalculation somewhere, I opine... The fact is, d' ye see," Vance added, with slow emphasis, "we found Montague's body just beyond the Clove—in one of the pot-holes."

Greeff's mouth sagged open, and his eyes contracted into small, shining discs.

"You found him, eh?" he iterated. "How did he die?"

"We don't know yet. The Medical Examiner is on his way up here now. But he wasn't a pleasant sight—a bad gash on the head and great claw-like scratches down his chest—"

"Wait a minute—wait a minute!" There was a tense huskiness in Greeff's demand. "Were there three scratches close together?"

Vance nodded, scarcely looking at the man.

"Exactly three—and they were a uniform distance apart."

Greeff staggered backward toward his chair and fell into it heavily.

"Oh, my God—oh, my God!" he muttered. After a moment he moved his thick fingers over his chin and looked up abruptly, fixing his eyes on Vance in furtive inquiry. "Have you told Stamm?"

"Oh, yes," Vance replied abstractedly. "We gave him the glad tidings as soon as we returned to the house, less than an hour ago." Vance appeared to reflect; then he put another question to Greeff. "Did you ever accompany Stamm on any of his treasure hunts or fishing expeditions in the tropics?"

Obviously Greeff was profoundly puzzled by this change of subject.

"No—no," he spluttered. "Never had anything to do with such silly business—except that I helped Stamm finance and equip a couple of his expeditions. That is," he amended, "I got some of my clients to put up the money. But Stamm paid it all back after the expeditions had fizzled..."

Vance arrested the other's explanations with a gesture. "You're not interested in tropical fish yourself, I take it?"

"Well, I wouldn't go so far as to say I'm not interested in them," Greeff returned in a matter-of-fact voice; but his eyes were still narrowed, like those of a man deeply perplexed. "They're nice to look at—grand colors and all that..."

"Any Dragonfish in Stamm's collection?"

Greeff sat up again, his face paling.

"My God! You don't mean—"

"Purely an academic question," Vance interrupted, with a wave of the hand.

Greeff made a throaty noise.

"Yes, by Gad!" he declared. "There are some Dragonfish here. But they're not alive. Stamm has two of them preserved some way. Anyway, they're only about twelve inches long— though they're vicious-looking devils. He has some long name for them—"

"*Chauliodus sloanei?*"

"Something like that... And he's also got some Sea-horses and a coral-red Sea-dragon... But see here, Mr. Vance, what have these fish got to do with the case?"

Vance sighed before answering.

"I'm sure I don't know. But I'm dashed interested in Stamm's collection of tropical fish."

At this moment Stamm himself and Doctor Holliday crossed the hall to the drawing-room.

"I'm going, gentlemen," Doctor Holliday announced quietly. "If you want me for anything, Mr. Stamm knows where to reach me." Without further ado he went toward the front door, and we heard him go out and drive away in his little coupé.

Stamm stood for several moments, glowering at Greeff.

"Adding more fuel to the fire?" he asked, with an almost vicious sarcasm.

Greeff shrugged hopelessly and extended his hands in a futile gesture, as if unable to cope with the other's unreasonable attitude.

It was Vance who answered Stamm.

"Mr. Greeff and I have just been discussing your fish."

Stamm looked skeptically from one to the other of them, then turned on his heel and went from the room. Vance permitted Greeff to go also.

He had no sooner passed the portières than there came the sound of a car on the front drive; and a few moments later Detective Burke, who had been stationed at the front door, ushered in the Medical Examiner.

CHAPTER THIRTEEN

Three Women
(Sunday, August 12; 3.30 p.m.)

DOCTOR **DOREMUS LOOKED** us over satirically, then fixed his gaze on Sergeant Heath.

"Well, well," he said, with a commiserating shake of the head. "So the corpse has returned. Suppose we have a look at it before it eludes you again."

"It's down the East Road a bit." Vance rose from his chair and went toward the door. "We'd better drive."

We went out of the house and, picking up Detective Burke, got into Vance's car. Doremus trailed us in his own car. We swung round to the south of the house and turned down the East Road. When we were opposite the pot-holes, where Snitkin was waiting, Vance drew up and we got out.

Vance led the way to the cliff and pointed to the rock wall of the pot-hole in which Montague's body lay.

"The chap's in there," he said to Doremus. "He hasn't been touched."

Doremus made a grimace of annoyed boredom.

"A ladder would have helped," he grumbled, as he climbed up to the low parapet and seated himself on its rounded top. After leaning over and inspecting the huddled body cursorily, he turned back to us with a wry face and mopped his brow.

"He certainly looks dead. What killed him?"

"That's what we're hoping you can tell us," answered Heath.

Doremus slid down from the wall.

"All right. Get him out of there and put him down on the ground."

It was not an easy matter to move Montague's body from the pot-hole, as *rigor mortis* had set in, and it required several minutes for Heath and Snitkin and Burke to accomplish the task. Doremus knelt down and, after straightening out the dead man's distorted limbs, began to make an examination of the wound in his head and the gashes down the breast. After a while he looked up and, pushing his hat back, shook his head in obvious uncertainty.

"This is a queer one," he announced. "The man's been struck on the head with a blunt instrument of some kind, which has ripped his scalp open and given him a linear fracture of the skull. It could easily have been the cause of death. But, on the other hand, he's been strangled—look at the ecchymosis on either side of the thyroid cartilage. Only, I'd swear those discolorations are not the marks of a human hand, or even of a rope or cord. And look at those bulging eyes, and the thick black lips and tongue."

"Could he have been drowned?" asked Heath.

"Drowned?" Doremus cocked a pitying eye at the Sergeant. "I've just finished telling you he was bashed over the head and also strangled. If he couldn't get air in his lungs, how could he get water in 'em?"

"What the Sergeant means, doctor," put in Markham, "is whether it's possible that the man was drowned before he was mutilated."

"No." Doremus was emphatic. "In that case he wouldn't show the same type of wound. There wouldn't have been the hemorrhage in the surrounding tissues; and the contusions on the throat would be superficial and circumscribed and not of such a deep color."

"What about those marks on his chest?" asked Vance.

The doctor pursed his lips and looked puzzled. Before replying he studied the three gashes again, and then rose to his feet.

"They're nasty wounds," he said. "But the lacerations are not very serious. They laid open the pectoralis major and minor muscles without penetrating the chest walls. And they were made before he died: you can tell that by the condition of the blood on them."

"He certainly had rough handling." Heath spoke like a man caught in a wave of wonder.

"And that's not all," Doremus went on. "He has some broken bones. The left leg is bent on itself below the knee, showing a fracture of both the tibia and the fibula. The right humerus is broken, too. And from the depressed look of the right side of his chest, I'd say a couple of the lower ribs are smashed."

"That might be the result of his having been thrown into the pot-hole," Vance suggested.

"Possibly," agreed Doremus. "But there are also dull open abrasions—made after death—on the posterior surfaces of both heels, as if he'd been dragged over a rough surface."

Vance took a long, deliberate inhalation on his cigarette.

"That's most interestin'," he murmured, his eyes fixed meditatively ahead of him.

Markham shot him a quick glance.

"What do you mean by that?" he asked, almost angrily.

"Nothing cryptic," Vance returned mildly. "But the doctor's comment opens up a new possibility, don't y' know."

Heath was staring raptly at Montague's body, and I detected something of both awe and fright in his attitude.

"What do you think made those scratches on his chest, doc?" he asked.

"How should I know?" snapped Doremus. "Haven't I already told you I'm a doctor and not a detective? They might have been made by any kind of a sharp instrument."

Vance turned with a smile.

"It's very distressin', doctor, but I can explain the Sergeant's uneasiness. There's a theory hereabouts that this johnny was killed by a dragon that lives in the pool."

"A dragon!" Doremus was bewildered for a moment; then he looked at Heath, and laughed derisively. "And I suppose the Sergeant is figuring out just how the naughty dragon scratched him with his claws—is that it?" He shook his head and chuckled. "Well, well! That's one way of solving a murder:—*cherchez le dragon*. Good Gad, what's the world coming to!"

Heath was piqued.

"If you'd been up against what I have the last coupla days, doc," he growled, "you'd believe anything, too."

Doremus lifted his eyebrows ironically.

"Have you thought of leprechawns?" he asked. "Maybe they did the fellow in. Or the satyrs may have butted him to death. Or the gnomes may have got him. Or perhaps the fairies tickled him to death with pussy-willows." He snorted. "A sweet-looking medical report it'd be if I put down death due to dragon scratches…"

"And yet, doctor," said Vance with unwonted seriousness, "a sort of dragon did kill the chap, don't y' know."

Doremus raised his hands and let them fall in a hopeless gesture.

"Have it your own way. But, as a poor benighted medico, my guess is this guy was first hit over the head and ripped open down the front; then he was strangled, dragged to this rock hole, and dumped into it. If the autopsy shows anything different, I'll let you know."

He took out a pencil and a pad of blanks, and wrote for a moment. When he had finished he tore off the top sheet and handed it to Heath.

"Here's your order for removal, Sergeant. But there's going to be no *post mortem* till tomorrow. It's too blooming hot. You can play Saint George and go dragon hunting till then."

"That's precisely what we're going to do," Vance smiled.

"Just as a matter of record—" began Heath; but the doctor interrupted him with an impatient gesture.

"I know, I know!—'How long has he been dead?'... When I die and go to hell, along with the rest of the medical fraternity, that's the query that'll be eternally drummed into my ears... All right, Sergeant: he's been dead over twelve hours and less than twenty-four. Satisfactory?"

"We have reason to believe, doctor," said Markham, "that the man was killed around ten o'clock last night."

Doremus looked at his watch.

"That would make eighteen hours. Just about right, I'd say." He turned and walked toward his car. "And now I'm on my way—back to a mint julep and an easy chair. Gad, what a day! I'll be having a sunstroke and a brain-storm, like the rest of you, if I don't hurry back to town." He got into his car. "But I'm going home by way of Spuyten Duyvil and Payson Avenue. Taking no chances on going back past the pool." He leered at Heath. "I'm afraid of running into that dragon!" And, with a cheerful wave of the hand, he shot down the East Road.

Heath ordered Snitkin and Burke to remain with Montague's body until it was called for, and the rest of us returned to the Stamm residence, where Heath telephoned to the Department of Public Welfare to send a wagon to the pot-holes.

"And where are we now?" asked Markham hopelessly, when we were again seated in the drawing-room. "Every discovery seems to throw this case deeper into the realm of impenetrable mystery. There's apparently no line of investigation that leads anywhere except into a blank wall."

"I wouldn't say that," Vance replied cheerfully. "Really, y' know, I thought things were shaping up rather well. Doremus gave us many revealin' items. The technique of the murder was unique,—the very brutality and insanity of it holds amazin' possibilities. Y' know, Markham, I've an idea we weren't expected to find the body. Otherwise, why should it have been so carefully hidden? The murderer wanted us to think Montague merely chose to disappear from his present haunts."

Heath nodded ponderously.

"I get what you mean, Mr. Vance. That note in Montague's clothes, for instance. My idea is that this dame who wrote the note had an accomplice in the car at the gate, who did the dirty work and threw the bird in that pot-hole…"

"That won't do, Sergeant," Vance interrupted in a kindly but firm voice. "Were that the case, we'd have found Montague's footprints leading out of the pool."

"Well, why didn't we find them?" demanded Markham with exasperation. "Montague's body was found down the East Road. He must have got out of the pool some way."

"Yes, yes; he got out some way." Vance frowned at his cigarette: something was troubling him deeply. "That's the devilish part of it… Somehow I think, Markham, that Montague didn't leave any footprints *because he wasn't able to.* He may not have wanted to escape from the pool—he may have been carried out…"

"My God!" Markham rose nervously and took a deep breath. "You're not reverting to that hideous flying-dragon theory, are you?"

"My dear fellow!" Vance spoke in soothing reprimand. "At least not the kind of dragon you imagine. I was merely intimatin' that the hapless Montague was killed in the pool and carried to the pot-hole."

"But that theory," protested Markham, "only involves us in deeper complications."

"I'm aware of that fact," sighed Vance. "But, after all, the chappie *did* travel, in some manner, from the pool to the pot-hole. And it's obvious he didn't go voluntarily."

"What about the car that was heard on the East Road?" The practical Sergeant projected himself again into the discussion.

"Quite." Vance nodded. "That car puzzles me no end. It may have been Montague's means of transportation. But, dash it all! how did he get from the pool to the car? And why was he mutilated in such shockin' fashion?"

He smoked a while in silence, and then turned to Markham.

"Y' know, there are several persons here who have not yet heard of the finding of Montague's body—Ruby Steele, and Mrs. McAdam, and Bernice Stamm. I think the time has come to inform them. Their reactions may be helpful..."

The three women were sent for, and when they had joined us Vance told them briefly of the circumstances surrounding the discovery and examination of the dead man. He spoke in a matter-of-fact manner, but I noticed he was watching his listeners closely. (At the time I could not understand his reason for the procedure, but it was not long before I realized why he had chosen this means of apprising the various members of the household of our gruesome find in the pot-hole.)

The three women listened intently; and there was a short silence following the conclusion of his information. Then Ruby Steele said, in a low, sententious voice:

"It really bears out what I told you last night. The fact that there were no footprints leading from the pool means nothing. A man like this half-breed, Leland—with all his hidden powers—could accomplish seeming miracles. And he was the last person to return to the house here!"

I expected Bernice Stamm to resent these remarks, but she merely smiled musingly and said with troubled dignity:

"I'm not surprised that poor Monty has been found; but I doubt if miracles are needed to explain his death..." Then the pupils of her eyes dilated, and her breast rose and fell with accelerated respiration. "But," she went on, "I don't understand the marks on Monty's chest."

"Do you understand the other features of the case, Miss Stamm?" Vance asked quietly.

"No—no!" Her voice became almost hysterical. "I don't understand any of it." Tears came into her eyes, and she was unable to continue.

"Don't let it worry you," Vance consoled her. "You're frightfully wrought up, don't y' know."

"May I go now?" she asked pleadingly.

"Of course." Vance rose and escorted her to the door.

When he returned to his chair Teeny McAdam spoke. She had been smoking with tense abstractedness for some time; I doubt if she had even heard any of Bernice Stamm's remarks. Suddenly she wheeled toward Vance, her features contracted and set.

"Listen!" she began, with peremptory desperation. "I'm sick of this whole miserable affair. Monty's dead and you've found his body—and I've got something to tell you. Alex Greeff hated Monty. And he said to Monty Friday night—I heard him—'You're not going to marry Bernice if I can help it.' Monty laughed at him and retorted: 'What are you going to do about it?' Mr. Greeff said: 'Plenty—*if the dragon doesn't get you first.*' Then Monty called him a foul name and went up to bed..."

"What do you think Mr. Greeff was referring to when he mentioned the dragon?"

"I don't know. But later that night it occurred to me he might have been referring to Mr. Leland."

"Was it because of these remarks you screamed when Montague failed to come up after his dive?"

"Yes! I'd been worrying all day yesterday. And when Mr. Greeff jumped into the pool and made a pretense of looking for Monty I kept my eyes on him. But he immediately swam out of sight toward the cliffs on the other side—"

"And you kept your eyes strained in that direction?"

Mrs. McAdam nodded jerkily.

"I didn't know what he was up to—and I didn't trust him... Later, when he came back he whispered to me: 'Montague's gone—and good riddance.' Even then I couldn't see how he'd accomplished the thing. But now that you've found Monty's body in the pot-hole, I had to tell you what I know."

Vance nodded sympathetically.

"But why were you upset when I told you of the splash in the pool late last night?"

"I don't know—exactly." The woman spoke hurriedly and excitedly. "But I thought it might be part of the plot to kill Monty—or maybe Monty's body being thrown from the cliff— or some one in the water *doing dreadful things to him*... Oh, I didn't know what it might be, but I was afraid...afraid—" Her voice died away, and she caught her breath.

Vance rose and regarded her rather coldly.

"Thank you for your information," he said, bowing. "I'm sorry, and all that, to have upset you. You and Miss Steele may return to the library now. There are a few other matters to be attended to. And if we need your assistance later I'm sure you'll both be good enough to give it."

When they had gone a brief discussion followed as to the best means of proceeding with the case. The greatest difficulty lay in the fact that there seemed to be nothing tangible to take hold of. Montague's murdered body was a reality, of course, and there were various suspects—that is, persons with a motive for killing the man. But there were no connecting links, no indicated lines of investigation, and no clues pointing in any specific direction. The actual *modus operandi* of the murder was in itself an incalculable mystery. And over the whole situation hung the sinister mythology of a dragon.

Routine police work was, however, in order; and the Sergeant, with his trained official mind, insisted on carrying this work through without further delay. Markham agreed with him; and Vance, who, for the solution of criminal problems, depended largely upon intuitive processes and psychological reasoning, finally acquiesced. The case had deeply impressed him: it held elements that profoundly appealed to his nature, and he was loath to spare even an hour for the Sergeant's routine activities. Moreover, he had, I knew, several definite, even if only vaguely formulated, ideas concerning the case.

"A very simple key," he said, "is all that's needed to unlock the door of this fantastic mystery. But without that key we're helpless…My word, what an amazin' situation! There are any number of people who admit that they are delighted with Montague's translation into the Beyond, and each one accuses one of the others of having manipulated his transit. But, on the other hand, the circumstances surrounding Montague's death seem to preclude the possibility of his having been killed at all. It was he who suggested the swim, and he dived into the pool in sight of every one… And yet, Markham, I'm thoroughly convinced the whole affair was carefully planned—deliberately enciphered with commonplace numerals to make it appear fortuitous."

Markham was weary and on edge.

"Granted all that, how would you propose going about deciphering the riddle other than by the usual measures which the Sergeant intends to take?"

"I have no suggestions at the moment." Vance was gazing meditatively into space. "I was hopin', however, to inspect Stamm's collection of tropical fish today."

Markham snorted with exasperation.

"The fish will keep till tomorrow. In the meantime, the Sergeant can clear up the routine matters."

CHAPTER FOURTEEN

An Unexpected Development
(Sunday, August 12; 5.30 p.m.)

IT WAS NEARLY half-past five when Markham and Vance and I left the old Stamm mansion and drove back to Vance's apartment. All the guests and members of the household had been given instructions to remain until the following day and not to leave the grounds of the estate. Stamm had generously cooperated with us in this respect. Greeff had raised objections, and even threatened us with his lawyer; but finally he had agreed to remain another twenty-four hours, in view of the complications that had arisen with the finding of Montague's body. The other guests had accepted Markham's decision without protest.

All the main entrances to the grounds were to be guarded; and the servants in the house were to be questioned for any possible suggestions, although nothing of importance was expected from their testimony.

Heath had decided to remain at the Stamm estate during this investigation and direct the activities. Other members of the Homicide Bureau were to take a hand in the case. Montague's associations were to be looked into; an attempt was to be made to find Ellen Bruett; and a canvass of Inwood was planned, in the hope of unearthing some information about the automobile which had been heard on the East Road. In short, the usual police procedure was to be intensively followed, with Sergeant Heath in charge.

"I see no other way to handle the case," Markham said despondently, as we settled ourselves in the sprawling wicker chairs on Vance's roof-garden.

Vance was troubled and distrait.

"You may be right. But the factors of this case are far from ordin'ry. The answer to the whole problem lies somewhere in the Stamm residence. That's a strange place, Markham. It's full of infinite possibilities—with its distorted traditions, its old superstitions, its stagnant air of a dead and buried age, its insanity and decadence, and its folk-lore and demonology. Such a place produces strange quirks of the mind: even casual visitors are caught in its corroding atmosphere. Such an atmosphere generates and begets black and incredible crimes. You have seen, in the last two days, how every one with whom we talked was poisoned by these subtle and sinister influences."

For a moment Markham studied Vance intently.

"Have you any particular person in mind?" he asked.

Vance rose and rang for Currie.

"I wasn't thinking of individuals so much as of the perverted psychological combinations of the problem. And no explanation can be reached without a recognition and consideration of this fantastic dragon—".

"Vance! For the love of Heaven!"

"Oh, I'm quite serious. We'll go far afield if we do not recognize that fact." He looked up. "There are various types of dragons, don't y' know."

Currie appeared, and Vance ordered Moraine Coolers.*

---

* The Moraine Cooler was one of Vance's favorite summer drinks. It is ordinarily made with Rhine wine, lemon juice (with the rind), Curaçao, and club soda; but Vance always substituted Grand Marnier for the Curaçao.

"The dragon," Vance continued, "has always had a powerful hold on the imagination of man. We find the dragon, in some form, in most religions; and all folk-lore is peppered with dragons. The dragon goes deeper than a mere myth, Markham: it has become a part of man's inheritance from the earliest times; it has enhanced his fears; it has guided and shaped his symbolism; it has put strange notions in his head by coloring and distorting his imagination. Without the dragon the history of man would be a very different record from what it is today. None of us can entirely escape the dragon myth: it is too much an integral part of our deeper and more primitive natures. That's why I say that we cannot ignore the dragon in dealing with a criminal case which is, at bottom, dragonish..."

Vance moved a little in his chair, and his eyes roamed dreamily over the hazy skyline of Manhattan.

"Where the conception of the dragon originated no one knows; but it is probably the most tenacious of all ancient superstitions. The Christian devil is nothing but a modified dragon of ancient folk-lore. There have, of course, been many speculations as to the origin of this supernatural monster, and Moncure Conway, in his 'Demonology and Devil-Lore,' says it is the result of a confused memory of prehistoric saurians. But other researchers—Sir James George Scott, for instance—take issue with Conway and attribute the conception of the dragon to the primitive imagination in connection with snakes. But whatever the origin, it is a persistent and varied superstition. The dragon has taken many forms in man's mind. It is a far cry, for example, from the Indian Vrtra and the Greek Hydra to the mild Burmese dragon and the *drakos* of the European Gipsies. And neither of these conceptions is comparable with the enormous tortoise which King Thai-to saw swimming toward his royal bark."

Vance sipped his drink, which Currie had just served.

"Every land and every people, Markham, has had its dragons. Even in ancient Egypt the dragon became more or less identified with Seth and fought against Horus in the form of water-monsters. And in the Papyrus of Ani—or Book of the Dead—we read of the fire-breathing dragon Apop, to whom the wicked were thrown. But the dragon was not always a monster. A dragon-horse brought Fu Hsi the Eight Diagrams nearly 3000 years B.C.; and whenever the Yellow Emperor saw dragons he knew that prosperity was at hand. Chinese mythology, in fact, is filled with dragons, both benevolent and malevolent. The Fifth Moon Feast in memory of Ch'ü Yüan's suicide is called the Dragon Festival; and Fei Ch'ang-fang's magic rod turned into a dragon and aided him in conquering the ogres of darkness. In the Buddhist myths we find many references to the dragon as associated with fish; and there is at least one instance where the Dragon King himself was carried off to sea in the body of a fish…"

Markham looked up sharply.

"Are you insinuating—" he began; but Vance interrupted him.

"No, oh no," he said. "I am not referring to Stamm's collection of tropicals. It's the dragon myth itself that fascinates me… In all the Indo-Chinese countries we find the snake—not the fish—as the basis of the dragon. Probably this conception was brought from China and Japan, where the water-snake was formerly worshipped as a god. In Indo-Chinese mythology there are any number of dragon-myths, after the fashion of the Chutia Nagpur tradition. There is the Naga Min, who is at times represented with coils long enough to embrace an entire pagoda; and Galon, the Burmese dragon who appeared like the Indian Garuda; and Bilu, a dragon ogre who fed on human flesh and never cast a shadow. And you perhaps recall the myth of Hkun Ai and his Naga princess who was the daughter of the King of the Dragons, and how he spied upon her and her court one night, only to find that the entire countryside and all the lakes around were filled with these gigantic writhing creatures… In the Han Dynasty the Spirit of the East was Thang-long, the Blue Dragon; and in the legends of the Karens we find the spirit of Satan symbolized as a dragon.

The mythology of the Tongkingese abounds in dragons; and their secret hiding-places exist to this day. Buddhist and Taoist tales are filled with dragon lore. Even the great Temple of Linh-lanh was supposed to have been built on a dragon's head. There was a dragon guardian of the city of Hanoi; and in the Ly Dynasty King Thaiton named the capital Thanh-long, meaning the Dragon City. The protective idea of the dragon, d' ye see, is also well established in folk-lore. At Pokhar in Rajputana there is a sacred lake which, tradition tells us, was once inhabited by a dragon who guarded the Burmese Temple nearby... And the dragon permeates the legends of Siam—he was probably brought from India along with Brahmanism and serpent worship. Siamese dragons lived in caves and under the water..."

Vance gazed up meditatively at the sky.

"You will note how the water motif runs through these ancient superstitions," he continued. "Perhaps one of the most significant tales—this is from the Japanese—is that of Kobo Daishi, the founder of Shingon Buddhism in the ninth century, who drew the ideogram for dragon on the waters of a stream in the Kozuke district. When he had finished the ideogram it became an actual dragon which rose over the water; and it is supposed to have hovered there ever since—a superstition no doubt based on the dense vapors which constantly rise from this mountain stream. And similar to this tale is the one in which Le-loi's sword turned into a jade-colored dragon and disappeared in the waters of the sacred lake which, to this day, is called the Lake of the Great Sword. Then, there's the legend of the province of Izumo, in Japan, which tells of a water-dragon who demanded the sacrifice of a virgin each year, and of how Susa-no-wo slew him when he came up out of the river. The hero of course married the young lady he had thus saved... Japanese mythology, like the Chinese, is filled with Dragon Kings: we find many tales of them in the Shinto chronicles. One of the most significant legends connected with the Dragon Kings was that of a Chinese emperor who sent a shipload of treasures to Japan. During a storm a priceless crystal, which perpetually held the image of Buddha, was lost. It was supposed to have been stolen by the Dragon King who lived in the deep waters off the coast of Sanuki. The crystal was recovered from the Dragon Palace by a poor fisher-woman who, as a reward, had her only child brought up by the noble Fujiwara family. The water motif again, Markham... And do you recall how Toda saved the dragon folk in Lake Biwa by slaying the giant centipede with poisoned arrows?"

"No, I don't recall it," growled Markham. "And anyway, what's the point of all this?"

"The dragon myth, old dear—a most engagin' subject," Vance returned. Then he went on blandly: "Iranian mythology is filled with dragons, and they too are related, to a great extent, to water. In fact, the water of the earth was supposed to be the result of a god slaying a dragon who was hidden in the clouds. Indra, with his thunderbolt, slew the dragon of drought. Trita, the son of Aptya, also slew a tri-headed dragon named Visvarupa. And there's the story of Keresaspa who slew the dragon Srvra and for whom Zarathustra intervened. Saam, the vassal of Minucihr, met many a dragon, but his great battle was with the one that haunted the river Kashaf. Then there's the Iranian tale which relates of Ahura Mazda and the monster Azhi with the serpents springing from his shoulders. And in a Persian manuscript of the *Shahnamah*, in the Metropolitan Museum of Art, there is a vivid picture of Gushtasp battling with a dragon."

"I do hope," sighed Markham, "you're not going to ask me to go to the Metropolitan Museum to inspect the manuscript."

Vance ignored Markham's sarcasm and continued his treatise.

"In Armenian mythology we have the Median king, Azdahak—a name which means 'dragon'—who fought Tigranes and who, after his defeat, was compelled to bring his family and settle in Armenia. Anush, who was the Mother of Dragons, was, we are told, Azdahak's first queen. And here we have, perhaps, the origin of the dragon children about whom the old songs were written... Vahagn, the most popular of all the Armenian deities, was known far and wide as the 'dragon-reaper,' and in later syncretistic times he was identified with Heracles. Then there was the dragon of the Macedonians, closely related to the Indian Vrtra and the Armenian Vishap. This dragon was a gigantic and terrible monster. But in all Armenian mythology the dragon was, as with other primitive peoples, associated with meteorology and was supposed to represent the whirl-wind, the water spout, thunder and lightning, and heavy rain; and often the meteorological and the eschatological dragon were confused... The water idea connected with the dragon is found also in the records of the Mayas. The great ceremonial monolith at Quirigua is known as the Great Turtle or the Dragon, and played an important part in the Mayan religion."

Vance sipped his drink and glanced up at Markham.

"Am I borin' you horribly?" he asked.

Markham compressed his lips and said nothing; and Vance, with a sigh, settled himself more comfortably in his chair.

"In Semitic mythology," he went on, "the dragon played an important and sinister part. In the Babylonian Epic of Creation we read of the dragons which issued from the belly of Tiamat, released by Bêl and the Imhullu wind. These eleven dragons became gods of the lower regions and were later identified by the astrologers with various constellations. The Assyrian fish-man was one of the dragons of Chaos and represented the constellation Aquarius; and Ninurta, in the creation myth, was commanded by Anu and Enlil to conquer the *ushumgal*, or Great Sea Serpent..."

Vance smoked a while in silence.

"The Greeks, and also the Romans, had their dragons. The Chimera, with her devastating breath of fire, whom Bellerophon slew, was part lion, part goat, and part dragon. The Golden Apples of the Hesperides were guarded by a hydra-headed deathless dragon; and, of course, there was the dragon that Cadmus destroyed and whose teeth he strew over the earth… And throughout Celtic mythology we find dragons called *péist* or *béist*—probably from the Latin *bestia*—living in lochs in various reptilian forms. The saints destroyed many of these monsters; and if a dragon shrieked on May-Eve the land was barren until Lludd buried him alive. And there were the dragons which encircled the oaks in the grove of which Lucan wrote; and the two dragons of Merlin, who slept in hollow stones and, when dug up, did battle with each other. Also there's the dragon who issued from the earth at the sound of Cliach's harp playing…"

"But we have no harps," protested Markham wearily.

Vance shook his head sadly.

"My dear Markham! I fear you have no soul for classical lore. But we are dealing with a dragon of some sort, and the dragon superstition should not be entirely ignored. The conception of the dragon 5000 years ago, for instance, was that he could change his aspect whenever he chose. The five-clawed dragon of the Manchus was benevolent and symbolic of power, but the three-clawed dragon was inimical to man—the symbol of death and destruction."

"Come, come!" Markham looked up alertly. "Are you trying to get me stirred up by that imprint with the three claws?"

"Not at all. I'm simply borin' you with a few historical details which may, or may not, prove illuminatin' in our investigation. There are, however, many variations in the pattern of the dragon: some are depicted with bearded heads, some with scaly bodies, some with horns; but all with claws not unlike the marks we have found on the basin of the pool."

Vance shifted his position a little and went on.

"And there were many winged dragons in mythology, Markham. Though they lived in lonely pools and lakes and beneath the waters, they nevertheless could fly, and they often bore their victims incredible distances. For instance, there were the winged dragons who bore the chariot of Triptolemus through the skies. And Medea, as you remember, after slaying her children, fled to Athens in a chariot hitched to winged dragons which had been sent to her by Helios."

Markham rose and paced back and forth for a moment.

"What has all this dragon lore to do with Montague's death?" he asked at length.

"Really, y' know, I haven't the vaguest notion," Vance sighed. "But the myths of the Algonkian Indians are quite in line with the classical dragon myths; and it was these Indians who named the Dragon Pool in Inwood and are responsible for the superstition that attaches to it. The important character of the Algonkian myths is the Great Hare, whose name was Manabozho, and he did valiant battle with giants and cannibals and witches. But his outstanding vict'ry was when he slew the Great Fish or Snake that preyed on man. This monster was a water-dragon— *Amangemokdom.* He ruled the Powers of the Deep, and one of his favorite pastimes was to destroy and devour fishermen.... You see how interestin' the parallel is? And, Markham, we're dealing not only with cold-blooded practical facts, but with a sinister superstition; and we cannot afford to ignore either one."

Markham was restless and disturbed. He walked to the parapet of the roof and looked out over the city for several moments. Then he returned and stood facing Vance.

"Well," he said with a hopeless gesture, "granted what you say is true, what procedure do you suggest?"

"Really now," answered Vance sombrely, "I have no definite plans. But I do intend to go to the Stamm estate early tomorrow morning."

Markham nodded grimly.

"If you think it necessary, go by all means," he said. "But you'll have to go alone, for I have a busy day at the office tomorrow."

But Vance did not go alone. Strange and uncanny things happened on the Stamm estate that night. Shortly after nine o'clock the next morning Markham telephoned to Vance. Heath, it seemed, had called the District Attorney's office and reported that Greeff had mysteriously disappeared.

CHAPTER FIFTEEN

Noises in the Night
(Monday, August 13; 9.30 a.m.)

WE ARRIVED AT the Stamm estate before ten o'clock. Immediately after calling Vance Markham had left his office and stopped in 38th Street to pick him up. The murder of Montague had taken a powerful hold on Markham's imagination, and the news of Greeff's disappearance had made an irresistible demand on his activities. As he explained to us, driving out in the car, he saw in this new development the first tangible element in the whole affair; and he had now put all his other work aside to take personal charge of the case.

"I've had my suspicions about Greeff from the first," he said. "There is something sinister in the man; and he has impressed me all along as being involved in Montague's death. Now that he has escaped we can go forward with the investigation with something like a definite aim."

"I'm not so sure," Vance demurred. He was frowning and smoking thoughtfully. "The case is not going to be so simple even now. Why should Greeff attract suspicion to himself by taking leave of the party? We had no evidence against him; and he must have known that by bolting he would put in operation all the police machinery in the city. Very silly of him, Markham—distressingly silly. And Greeff does not strike me as a silly man."

"Fear—" Markham began.

"The man is fearless," Vance interrupted. "It would have been more logical for any other member of the party to have run away... It's most confusin'."

"The fact remains he's gone," Markham retorted testily. "However, we'll know more when we get there."

"Oh, quite." And Vance lapsed into silence.

When we reached the Stamm house Heath greeted us sourly at the entrance.

"A sweet mess," he complained. "The only guy I had my eye on has made his get-away."

"Sad...sad," sighed Vance. "But console yourself, Sergeant, and unfold your story."

Heath led the way into the drawing-room and planted himself aggressively before the mantelpiece.

"First," he said, addressing Markham, "I'd better report on what's been done since yesterday afternoon.—We checked up as best we could on this Bruett woman, but haven't got a trace of her. Furthermore, there hasn't been a boat to South America for four days; so I guess her story to Stamm about sailing was phony. We've checked on all the likely hotels, without any result. And here's a funny one:—she wasn't on the passenger lists of the boats that've arrived from Europe during the past two weeks. Think that over. There's something wrong about that dame, and she'll have a lot of explaining to do when my men locate her."

Vance smiled tolerantly.

"I don't wish to dampen your official ardor, Sergeant; but I fear you're not going to find the lady. She's far too sketchy."

"What do you mean?" snapped Markham. "The automobile on the East Road at the time stated in the note—"

"It's wholly possible, don't y' know," returned Vance mildly, "that the lady in question wasn't at the wheel... Really, Sergeant, I wouldn't wear my nerves out about her."

"I'm looking for her, and I'm going to keep on looking for her," Heath asserted with a show of belligerence. Then he turned back to Markham. "We didn't find out anything about Montague except what we already know. Always mixed up with some woman—but what good-looking actor isn't? He always seemed to have money—lived high and spent a lot—but he didn't have many jobs, and no one seems to know where his money came from."

"Any news about the car on the East Road Saturday night?" asked Markham.

"Nothing." Heath was disgusted. "We couldn't find any one in Inwood who'd seen it or heard it. And the officer on duty on Payson Avenue says no car came out of Inwood after nine o'clock that night. He was patrolling from eight o'clock on, and could have seen any car that came down the hill... Anyway," Heath added, "it may have coasted down the hill with the lights out."

"Or," suggested Vance vaguely, "it may never have left Inwood."

Markham shot him a quick look.

"What's back of that remark?" he demanded.

Vance made a slight gesture and shrugged.

"Oh, I say! Must there be hidden meanings in all my observations?... I was merely offering a counter supposition regarding the elusive vehicle."

Markham grunted.

"Anything else, Sergeant?"

"Well, we put the servants here on the carpet—the cook and the maid; and I went over that pasty-faced butler again." Heath made a wry face. "But all I got was the same line of gossip that we've been hearing for a coupla days. They don't know anything, and we can check 'em off the list."

"The butler," put in Vance, in a quiet tone, "is not without possibilities, Sergeant. He may not know anything, but no one with eyes like his can be devoid of suspicions."

Heath looked at Vance with a canny squint.

"You said something, Mr. Vance," he remarked. "But he's too slippery for me. And he's not giving anything away if he can help it."

"I didn't want to infer, Sergeant," Vance amended, "that you are to pin your faith on him for a solution to the case. I was merely implyin' that the fish-loving Trainor is full of ideas... But, I say, what about the amazin' disappearance of Alex Greeff? His truancy fascinates me."

Heath drew himself up and took a deep breath.

"He sneaked away some time during the night. And he was damn slick about it. I stayed here till eleven o'clock, after everybody had gone to their rooms. Then I went home, leaving Snitkin in charge. There was a man at the east gate and one at the front gate all night. Hennessey covered the south border of the estate, and another man from the Bureau was down below the dam watching Bolton Road. I got back here at eight-thirty this morning; and Greeff was gone. I've been in touch with his apartment and his office; but he hasn't showed up at either place. Skipped out clean..."

"And who," asked Vance, "apprised you of his dis-appearance?"

"The butler. He met me at the door—"

"Ah! The butler—eh, what?" Vance thought a moment. "Suppose we let him chant his own rune."

"Suits me."

Heath went from the room, and returned a few minutes later with Trainor. The man's face was ashen. There were deep hollows under his eyes, as if he had not slept for nights; and the flabbiness of his face was like a plastic mask.

"Was it you, Trainor," asked Vance, "who first discovered Mr. Greeff's absence?"

"Yes, sir—in a manner of speaking, sir." (He did not meet Vance's direct gaze.) "When Mr. Greeff did not appear for breakfast, Mr. Stamm sent me up-stairs to call him..."

"What time was that?"

"About half-past eight, sir."

"Was every one else down at the time?"

"Every one, sir. They were all in the dining-room. It was unusually early—if you understand me—but I surmise that no one slept very well last night. Mr. Leland and Miss Stamm were down-stairs before seven; and the others followed shortly afterward. Every one but Mr. Greeff, you understand, sir."

"And they all retired to their rooms early last night?"

"Yes, sir. Quite early. I put out the down-stairs lights about eleven."

"Who was the last to retire?"

"Mr. Stamm, sir. He had been drinking heavily again—if you will forgive me for saying so. But this is no time for reticence—is it, sir?"

"No, Trainor." Vance was studying the other closely. "Any little detail may be of vital help to us; and I'm sure Mr. Stamm would not construe your information as disloyalty."

The man seemed relieved.

"Thank you, sir."

"And now, Trainor," continued Vance, "tell us about this morning. At half-past eight Mr. Stamm sent you to call Mr. Greeff. And then?"

"I went to his room, sir—it is just down the hall from Mr. Stamm's—and I knocked. I got no answer, and I knocked again. After I had knocked several times, I got a little worried,—strange things have been happening around here, sir—"

"Yes, yes. Very strange things, Trainor. But continue. What did you do then?"

"I—I tried the door, sir." The man's eyes rolled, but he did not look at any one of us. "It was unlocked; and I opened it and looked into the room... I noticed the bed had not been slept in; and I felt a most peculiar sensation—"

"Spare us your symptoms, Trainor." Vance was becoming impatient. "Tell us what you did."

"I entered the room, sir, and made sure that Mr. Greeff was not there. Then I returned to the dining-room and indicated to Mr. Stamm that I wished to speak to him alone. He came into the hall, and I informed him of Mr. Greeff's absence."

"What did Mr. Stamm say?"

"He didn't say anything, sir. But he had a very queer look on his face. He stood at the foot of the stairs frowning. Then, after a few moments, he pushed me to one side and ran up-stairs. I went back into the dining-room and continued serving the breakfast."

Heath took up the story at this point.

"I was in the front hall when Stamm came down," he said. "He was looking queer, all right. But when he saw me he came right up to me and told me about Greeff's being gone. I did a little looking around, and questioned the men on post duty; but they hadn't seen any one leave the estate. Then I phoned to Mr. Markham."

Vance, for some reason, appeared deeply troubled.

"Amazin'," he murmured, busying himself with a cigarette. When it was lighted he turned back to the butler. "What time did Mr. Greeff go up-stairs last night?" he asked.

"I couldn't say exactly, sir." The man was growing noticeably more nervous. "But Mr. Greeff was one of the last to retire."

"And what time did you yourself go to your quarters?"

The butler moved forward, thrust out his head, and swallowed with difficulty.

"Shortly after eleven, sir," he replied in a strained voice. "I closed up the house as soon as this gentleman"—indicating Heath—"had gone. Then I went to my room—"

"Where is your room?"

"At the rear of the house, sir, on this floor—next to the kitchen." There was a peculiar intonation in his voice that puzzled me.

Vance sank deeper into his chair and crossed his knees.

"I say, Trainor," he drawled, "what did you hear last night, after you had gone to your room?"

The butler gave a start and sucked in his breath, and his fingers began to twitch. It was several moments before he answered.

"I heard"—he spoke with a curious mechanical precision—"some one slide the bolt on the side door."

"The door that leads out to the steps to the pool?"

"Yes, sir."

"Did you hear anything else? Any footsteps?"

Trainor shook his head.

"No, sir—nothing else." The man's eyes moved vaguely about the room. "Nothing, sir, until an hour or so later—"

"Ah! And what did you hear then?"

"I heard the bolt being thrown—"

"What else?" Vance had risen and was confronting the man sternly.

Trainor retreated a step or two, and the twitching of his fingers increased.

"I heard some one go up-stairs—very softly."

"To which room?"

"I—I couldn't say, sir."

Vance gazed at the man indifferently for several seconds; then he turned and walked back to his chair.

"Who did you think it was?" he asked lazily.

"It occurred to me that perhaps Mr. Stamm had gone out for a little walk."

Vance smiled indulgently.

"Really, y' know, Trainor, if you thought it was Mr. Stamm you wouldn't be so frightfully upset."

"But who else could it have been, sir?" the man protested weakly.

Vance was silent for a while.

"That will be all, Trainor," he said at length. "Tell Mr. Leland we're here and would like to see him."

"Yes, sir."

The butler went out, obviously relieved to have the interrogation over; and shortly afterward Leland entered the drawing-room. He was smoking his pipe calmly, and greeted us with more than his usual reserve.

"You know, of course, Mr. Leland," Vance began, "that Greeff isn't around this morning. Can you suggest any possible explanation for this?"

Leland appeared worried and sank into a chair by the table.

"No," he said, "I can see no reason why he should have run off. He is not the kind to run away from anything."

"Exactly my impression," nodded Vance. "Have you spoken to any of the other persons in the house about it?"

Leland nodded slowly.

"Yes, we all discussed it at breakfast and afterwards. Every one seems to be mystified."

"Did you hear anything during the night that might have indicated when he left the house?"

Leland hesitated before answering.

"Yes," he replied finally. "But I also heard something that would indicate that it was not Greeff who went out."

"You mean the rebolting of the side door an hour or so after it had been unbolted?"

Leland looked up in mild surprise.

"Yes," he said. "Just that. Shortly after midnight some one went out the side door, but later some one re-entered the house. I had not been able to go to sleep—and my hearing is particularly keen..."

"Trainor, too, heard some one go out and come in last night," Vance told him. "But he couldn't tell to what room the midnight prowler returned. Perhaps you are able to enlighten us on that point?"

Again Leland hesitated, and shook his head slowly.

"No, I am afraid not," he said. "My room is on the third floor, and several people were moving about below me. I will say this, however: whoever it was that came back to the house was very careful not to make any unnecessary noise."

Vance had scarcely looked at Leland during the questioning, and he now rose and walked to the front window and back.

"Is the room you occupy," he asked, "on the side of the house facing the pool?"

Leland took his pipe leisurely from his mouth and moved uneasily in his chair.

"Yes, it is just across the side passageway from Mrs. Stamm's quarters."

"Did you hear any one outside the house after the side door had been opened?"

"Yes, I did!" Leland sat upright in his chair and carefully repacked his pipe. "I heard voices, as if two people were talking in low tones. But it was only the merest murmur, and I could not distinguish what they were saying or who it was."

"Could you tell whether it was a man or woman speaking?"

"No. It seemed to me that they were deliberately pitching their voices to a whisper, to avoid being overheard."

"How long did this whispered conversation last?"

"Only a few seconds. Then it faded away."

"As if the two holding converse were walking away from the house?"

"Exactly."

Vance swung about quickly and faced Leland.

"What else did you happen to hear last night, Mr. Leland?"

Once again Leland hesitated, and busied himself with relighting his pipe.

"I am not sure," he answered reluctantly. "But there was a scraping sound at the far side of the pool, toward the East Road."

"Most interestin'." Vance did not relax his steady gaze. "Will you describe, as nearly as possible, just what you heard."

Leland looked down at the floor, and smoked intently for a moment.

"First," he said, "I heard a faint grating noise, as of one piece of metal being rubbed against another—at least, such was my impression. Then all was silence for several minutes. A little later the same sound was repeated and, still later, I could distinguish a low, continuous noise, as of something heavy being dragged over a sandy surface. This noise became fainter and fainter, until finally it died away altogether... I heard nothing more until perhaps half an hour later, when some one re-entered the house through the side door and replaced the bolt."

"Did these noises strike you as peculiar in any way?"

"No, I cannot say that they did. We had all been told we had access to the grounds, and I took it for granted, when I heard the side door open, that some one was going out for a walk in the air. The other noises—those on the other side of the pool—were very indistinct and might have been explained in various ways. I knew, of course, that a man had been stationed at the gate on the East Road, and I suppose I assumed— without giving the matter any particular thought—that it was he whom I heard across the pool. It was not until this morning, when I learned of the disappearance of Greeff, that I attached any importance to what I had heard during the night."

"And now, knowing that Mr. Greeff is gone, can you offer any explanation for the noises you heard?"

"No, I cannot." Leland thought a moment. "They were not familiar sounds; and while the metallic noise might have been the creaking of the hinges of the gate, there would have been no point in Greeff's opening the gate to make his escape, for he could very easily have climbed over, or walked round it. Moreover, the sound seemed to be much nearer to the house than the gate is. In any event, there was some one guarding the gate, and Greeff would not have chosen that avenue of escape—there are too many other ways of leaving the estate, if he really wished to do so."

Vance nodded as if satisfied, and again strolled toward the front window.

"Did you, by any chance," he asked casually, "hear an automobile on the East Road last night?"

"No." Leland shook his head with emphasis. "I can assure you no car traversed the East Road in either direction up to the time I fell asleep—which, I should say, was about two o'clock in the morning."

Vance turned leisurely at the window.

"Did Mr. Greeff," he asked, "by any action or any remark, give you the impression that he contemplated leaving the estate?"

"Quite the contrary," Leland returned. "He did grouse a bit about being detained here. He said it might mean the loss of some business at his office this morning; but he seemed resigned to seeing the affair through."

"Did he have any words with any one last night?"

"No, he was in unusually good humor. He drank a bit more than is his custom, and spent most of the evening, after dinner, discussing financial matters with Stamm."

"Any evidences of animosity between them?"

"None whatever. Stamm seemed to have forgotten completely his outburst of the night before."

Vance walked back and stood before Leland.

"What of the other members of the party?" he asked. "How did they disport themselves after dinner?"

"Most of them went out on the terrace. Miss Stamm and I walked down to the pool, but we returned immediately—a pall seemed to hang over it. When we came back to the house, Mrs. McAdam and Miss Steele and young Tatum were sitting on the steps of the terrace, drinking some sort of punch that Trainor had made for them."

"Where were Greeff and Stamm?"

"They were still in the library. I doubt if they had gone outdoors at all."

Vance smoked a moment in thoughtful silence; then he resumed his chair and lay back languidly.

"Thanks awfully," he said. "That will be all for the present."

Leland rose.

"If I can be of any help—" he began, and then contemplated his pipe. Without finishing the sentence he went from the room.

"What do you make of it, Vance?" Markham asked with a puzzled frown, when we were alone.

"I don't like it," Vance returned, his eyes on the ceiling. "Too many strange things have been happening in these ancient purlieus. And it's not like Greeff to walk out in the middle of the night..."

At this moment some one came hurrying down from up-stairs, and a few seconds later we heard Stamm telephoning to Doctor Holliday.

"You'd better come as soon as you can," he was saying nervously. Then, after a pause, he hung up the receiver.

Vance had risen and gone to the door.

"May we see you a moment, Mr. Stamm." His request was practically a command.

Stamm crossed the hall and entered the drawing-room. It was obvious that he was laboring under some suppressed excitement. The muscles of his face were twitching, and his eyes were staring and restless.

Before he could speak Vance addressed him.

"We heard you phoning to the doctor. Is Mrs. Stamm ill again?"

"The same trouble," Stamm answered. "And it's probably my own fault. I went up to see her a while ago, and I mentioned that Greeff was missing. Then she started in with her pet hallucination. Said he was missing because the dragon had got him. Insisted she saw the dragon rise out of the pool last night and fly down toward Spuyten Duyvil."

"Most interestin'." Vance leaned against the edge of the table and looked at Stamm through half-closed eyes. "Have you yourself any more rational explanation of Greeff's disappearance?"

"I can't—understand it." Stamm appeared nonplussed. "From what he said last night he had no intention of leaving the place till you gentlemen gave him permission to go. Seemed quite content to remain here."

"By the by, did you happen to go outdoors late last night?"

Stamm looked up with considerable surprise.

"Didn't leave the house after dinner," he said. "Greeff and I sat in the library chatting till he went up-stairs. I had a nightcap and went to bed very soon after he did."

"Some one," mused Vance, "let himself out by the side door around midnight."

"Good God! That must have been when Greeff walked out."

"But it seems some one came back through the side door an hour or so later."

Stamm stared with glassy eyes, and his lower lip sagged.

"You—you're sure?" he stammered.

"Both Mr. Leland and Trainor heard the bolt being opened and closed," Vance returned.

"Leland heard it?"

"So he told us a few minutes ago."

A change came over Stamm. He drew himself up and made a deprecatory gesture.

"Probably some one went out for an airing."

Vance nodded indifferently.

"That's quite reasonable... Sorry to have bothered you. I presume you want to return to your mother."

Stamm nodded gratefully.

"If you don't mind. Doctor Holliday is coming right over. If you want me I'll be up-stairs." And he hurried from the room.

When the sound of his footsteps had died out up the stairs, Vance suddenly rose and threw his cigarette into the grate.

"Come, Markham," he said with animation, moving toward the door.

"Where are you going now?" Markham demanded.

Vance turned at the portières. His eyes were cold and hard.

"To the pot-holes," he said quietly.

CHAPTER SIXTEEN

Blood and a Gardenia
(Monday, August 13; 10.15 a.m.)

Markham SPRANG TO his feet.

"Good God! What do you mean?"

But Vance was already on his way to the front door, and without answering, he ran quickly down the steps and took his place at the wheel of his car. Markham and Heath, silent and, I thought, a little dazed, got into the tonneau, and I followed. Something in Vance's manner when he mentioned the pot-holes sent a chill up my spine, and I wondered vaguely—without admitting to myself the hideous suspicion that had been roused in me by his sudden decision—what it was that he hoped to learn at the scene where he had discovered Montague's body.

We sped down the East Road, through the gate, and on toward the Clove. When we were opposite the pot-holes Vance threw on the brakes and sprang down to the ground. We followed him as he hastened to the foot of the rocks and drew himself up to the top of the low wall of the hole where Montague's remains had been found.

He gazed over the edge a moment and then turned back to us, his face grave. He said nothing but merely made a gesture toward the hole. Heath was already climbing to the top of the wall, and Markham and I were close behind him. Then came a tense moment of silence: we were all too horrified at the sight to speak.

Heath slid down from the wall, a look of combined anger and fear on his grim face.

"Mother of God!" he mumbled, and crossed himself.

Markham stood at the foot of the wall with a far-away look of horror and bafflement. And I found it difficult, in the peaceful atmosphere of that calm summer morning, to adjust my mind and emotions to the hideous thing I had just beheld.

There, in the depths of the pot-hole, lay the crumpled dead body of Alex Greeff. His position, like that of Montague, was unnatural and distorted, as if he had been dropped from a height into this narrow rock grave. Across the left side of his head ran a gaping wound, and there were black bruises on his neck. He wore no waistcoat, and his coat was open, exposing his breast. His shirt had been ripped down the front, like the jersey of Montague's bathing suit, and there were three long gashes in the flesh, as if a monster's claw had torn him downward from the throat. The moment I looked at him, mutilated in exactly the same manner as Montague, all the wild stories of the dragon of the pool came back to me and froze my blood.

Markham had brought his gaze back from the distance and looked wonderingly at Vance.

"How did you know he was here?" he asked huskily.

Vance's eyes were focused on the tip of his cigarette.

"I didn't know," he answered softly. "But after Stamm told us of his mother's comment when she heard Greeff had disappeared, I thought it best to come down here..."

"The dragon again!" Markham spoke angrily, but there was an undertone of awe in his voice. "You're not trying to intimate, are you, that the ravings of that crazy woman are to be taken seriously?"

"No, Markham," Vance returned mildly. "But she knows a great many things, and her predictions thus far have all been correct."

"That's sheer coincidence," Markham protested. "Come, come, let's be practical."

"Whoever killed Greeff was certainly practical," observed Vance.

"But, good Heavens! where do we stand now?" Markham was both baffled and irritable. "Greeff's murder only complicates the case. We now have two hideous problems instead of one."

"No, no, Markham." Vance moved slowly back to the car. "I wouldn't say that, don't y' know. It's all one problem. And it's clearer now than it was. A certain pattern is beginning to take shape—the dragon pattern."

"Don't talk nonsense!" Markham fairly barked the reprimand.

"It's not nonsense, old dear." Vance got into the car. "The imprints on the bed of the pool, the talon-like marks on Montague and now on Greeff, and—above all—the curious prognostications of old Mrs. Stamm—these must all be accounted for before we can eliminate the dragon theory. An amazin' situation."

Markham lapsed into indignant silence as Vance started the car. Then he said with sarcasm:

"I think we'll work this case out on anti-dragon lines."

"That will depend entirely on the type of dragon you have in mind," Vance returned, as he guided the car round and started back up the East Road to the Stamm estate.

When we reached the house Heath went immediately to the telephone and notified Doctor Doremus of our second gruesome find. As he hung up the receiver he turned to Markham with a look of hopeless desperation.

"I don't know how to handle this job, Chief," he admitted in an appealing tone.

Markham looked at him a moment and slowly nodded his head appreciatively.

"I know just how you feel, Sergeant." He took out a cigar, carefully clipped the end, and lighted it. "The usual methods don't seem to get us anywhere." He was profoundly perplexed.

Vance was standing in the middle of the hall, gazing at the floor.

"No," he murmured, without looking up. "The usual methods are futile. The roots of these two crimes go down much deeper than that. The murders are diabolical—in more than one sense; and they are closely related, in some strange way, to all the sinister factors which go to make up this household and its influences..." He ceased speaking and turned his head toward the staircase.

Stamm and Leland were descending from the second floor, and Vance immediately approached them.

"Will you gentlemen please come into the drawing-room," he said. "We have a bit of news for you."

A breath of air stirred in the room: the sun had not yet reached that side of the house. Vance turned to the west window and gazed out a few moments. Then he turned back to Stamm and Leland who were standing just inside the portières.

"We have found Greeff," he said. "He is dead—in the same pot-hole where Montague's body was chucked."

Stamm paled perceptibly and caught his breath. But Leland's expression did not change. He took his pipe from his mouth.

"Murdered, of course." His remark was half question and half statement.

"Murdered, of course." Vance repeated the words, nodding. "A messy affair. The same sort of wounds we found on Montague. A perfect duplication of the technique, in fact."

Stamm wavered on his feet, as if he had been struck a physical blow.

"Oh, my God!" he muttered, with a sucking intake of breath.

Leland grasped him quickly by the arm and led him to a chair.

"Sit down, Rudolf," he said kindly. "You and I have been expecting this ever since we knew that Greeff was missing."

Stamm slumped into the chair and sat glaring before him with unseeing eyes. Leland turned back to Vance.

"I feared all morning," he said simply, "that Greeff did not absent himself voluntarily... Have you learned anything else?"

Vance shook his head.

"No—nothing else. But I think we'll take a look around Greeff's room. Do you know which one it is?"

"Yes," Leland answered quietly. "I will be very glad to show you."

We had barely passed over the threshold of the drawing-room door when Stamm's strained, husky voice halted us.

"Wait a minute—wait a minute!" he called, struggling forward in his chair. "There's something I should have told you. But I was afraid—God help me, I was afraid!"

Vance regarded the man quizzically.

"What is it?" he asked, in a curiously stern voice.

"It's about last night." Stamm's hands clutched the arms of the chair, and he held himself rigid as he spoke. "After I had gone to my room Greeff came and tapped on my door. I opened it and let him in. He said he did not feel like sleeping and thought he would join me in another drink, if I did not mind. We talked for an hour or so—"

"About what, for instance?" interrupted Vance.

"Nothing of importance—generalities about finance, and the possibilities of a new expedition to the South Seas next spring... Then Greeff looked at his watch. 'It's midnight,' he said. 'I think I'll take a stroll before I turn in.' He went out and I heard him go down to the lower hall, unbolt the side door—my room, you know, is just at the head of the stairs. I was tired and I got into bed, and—and—that's all."

"Why were you afraid to tell us this before?" Vance asked coldly.

"I don't know—exactly." Stamm relaxed and settled back in his chair. "I didn't think anything of it last night. But when

Greeff failed to put in an appearance this morning, I realized that I was the last person to see him and talk to him before he went out. I saw no reason for mentioning the fact this morning, but after what you've just told us—about his body being found in the pot-hole—I felt that you ought to know—"

"It's quite all right," Vance assured him, in a somewhat softened tone. "Your feelings are quite natural in the circumstances."

Stamm lifted his head and gave him a grateful look.

"Would you mind asking Trainor to bring me some whisky?" he asked weakly.

"Not at all." And Vance turned and walked into the hall.

After sending the butler to Stamm we went up-stairs. Greeff's room was the second one from Stamm's on the same side of the hall. The door was unlocked and we went in. As Trainor had told us, the bed had not been slept in; and the window shades were still drawn. The room was somewhat similar to Montague's, but it was larger and more luxuriously furnished. A few toilet articles lay neatly on the dressing-table; a pongee robe and a pair of pajamas were thrown over the foot of the bed; and on a chair near the window lay Greeff's dinner suit, in a rumpled heap. On the floor, near an end-table, was a gaping Gladstone bag.

The inspection of Greeff's belongings took but a short time. Vance went first to the clothes-closet and found there a brown business suit and a sport suit; but the pockets held nothing of any importance. The dinner suit was then investigated, without any enlightening result: its pockets contained merely an ebony cigarette holder, a cigarette-case of black moiré silk, and two elaborately monogrammed handkerchiefs. There was nothing belonging to Greeff in the drawers of the dressing-table; and in the cabinet of the bathroom were only the usual toilet accessories—a toothbrush and paste, a shaving outfit, a bottle of toilet water and a shaker of talcum powder. Nor did the Gladstone bag yield anything significant or suggestive.

Vance had said nothing during the search, but there was an intent eagerness in his attitude. He now stood in the middle of the room, looking down, his eyes half closed in troubled thought. It was patent that he was disappointed.

Slowly he lifted his head, shrugged slightly, and started toward the door.

"I'm afraid there's nothing here that will help us," he said; and there was something in his voice that made me feel that he was referring to some specific, but unnamed, object which he had hoped to find.

Markham, too, must have caught the undertone in Vance's voice which had conveyed this impression to me, for he asked crisply:

"Just what, Vance, were you expecting to discover in this room?"

Vance hesitated and turned slowly back to us.

"I am not quite sure... There should have been something here. But don't ask me to say what—there's a good fellow. I wouldn't know exactly how to answer." He smiled ingratiatingly and, turning, went out into the hall. The rest of us followed him.

As we reached the head of the stairs Doctor Holliday was just coming up from the main floor. He greeted us with reserved cordiality, and we were about to start down the stairs when, with what seemed a sudden impulse, Vance halted.

"I say, doctor," he asked, "would you mind if we went up with you? There's something of vital importance I would like to ask Mrs. Stamm. I sha'n't disturb her..."

"Come along," Doctor Holliday nodded, as he turned on the landing and swung his bulky frame up toward the third floor.

When Mrs. Schwarz opened the door for us Mrs. Stamm was standing at the open window overlooking the pool, her back to us. As we entered the room she turned slowly until her fiery eyes rested on us. There seemed to be a new glittering quality in her gaze, but there was no smile on her lips: her mouth was at once grim and placid.

Vance walked directly toward her, halting only when he was within a few feet of her. His expression was severe; his eyes were determined.

"Mrs. Stamm," he said, in a stern, quiet tone, "terrible things have happened here. And more terrible things are going to happen—*unless you help us*. And these other terrible things will not be of a nature that will please you. They will befall those who are not enemies of the Stamms; and, therefore, your dragon—that protector of your household—could not be held responsible."

A frightened look came into the woman's eyes as she stared raptly at Vance.

"What can I do to help you?" Her voice was a hollow monotone, as if she had merely thought the words and her lips had automatically articulated them.

"You can tell us," Vance answered, without relaxing his severity of tone, "where you have hidden the key to the family vault."

The woman's eyes closed slowly, as if from some great physical reaction, and she took a long, deep breath. I may have imagined it, but I received the strong impression that Vance's words had brought her a sense of relief. Then her eyelids went up quickly: a certain calm had come into her gaze.

"Is that all you wish to know?" she asked.

"That is all, madam—but it is vitally important. And I give you my word that the tomb of your dead will not be desecrated."

The woman studied Vance appraisingly for several moments. Then she moved to the large chair by the window and sat down. With slow but resolute determination she reached into the bosom of her black lace dress and drew forth a small rectangular scapular on which I could see the faded image of a saint. The stitching, which held the linen and chamois-skin together, was open at the top, so that the scapular was in actuality a small bag. Turning it upside down, she shook it; and presently there fell out into her hand a small flat key.

"Mrs. Schwarz," she commanded dictatorially, "take this key and go to my old steamer trunk in the clothes-closet."

Mrs. Schwarz took the key, turned stoically and, opening the small door in the east wall of the room, disappeared into the semi-darkness beyond.

"*Ja*, Frau Stamm," she called from within.

"Now unlock the trunk and lift out the tray," Mrs. Stamm instructed her. "Carefully turn up all the old linen you see there. In the right-hand back corner there is an old jewel box, wrapped in a damask tablecloth. Bring out the box."

After a few moments, during which Vance stood in silence looking out the window at the cliffs beyond the pool, Mrs. Schwarz emerged from the closet, carrying a beautiful Venetian box, about eight inches long and six inches wide, with a rounded top. It was covered in faded mauve brocaded velvet, surmounted with hammered-metal scroll-work.

"Hand it to this gentleman." Mrs. Stamm made an awkward gesture toward Vance. "The vault key is inside."

Vance came forward and took the box. He threw the catch and opened the lid. Markham had stepped up to him and stood looking over his shoulder. After a moment's inspection Vance closed the box and handed it back to Mrs. Schwarz.

"You may put it away again," he said, in a tone and with a look which constituted a command. Then he turned to Mrs. Stamm and, bowing, said: "You have helped us no end. And I want you to know that we deeply appreciate your confidence."

A faint smile of cynical gratification distorted the contour of Mrs. Stamm's mouth.

"Are you entirely satisfied?" she asked. (There was an undertone of both sarcasm and triumph in her voice.)

"Quite," Vance assured her.

He took his leave at once. Doctor Holliday remained with his patient. When we were again in the hallway and Mrs. Schwarz had closed the door behind us, Markham took Vance by the arm.

"See here," he said, frowning deeply; "what was the idea? Are you going to let her put you off with an empty box?"

"But she hasn't, don't y' know," Vance returned dulcetly. "She didn't know the box was empty. She thought the key was there. Why upset her by telling her the box is empty?"

"What has the key got to do with it, anyway?" Markham demanded angrily.

"That's what I'm trying to ascertain." And before Markham could say anything more, Vance turned to Leland, who had watched the entire proceeding in puzzled silence. "Can you show us where Tatum's room is?" he asked.

We had now reached the second-story landing, and Leland drew himself up with a curious start: his habitual air of cool reserve momentarily deserted him.

"Tatum's room?" he repeated, as if he doubted that he had heard Vance correctly. But immediately he recovered himself and turned. "His room is just here, across the hall," he said. "It is the one between Stamm's room and Greeff's."

Vance crossed the hall to the door Leland indicated. It was unlocked, and he opened it and stepped inside the room. We followed him, puzzled and silent. Markham appeared even more surprised than Leland had been at Vance's sudden and unexpected query about Tatum's room. He now gave Vance a searching, inquisitive look, and was about to say something but checked himself and waited.

Vance stood in the middle of the room, glancing about him and letting his gaze rest for a moment on each piece of furniture.

Heath's expression was hard and determined. Without waiting for Vance to speak, he asked:

"Do you want me to get the guy's clothes out and make a search?"

Vance shook his head in a slow, thoughtful negative.

"I don't think that will be necess'ry, Sergeant. But you might look under the bed and on the floor of the clothes-closet."

Heath drew out his flashlight and went down on his hands and knees. After a brief inspection, he stood up with a grunt.

"Nothing there but a pair of slippers."

He went to the clothes-closet and made another inspection.

"Just some shoes, that's all," he announced upon emerging.

Vance, in the meantime, had gone to the low-boy beside the window and opened the drawers, examining them carefully. He then went to the dressing-table and repeated the operation. There was a look of disappointment on his face as he turned away from the table and slowly lit a cigarette. Again his eyes roamed about the room and finally came to rest on a Queen Anne night-table beside the bed.

"One more chance," he murmured, as he crossed the room and drew out the small drawer of burl walnut.

"Ah, quite!"

He reached into the drawer and withdrew some object which we could not see. Then he approached Leland and held out his hand.

"Is that the key to the vault, Mr. Leland?" he asked.

"That is the key," said Leland simply.

Markham strode forward, his face an ugly red.

"How did you know the key was here?" he demanded angrily. "And what does it mean?"

"I didn't know it was here, old dear," Vance returned with exaggerated sweetness. "And I don't know what it means... But I think we'll take a peep at the vault—eh, what?"

When we were again in the lower hall Vance turned to Leland with a serious and stern gaze.

"You will remain here, please," he said. "And you're to make no mention, to any one, of the fact that we have found the key to the vault."

Leland appeared nettled at Vance's tone. He bowed with considerable dignity.

"I will, of course, respect your wishes," he replied, and turned toward the library.

Vance went immediately to the front door. We circled the house to the north, descended the steps to the pool, traversed the coping of the filter, and turned into the narrow tree-lined cement walk which led to the East Road. When we had

reached a point where we were entirely hidden from observation, Vance led the way through the shrubbery toward the
ivy-covered vault. Taking the key from his pocket, he inserted it
in the keyhole and turned it. I was astonished to see how easily
the tumblers swung back and operated the bolt. Vance leaned
against the heavy door, and it moved slowly inward, rasping and
creaking on its rusty iron hinges.

A musty dead odor assailed us from the dimness within.

"Let's have your flashlight, Sergeant," Vance said, as he
passed over the threshold.

Heath complied with alacrity, and we stepped into the
ancient vault of the Stamms. Then Vance cautiously closed
the door and played the beam of the flashlight about the
walls and ceiling and floor. Even on that hot summer day
there was a damp and chilling atmosphere in this gruesome
half-buried tomb, with its encrusted walls of dank mortar, its
age-discolored marble floor, and its tiers of wooden coffins,
which stretched across the entire south side of the vault, from
the floor to the ceiling.

After a casual inspection Vance knelt down and examined
the floor carefully.

"Some one's been walking round here recently," he
remarked. He moved the circle of light along the marble tiles,
toward the coffins. On one of the tiles were two small dark
spots.

Stepping toward them, Vance leaned over. Then he moist-
ened a finger and touched one of them. When he moved his
finger directly into the light there was visible a dark red smudge.

"That will be blood, Markham," he commented dryly, as
he stood up.

Again he moved the flashlight back and forth across the
floor, systematically traversing each of the large marble tiles.
Suddenly he stepped forward, toward the north wall of the
vault and, reaching swiftly down, picked up something which
I had not even noticed, although my eyes had been following
the sweep of the light.

"Oh, my aunt! That's interestin'." He extended his hand in the circle of intense illumination cast by the flashlight.

We beheld there a small gardenia, still white and fresh-looking, with only the edges of the petals curled and browning.

"Greeff's gardenia, I imagine." Vance's tone was low and held a faint undercurrent of sinister awe. "You remember he wore one yesterday afternoon when we talked with him. And there was no gardenia in his coat lapel when we found him in the pot-hole this morning!"

CHAPTER SEVENTEEN

The Duplicated Death
(Monday, August 13; 11.15 a.m.)

W E CAME OUT of the chilly dank vault into the hot sunlight, and there was something benign and steadying in the vista of trees and shrubbery and the intimate, familiar objects of the outdoors.

"I think that will be all for the present," Vance said, in a curiously hushed voice, as he locked the ponderous iron door and dropped the key into his pocket. He turned, a deep frown on his forehead, and started back toward the house. "Bloodstains and a gardenia! My word!"

"But, Vance," protested Markham, "those marks on Greeff's body:—surely Greeff wasn't in the pool last night. His clothes were perfectly dry and showed no signs of having been wetted—"

"I know what's in your mind," Vance interrupted. "And you're quite right. Even if Greeff was murdered in the vault, the same cannot be said of Montague. That's the confusin' part of it... But let's wait a bit before we speculate." He made a slight gesture, as if to request silence, and continued his way across the coping of the filter.

When we had reached the south side of the pool and were about to mount the steps leading to the house, I happened to glance up. On the third-floor balcony sat old Mrs. Stamm, her elbows on the railing and her head buried between her hands. Behind her stood the imperturbable Mrs. Schwarz, gazing down at her.

Then suddenly there came drifting out of the library windows the blurred, cacophonic strains of a popular dance tune played *fortissimo* on the piano; and I assumed that Tatum was endeavoring to throw off the depressing pall that hung over the old house. But as suddenly as the raucous music had begun, it ceased; and at this moment Vance, who was leading the way up the steps, turned and spoke, with the air of one who had made a final decision on some moot and difficult problem.

"It would be best to say nothing to any one about our visit to the vault. The right time has not come yet." His eyes were troubled as they rested on Markham. "I can't fit the pattern together yet. But something horrible is going on here, and there's no telling what might happen if what we have just discovered became known."

He gazed at his cigarette speculatively, as if trying to make another decision. At length he added:

"I think, however, we had better speak to Leland about it. He knows we found the key to the vault... Yes, we had better tell Leland. And there's always the chance that he may have some explanation that will help us."

When we entered the house Leland was standing in the front hall, near the stairs. He turned quickly and looked at us uneasily.

"I had to leave the library," he explained, as if his presence in the hall required an apology. "Tatum started playing the piano. I am afraid I was a bit rough with him."

"He can endure it, I imagine," Vance murmured. "Anyway, I'm glad you're here. I wanted to ask you something about Tatum."

He led the way into the drawing-room.

"Did Tatum, by any chance," he inquired when we were seated, "accompany Stamm on any of his fishing or treasure-hunting expeditions?"

Leland looked up slowly, and there was a flicker of astonishment in his eyes.

"Funny you should ask that." His voice, though drab, was pitched a little higher than usual. "The truth is, Tatum did ship along with us to Cocos Island—an uncle of his, I believe, helped finance the trip. But he could not stick it out. He went all to pieces in the deadly climate there—too much alcohol, I imagine. We tried him on under-sea work for a while, but it was no go. He was just a burden to the expedition. We finally hailed a whaler and sent him to Costa Rica, where he picked up a liner back to the States."

Vance nodded abstractedly and dropped the subject. Slowly he took his cigarette-case from his pocket, chose a *Régie* with intent deliberation, and lighted it.

"We've been to the Stamm vault, Mr. Leland," he remarked, without looking up.

Leland glanced at Vance sideways, took his pipe from his mouth, and said indifferently: "I imagined as much. I have never been inside it myself. The usual thing, I suppose?"

"Quite the usual thing," Vance concurred. He looked up casually and smoked for a moment. "One or two little points of interest, however. There was a bit of blood on the floor—and the gardenia Greeff wore yesterday. Otherwise quite conventional."

Leland stiffened in his chair and then leaned forward. Presently he rose to his feet—it was obvious that he was deeply perturbed. He stood for several moments, gazing down at the floor.

"You found nothing else of an unusual nature?" he asked at last in a strained tone, without lifting his head.

"No," Vance replied, "nothing else. Do you feel that we overlooked something? There are no hidden nooks, y' know."

Leland glanced up quickly and shook his head with unwonted vigor.

"No, no, of course not. My query had no significance. I was merely shocked by what you told me. I cannot imagine what your discoveries portend."

"Could you not offer some explanation?" Vance asked quietly. "We would be most grateful for a suggestion."

Leland appeared bewildered.

"I have nothing to suggest," he said, in a low colorless tone. "I would be only too glad…" His voice trailed off and he stared again at the floor, as if weighing the possibilities of the situation.

"By the by," Vance went on, "that creaking noise you heard last night—as of one piece of metal against another I believe you expressed it—: might that have been the creaking of the iron hinges of the vault door?"

"It is quite possible," Leland returned, without taking his troubled gaze from the carpet. Then he added: "The sound certainly seemed to come from just that point."

Vance studied the man for some time without speaking. Then he said:

"Thanks awfully… I'd like to have a bit of a chat with Tatum. Would you mind asking him to come here?… Oh, and please don't make any mention to him—or to any of the others—for the present, of what you have just learned."

Leland moved uneasily, drew himself together, and studied Vance inquisitively.

"As you wish," he answered, and hesitated. "You found the key to the vault in Tatum's room:—do you think, perhaps, it was he who went to the vault last night?"

"I really couldn't say," Vance replied coldly.

Leland turned and started from the room; but he halted at the portières and looked round.

"May I inquire," he asked, "whether you left the vault door unlocked?"

"I took the precaution of relocking it," Vance informed him, in an offhand manner. After a slight pause he added: "I have the key in my pocket. I intend to keep it until this investigation is brought to a satisfact'ry close."

Leland regarded him for a moment in silence. Then he nodded slowly.

"I am glad of that. I think that is wise." He turned and walked across the hall toward the library.

When Tatum entered the drawing-room it was obvious that he was in a sullen, defiant mood. He did not greet any of us, but stood inside the door, looking us over with smouldering, cynical eyes.

Vance rose as he entered the room and, moving to the centre-table, beckoned to him peremptorily. When the man had swaggered to the table Vance took the vault key from his pocket and laid it down before the other's gaze.

"Did you ever see that key?" he asked.

Tatum looked at the key with a smirk, studied it for a few moments, and shrugged.

"No, I never saw it before," he replied flatly. "Any mystery attached to it?"

"A bit of a mystery," Vance told him, picking up the key and resuming his seat. "We found it in your room this morning."

"Maybe it's the key to the situation," Tatum sneered, with cold, half-closed eyes.

"Yes, yes, of course… Quite." Vance smiled faintly. "But, as I've said, it was found in your room."

The man smoked a minute, without moving. Then he raised his hand and took his cigarette from his lips. (I particularly noted that his fingers were as steady as steel.)

"What of it?" he asked, with exaggerated indifference. "You will probably find plenty of junk in the rooms of this rotting old house." He turned to Vance with a hard mirthless smile which barely contorted the corners of his mouth. "You know, I don't live here—I'm only a guest. Am I supposed to be frightened, or have the jitters, or go into hysterics, because you found an old rusty key in my room up-stairs?"

"Oh, no, nothing like that," Vance' assured him lightly. "You're acting in the most highly approved manner."

"Well, where do we go from here?" Tatum's tone was contemptuous.

"Figuratively speaking, we go to the vault." Vance spoke with unusual mildness.

Tatum appeared puzzled. "What vault?"

"The ancestral vault of the Stamms."

"And where might that be?"

"Just the other side of the pool, hidden in the spruce trees, beyond the little cement walk."

Again Tatum's eyes narrowed, and the contours of his face formed into a rigid defensive mask.

"Are you trying to spoof me?" he asked, in a metallic voice.

"No, no," Vance assured him. "I'm merely answering your question... I say, don't you know about the vault?"

Tatum shifted his eyes and grinned.

"Never saw it and never heard of it." Suddenly he wheeled round, crushed out his cigarette, and glared truculently at Vance. "What's the idea?" he demanded. (His nerves seemed to have snapped.) "Are you trying to pin something on me?"

Vance studied the man indifferently for a while and then shook his head.

"Not even a gardenia," he replied sweetly.

Tatum started, and his eyes closed to mere slits.

"I know what you mean by that!" His face paled, and his long flat fingers began to twitch. "Greeff was wearing a gardenia last night, wasn't he? Maybe you're going to tell me that you also found a gardenia in my room."

Vance seemed puzzled for a moment at the man's words, but in an instant his face cleared.

"No," he said, "the gardenia was not in your room. But really, y' know, the possible presence of Greeff's posy in your boudoir shouldn't be so upsetting—unless, of course, Greeff has met with foul play."

Another grim, ironic smile moved the muscles of Tatum's mouth.

"He met with foul play all right—the same as Montague. Greeff didn't run away; and there are too many people round here that would be glad to see him smeared out."

"And you're one of those people, aren't you?" Vance returned dulcetly.

"Sure I am." Tatum thrust out his jaw, and his eyes became venomous. "But that doesn't mean that I did it."

"No, that doesn't mean that you did it." Vance rose and waved his hand in dismissal. "That will be all for the present. But, if I were you, I would control my musical impulses. Leland might decide that you too were due for a bit of killin'."

Tatum grinned viciously.

"That half-breed!" And, with an awkward gesture of contempt, he went from the room.

"A hard-bitten character," Markham commented when the man was out of hearing.

"True," Vance nodded. "But shrewd."

"It seems to me," said Markham, rising, and pacing nervously up and down, "that if we could learn who managed to get the vault key from old Mrs. Stamm's trunk, we'd know a lot more about the deviltry that went on here last night."

Vance shook his head.

"I doubt if the key has been in the trunk for years. It may never have been there, Markham. The hiding of the key, and all the secrecy, may be just another hallucination on Mrs. Stamm's part—an hallucination closely connected with the dragon..."

"But why, in Heaven's name, was the key in Tatum's room? Tatum struck me as telling the truth when he said he'd never seen it before."

Vance gave Markham a quick, curious look.

"The chap was certainly convincing..."

Markham halted and looked down at Vance.

"I can't see any way of tackling this case," he remarked despondently. "Every factor in it that we try to touch turns out to be a sort of *Fata Morgana*. There's nothing tangible to take hold of. The situation even precludes plausible theorizing."

"Don't give way to discouragement, old dear," Vance consoled him. "It's not as Cimmerian as it appears. The whole difficulty is that we've been attacking the problem from a too rational and ordin'ry point of view. We've been trying to make a conventional peg fit into a sinister and bizarre hole. There are extr'ordin'ry elements in this case..."

"Damn it, Vance!" Markham uttered the expletive with unwonted passion. "You're not reverting to that incredible dragon theory, I hope."

Before Vance could reply there was the sound of a car swinging into the parking-space before the house; and a minute later Snitkin threw open the front door and led Doctor Doremus into the drawing-room.

"Another body, eh?" the Medical Examiner grumbled, with a casual wave of the hand in greeting. "Can't you get all of your corpses together at one time, Sergeant?... Well, where is it? And what's all the excitement?" He grinned at Heath with sardonic good humor. "Your dragon again?"

Vance rose.

"It looks that way," he said soberly.

"What!" Doremus was puzzled. "Well, where's the new victim?"

"In the same pot-hole." Vance took his hat and went into the hall.

Doremus squinted, and followed without a word.

The Sergeant ordered Snitkin to join us, and once again we drove round the house and down the East Road. At the pot-holes we stood back while Doremus looked over the wall into the shallow chasm beyond. After a cursory glance he slid back to the ground, and turned to us. There was a strange, startled look on his face: he had completely lost his cynicism and jauntiness.

"Good Gad! Good Gad!" he repeated. "What kind of a case is this?" He compressed his lips and made a jerky motion in Heath's direction. "Get him out," he ordered in a strained tone.

Snitkin and the Sergeant lifted Greeff's body from the pot-hole and laid it on the ground.

After a brief examination Doremus stood up and looked toward Markham.

"The same as that fellow yesterday," he said. "Same wounds exactly. Same fracture of the skull; same three scratches down his chest; same discoloration on his throat. Ripped wide open, bashed over the left side of the head, and strangled... Only," he added, "he hasn't been dead as long as the other one." He made a grimace at Heath. "That's what you want to know, isn't it?"

"How would twelve o'clock last night fit?" asked Vance.

"Midnight, eh?" Doremus bent down over Greeff's body and again tested the *rigor mortis*. "That'd make it about twelve hours... Right." He stood up and wrote out a removal blank. As he handed it to the Sergeant he said: "There was nothing found at the autopsy of the other fellow that changed what I told you yesterday, but you'd better get this one down to the morgue right away—I'll have time this afternoon to autopsy him." (I had never seen Doremus so serious.) "And I'm driving back again by Payson Avenue. I'm getting to believe in that dragon of yours, Sergeant... Damn queer," he muttered, as he walked to the road and got into his car. "That's no way to kill a man. And two of 'em!... I saw that stuff in the morning papers about Dragonfish.* Good Gad, what a story!" He released the brakes, letting his car roll down the road, and drove off toward Spuyten Duyvil.

Leaving Snitkin to watch Greeff's body, we returned to the house.

"And now what's to be done?" Markham asked hopelessly, as we entered the front door.

---

*   *The papers that day had carried spectacular accounts of Montague's murder; and the reporters had let their imaginations run riot over the possibilities of an actual aquatic monster having caused his death. A zoologist from one of the local universities had been interviewed and had expressed the opinion that such an explanation could not be scientifically refuted because of our scant knowledge of submarine life.*

"Oh, that's clearly indicated, don't y' know," Vance replied. "I'm going to take a peep at Stamm's fish collection. Really, you'd better come along. Tropicals are fascinatin', Markham." He turned to Trainor, who had taken Snitkin's place at the door. "Ask Mr. Stamm if we may see him."

Trainor glared at Vance fearfully; then drew himself up rigidly and went down the hall.

"See here, Vance," Markham protested irritably, "what's the point of this? We have serious work to do, and you talk of inspecting a fish collection! Two men have been murdered—"

"I'm sure," Vance interrupted, "that you'll find the fish highly educational..."

At this moment Stamm came out from the library and strode toward us.

"Would you be so good as to act as our *cicerone* among your aquaria?" Vance asked him.

Stamm evinced considerable surprise.

"Why, yes," he said, with an intonation of forced politeness. "Of course—of course. I'd be delighted. Come this way." And he turned and walked back toward the library.

CHAPTER EIGHTEEN

Piscatorial Lore
(Monday, August 13; 12.15 p.m.)

T HE LIBRARY WAS an unusually large room, severely but comfortably furnished in the Jacobean style, with great tiers of books reaching from the floor to the ceiling. There were windows to the east and west, and, in the north wall, facing us, was a large archway which led to the aquaria and terrarium beyond.

Leland was sitting on the davenport with one of the volumes of the Eumorphopoulos collection of ceramics on his knees. In one corner, at a small card-table, sat Mrs. McAdam and Tatum, a cribbage board between them. There was no one else in the room. All three looked up curiously as we entered, but made no comment.

Stamm led the way across the library and into the first aquarium. This room was even larger than the library, and had an enormous skylight as well as a row of high windows along both walls to the east and west. Beyond, through a second archway was still another aquarium, similar to the first; and beyond that was the terrarium with windows on three sides.

The aquarium in which we stood was lined with fish tanks of all sizes, reaching to the base of the high windows; and half-way between the walls, running the entire length of the room, were two double rows of additional tanks, set on a long metal rack. There were more than a hundred such tanks in the room, ranging in capacity from five to one hundred gallons.

Stamm, beginning at the tank nearest the door, on the left, led us about the room commenting on his living treasures. He pointed out the various types of *Platyœcilus maculatus*—*pulcher, ruber, auratus, sanguineus*, and *niger*; various *Xiphophorus hellerii* (the Mexican Swordtail) and the Red Helleri (a cross between the Swordtail and the Red Platy); *Mollienisia latipinna*, with their dotted mother-of-pearl sides; and Black Mollies, perfectly line-bred to enhance their original black mottled coloring. His collection of the genus *Barbus* was extensive: he had beautiful specimens of the opalescent red-finned *oligolepis*; the rosy *conchonius*; the *lateristriga*, with its chameleon-like golden, black and carmine coloring; the black-banded *pentazona*; the silvery *ticto*; and many others. After these came the species of the genus *Rasbora*, especially *heteromorpha* and *tæniata*; and still further were beautiful specimens of the Characinidæ, particularly of the sub-family Tetragonopterinæ—the Yellow, Red, Glass, Bronze, and Flag Tetras, and the *Hemigrammus ocellifer*, or Head and Tail Light fish.

In a series of tanks down the centre of the room Stamm pointed with pride to his specimens of the Cichlidæ—*Cichlasoma facetum, severum, nigrofasciatum, festivum* (the Flag Cichlid), *urophthalmus, aureum*, and so on. He also showed us several specimens of that enigmatical *Symphysodon discus*, about which so little is known, either as to its sex distinction or its habits.

"I'm working on this species," Stamm said, proudly indicating the blue-green brassy specimens. "They are closely related to the *Pterophyllum* and are the only one of their genus. I'll surprise the old-time aquarists yet."

"Have you succeeded in breeding any of the *Pterophyllum*?" Vance asked with interest.

Stamm chuckled.

"I was one of the first aquarists in the country to find out that secret... Look here." He pointed to an enormous tank of at least one hundred gallons. "That's the explanation. Plenty of swimming space, with heavy-stemmed Sagittaria for the eggs, and a good warm temperature." (There were many beautiful specimens in the tank, some of them twelve inches from dorsal to anal fin.)

He moved along the west wall, talking proudly and fluently of his fish, with the enthusiasm of a fanatic. Before we had completed the circuit he had shown us specimens of the *Æquidens portalegrensis* (the Blue Acara); tiny transparent glass fish (*Ambassis lala*); many species of *Panchax*, especially *lineatus* and the rare Nigerian species, *grahami*; a pair of pike-like *Belonesox belizanus*; the usual *Danio malabaricus*; such mouthbreeders as *Haplochromis multicolor, Astatotilapia moffati, Tilapia heudeloti,* and *Etroplus maculatus*; labyrinthine fishes, such as *Osphromenus, Macropodus, Anabas,* and *Ctenopoma*; and hundreds of *Lebistes reticulatus*.

Stamm waved his hand at this last large tank contemptuously.

"Scalare fodder," he muttered.

"Still," said Vance, "despite their commonness, there aren't many fish among the tropicals more beautiful than the Guppies."

Stamm snorted and moved on toward the room beyond.

"In here are the fish that really count," he said.

This second aquarium was similar to the one we had just quitted and contained quite as many tanks, but they were arranged differently.

"Here, for instance," said Stamm, standing before a tank at the right, "is the *Monodactylus argenteus*."

"Brakish water, of course," Vance remarked.

"Oh, yes." Stamm shot him a curious look. "Many of the tanks in this room are really marine aquaria, and, of course, I use brakish water also for my *Toxotes jaculator*—the Shooting Fish—and the *Mugil oligolepis*."

Vance leaned over the tank that Stamm had indicated.

"The *Mugil oligolepis* resembles the Barb, but it has two dorsals instead of one," he observed.

"Quite right." Stamm again looked at him curiously. "You've spent some time with fish yourself, haven't you?"

"Oh, I've dabbled a bit," returned Vance, moving on.

"Here are some of my best," Stamm said, going to a series of tanks in the middle of the room. And he pointed out to us some *Colossoma nigripinnis*, *Mylossoma duriventris*, and *Metynnis rooseveltii*.

"How do you manage to keep these rare Characins in such apparently good condition?" Vance asked.

"Ah, that's my secret," returned Stamm with a shrewd smile. "High temperatures, of course, and large tanks and live food…and other things," he added enigmatically, turning to another series of tanks along the west wall. "But here are a few fish about which even less is known." He put his hands in his pockets and regarded the tanks with satisfaction. "These are the Hatchet Fishes: the *Gasteropelecus sternicla*, the *Carnegiella strigata*, and the *Thoracocharax securis*. The so-called experts will tell you that the breeding habits of these species are not known, and that they cannot be bred in aquaria. Tommy-rot! I've done it successfully."

He moved further down the room.

"Here's an interesting one." He tapped on the front wall of a particularly attractive tank. "The Blow Fish—*Tetrodon cucutia*. Watch this."

He took one of the fish out of the water in a small net, and it inflated itself into the shape of a ball.

"Curious idea," Stamm commented, "—blowing oneself up to keep from being swallowed."

"Oh, quite human, I should say," Vance returned dryly. "All our politicians do the same thing."

Stamm grinned.

"I never thought of that," he chuckled... "And right next door here," he went on, "is the *Pantodon buchholzi*. Just look at those large transparent pectoral fins. I brought these Butterfly Fish with me from West Africa... And here are some beauties—the *Scatophagus*." He pointed to two tanks containing fairly large hexagonal fish—one tank of the spotted *argus* and the other of the striped *rubrifrons*. "And just here," Stamm continued, moving along the wall, "are a couple of *Luciocephalus pulcher*."

Vance looked at this fish closely and inquiringly.

"I've heard of them," he commented. "They are related to the Anabantidæ, I believe. But I didn't know any one was versed in their habits and care."

"No one but me," Stamm boasted. "And I might add that they are not bubble-nest breeders, as many believe, but viviparous—live-bearers."

"Astonishin'," Vance murmured.

Stamm directed our attention to a series of small individual tanks on the shelf above.

"Piranhas," he said. "A rare species. And savage devils:— take a squint at those wicked teeth. I believe these are the first ever to come to the United States alive. Brought them back myself from Brazil—in separate cans, of course: they'd kill each other if they were put together. Damned cannibals—the *Serrasalmus*. I had a couple that were nearly twenty inches long,—not the *spilopleura*: they rarely grow over a foot in length... And here," he went on, moving away, "is a nice collection of Sea-horses—the *Hippocampus punctulatus*. Better than those in the New York Aquarium..."

Stamm moved a little further on.

"Here's an interesting fish—pugnacious and dangerous. The *Gymnotus carapo*. Have to be kept separately. Known as the 'Electric Eel'—*Electrophorus electricus*. But that's all wrong, really. Though they have eel-like bodies, they are not eels at all, but related to the Characinidæ. These are only about eight inches long, but they grow to three feet."

Vance looked at the queer specimens closely: they were vicious-looking and repulsive.

"I have heard," he remarked, "that they are actually capable of electrocuting a man by a moment'ry contact."

Stamm pursed his lips.

"So they say, so they say."

At this point Tatum and Mrs. McAdam came into the room.

"How about a little battle?" Tatum asked of Stamm with a smirk. "Teeny and I are bored."

Stamm hesitated.

"I've wasted eight of my biggest Bettas on you now... Oh, all right."

He went to a wide niche in the east wall, where there were numerous quart tanks each containing one Siamese Fighting Fish. From the ceiling hung a globe of water, on three slender chains, at a height of about five feet from the floor. He took up a small round Brussels net and transferred two veil-tail fish—a beautiful blue-green and a purple one—to the suspended globe.

The two fish appeared to look at each other cautiously before attacking. Then, with brilliantly heightened color and with fins and tails twitching and spreading furiously, they rushed about. Coming close together and nearly parallel, they slowly rose, side by side, to the surface. Soon they seemed to relax, and sank to the bottom of the globe. These preliminary manœuvres continued for a few minutes. Then, with lightning swiftness, the fight was on. They dashed at each other viciously, ripping off scales, mutilating each other's tails and fins, and tearing bloody bits from the sides. Tatum was offering odds on the purple Betta, but no one paid any attention to him. The blue-green one fastened on the other's gill with a terrific grip, hanging on until he was compelled to rise to the surface for air. The other then attached himself savagely to his antagonist's mouth and relinquished his hold only when forced to go up for air himself. It was a terrible, but beautiful, sight.

Vance looked toward Tatum.

"You enjoy this sort of thing?" he asked.

"Too tame," Tatum complained, with an unpleasant laugh. "I prefer cock-fighting myself; but when there's nothing else to do…"

Leland had entered the room without our hearing him. He stood just behind Vance.

"I think it is a brutal sport," he said, his smouldering eyes on Tatum. "It is beastly."

The purple Betta was now at the bottom of the globe, mutilated and almost entirely stripped of its scales; and the other was attacking it to give the *coup de grâce*. Leland quickly picked up a small net and, reaching into the globe, removed the wounded loser and placed him in a small tank of Mercurochrome water. Then he went back to the library.

Tatum shrugged and took Mrs. McAdam's arm.

"Come on, Teeny, we'll play tiddledywinks. I'm sure Leland would approve of that."

And the two of them left the room.

"A pleasant little household," Stamm remarked with a sneer. He continued his rounds of the tanks, talking volubly and lovingly of his rare assortment of fish. That he had a wide and varied knowledge of them, and that he had done much important experimentation, was obvious. When he had come to the farther archway, he offered to show us his terrarium.

But Vance shook his head.

"Not today," he said. "Thanks awfully, and all that."

"I have some fascinating toads here—the *Alytes obstetricans*—the first ever to come from Europe," Stamm urged.

"We'll inspect the Midwives another time," Vance replied. "What I'm interested in at the moment are your bottled Devil Fish. I see some allurin' specimens over there."

Below one of the large east windows there were several shelves lined with jars of strange preserved sea-monsters of varying sizes, and Stamm led us immediately to them.

"There's a jolly little fellow," he remarked, pointing to a specimen in a long conical jar. "The *Omosudis lowi*. Look at those sabre-like fangs!"

"A typical dragon's mouth," Vance murmured. "But not as vicious as it looks. A fish one-third its size can conquer and swallow it—the *Chiasmodon niger*, for instance."

"That's right." Once more Stamm glanced sharply at Vance. "Any implication in that observation?"

"Really now," Vance protested, and pointed to a large glass receptacle containing a preserved fish of the most hideous and formidable aspect I had ever seen. "Is this one of the *Chauliodus sloanei*?"

"Yes, it is," Stamm answered, without shifting his gaze from Vance. "And I have another one here."

"I believe Greeff did mention two."

"Greeff!" Stamm's face hardened. "Why should he have mentioned them?"

"I'm sure I don't know." Vance moved along the row of bottles. "And what might this be?"

Stamm turned reluctantly, and glanced at the jar on which Vance had placed his finger.

"Another so-called Dragonfish," he said. "The *Lampro-taxus flagellibarba*." It was a wicked-looking, greenish-black monster, with blazing emerald markings.

Stamm showed us other specimens: the *Idiacanthus fasciola*, a serpent dragon with a long eel-like body, almost black, and with a golden tail; the wolf-like *Linophryne arborifer*, with a very large mouth and strong teeth, and what appeared to be a fungus-like beard; the *Photocorynus spiniceps* which, though very small, possessed a head half the length of its body, with an enormous jaw and serried teeth; the *Lasiognathus saceostoma*, known as the Angler Fish, with a jaw longer than the rest of its body, and equipped with a line and hooks for catching its prey; and other repulsive varieties of luminous Dragonfish. He also showed us a vermilion and yellow sea-dragon, with what appeared to be a coat of armor and waving plumes—a miniature dragon that looked as if it had been reconstructed from the imaginative pages of mythology...

"A most fascinatin' collection," Vance commented, as he turned from the jars. "With such an array of Dragonfish round the place, it's no wonder the old superstition of the pool persists."

Stamm drew up short and scowled: it was patent that Vance's last remark had upset him. He started to make a reply, but evidently thought better of it, and walked back toward the inner room without a word.

As we came again into the library Vance gazed about curiously at various potted plants in the room. "I see you have some unusual botanical specimens here," he remarked.

Stamm nodded indifferently.

"Yes, but I am not much interested in them. I brought them back with me on some of my trips, but only for the mater."

"Do they require any special care?"

"Oh, yes. And many of them have died. Too cold up here for tropical vegetation, though I keep the library pretty warm, and there's plenty of sunlight."

Vance paused beside one of the pots and studied it a moment. Then he moved on to another plant which looked like a dwarf evergreen but showed many tiny pale yellow berries— a most unusual plant.

"What might this be?" he asked.

"I'm sure I don't know. I picked it up in Guam."

Vance walked over to a rather high miniature tree in a large jardinière standing by the davenport on which Leland sat reading. This tree had large oblong glossy leaves, like the India-rubber plants that are cultivated in Europe for ornamental purposes, but these leaves were smaller and broader and seemed more profuse.

Vance regarded it a moment.

"*Ficus elastica*?" he asked.

"I imagine so," Stamm replied. (It was evident that his interest lay in fish rather than in plants.) "However, it's a curious type—maybe a cross of some kind. And it's undoubtedly stunted. Moreover, it's never had any pink buds. I got it in Burma three years ago."

"Amazin' how it has thrived." Vance bent over it closely and touched the dirt in the jardinière with his finger. "Any special soil required?"

Stamm shook his head.

"No. Any good fertilizer mixed with the earth seems to suffice."

At this point Leland closed his book. Then, with a sharp look at Vance, he rose and walked into the aquarium.

Vance drew out his handkerchief and wiped the moist earth from his finger.

"I think we'll be running along; it's nearly lunch time. We'll either be back or communicate with you later this afternoon. And we'll have to impose upon your hospitality a while longer. We do not want any one to leave here just yet."

"That will be perfectly all right," Stamm returned pleasantly, going to the hall door with us. "I think I'll rig up a windlass and get that rock out of the pool this afternoon. A little physical exercise, you know..." And with a genial wave of the hand he turned and went back to his beloved fish.

When we had returned to the drawing-room Markham turned on Vance angrily.

"What's the idea of wasting all that time on fish and plants?" he demanded. "There's serious work to be done."

Vance nodded soberly.

"I was doing serious work, Markham," he returned, in a low voice. "And during the last half-hour I've learned many important things."

Markham scrutinized him a moment and said nothing.

Vance took up his hat.

"Come, old dear. We're through here for the present. I'm taking you to my apartment for lunch. The Sergeant can carry on till we return." He addressed Heath who stood by the table, smoking in sour silence. "By the by, Sergeant, there's something I wish you would do for me this afternoon."

Heath looked up without change of expression, and Vance went on:

"Have your men make a thorough search of the grounds in the vicinity of the pot-holes—in the bushes and clusters of trees. I would be jolly well pleased if they could find some sort of grass-cart, or wheelbarrow, or something of that nature."

Heath's unhappy eyes slowly focused on Vance and became animated. He took his cigar from his mouth, and a look of understanding spread over his broad face.

"I get you, sir," he said.

CHAPTER NINETEEN

The Dragon's Tracks
(Monday, August 13; 1 p.m.)

On OUR DRIVE TO VANCE'S apartment we were caught in a sudden thunder-shower. Dark clouds had been gathering in the west for some time before we left the Stamm estate, though they had not appeared very menacing, and I thought they would pass us to the south. But the downpour was terrific, and our car was almost stalled on upper Broadway. When we reached Vance's apartment, however, a little before half-past one, the storm had passed over the East River, and the sun was shining again. We were, in fact, able to have our lunch on the roof-garden.

During the meal Vance deliberately avoided any discussion of the case, and Markham, after two or three futile efforts at conversation, settled into a glum silence.

Shortly after two o'clock Vance rose from the table and announced that he was leaving us for a few hours.

Markham looked up in exasperated surprise.

"But, Vance," he protested, "we can't let things remain as they are. We must do something immediately... Must you go? And where are you going?"

Vance ignored the first question.

"I am going shopping," he returned, moving toward the door.

Markham sprang to his feet resentfully.

"Shopping! What, in the name of Heaven, are you going shopping for, at such a time?"

Vance turned and gave Markham a whimsical smile.

"For a suit of clothes, old dear," he replied.

Markham spluttered, but before he could articulate his indignation Vance added:

"I'll phone you at the office later." And with a tantalizing wave of the hand, he disappeared through the door.

Markham resumed his chair in sullen silence. He finished his wine, lighted a fresh cigar, and went off to his office in a taxicab.

I remained at the apartment and tried to catch up on some of my neglected work. Unable, however, to concentrate on figures and balances, I returned to the library and began travelling round the world on Vance's specially built short-wave radio set. I picked up a beautiful Brahms symphony concert from Berlin. After listening to the *Akademische Fest-Ouvertüre* and the E-minor Symphony, I tuned off and tried to work out a chess problem that Vance had recently posed for me.

Vance returned to the apartment a little before four o'clock that afternoon. He was carrying a moderate-sized package, neatly wrapped in heavy brown paper, which he placed on the centre-table. He seemed unduly serious and scarcely nodded to me.

Currie, having heard him, came in and was about to take his hat and stick, when Vance said:

"Leave them here. I'll be going out again immediately. But you might put the contents of this package in a small hand-bag for me."

Currie took the package from the table and went into the bedroom.

Vance relaxed in his favorite chair in front of the window and abstractedly lighted one of his *Régies*.

"So Markham hasn't shown up yet—eh, what?" he murmured, half to himself. "I phoned him from Whitehall Street to meet me here at four." He glanced at his watch. "He was a bit annoyed with me over the wire… I do hope he comes. It's most important." He rose and began pacing up and down the room; and I realized that something momentous was occupying his thoughts.

Currie came back with the hand-bag and stood at the door, awaiting orders.

"Take it down-stairs and put it in the tonneau of the car," Vance directed, hardly lifting his eyes.

Shortly after Currie had returned, the door-bell rang and Vance came to an expectant halt.

"That should be Markham," he said.

A few moments later Markham entered the library.

"Well, here I am," he announced irritably, without a word of greeting. "I answered your curt summons, though God knows why."

"Really, y' know," Vance returned placatingly, "I didn't mean to be curt…"

"Well, did you have any success in getting your suit?" Markham asked sarcastically, glancing round the room.

Vance nodded.

"Oh, yes, but I didn't bring all of the new integuments with me—only the shoes and gloves. They're in the car now."

Markham waited without speaking: there was something in Vance's manner and tone which belied the trivial significa- tion of his words.

"The truth is, Markham," Vance went on, "I think—that is, I hope—I have found a plausible explanation for the horrors of the last two days."

"In a new sartorial outfit?" Markham asked, with irony.

Vance inclined his head soberly.

"Yes, yes. Just that—in a new sartorial outfit... If I am right, the thing is fiendish beyond words. But there's no other rational explanation. It's inevitable from a purely academic point of view. But the problem is to prove, from a practical point of view, that my theory fits the known facts."

Markham stood by the library table, resting both hands on it and studying Vance with interrogative sharpness.

"What's the theory—and what are the facts you've got to check?"

Vance shook his head slowly.

"The theory can wait," he replied, without looking at Markham. "And the facts cannot be checked here." He drew himself up, threw his cigarette into the fireplace, and picked up his hat and stick. "Come, the car awaits us, old dear," he said, with an effort at lightness. "We're proceeding to Inwood. And I'd be deuced grateful if you'd refrain from plying me with leading questions on our way out."

I shall never forget the ride to the Stamm estate that afternoon. Nothing was said en route and yet I felt that terrible and final events were portending. A sense of awe-stricken excitement pervaded me; and I think that Markham experienced the same feeling to some degree, for he sat motionless, gazing out of the car window with eyes that did not focus on any of the immediate objects we passed.

The weather was almost unbearable. The terrific storm that had broken over us during our drive to Vance's apartment had neither cleared nor cooled the atmosphere. There was a sultry haze in the air and, in addition to the suffocating humidity, the heat seemed to have increased.

When we arrived at the Stamm residence, Detective Burke admitted us. As we came into the front hall, Heath, who had evidently just entered through the side door, hurried forward.

"They've taken Greeff's body away," he reported. "And I've kept the boys busy on the usual routine stuff. But there's no new information for you. We're up against a blank wall, if you ask me."

Vance looked at him significantly.

"Nothing else on your mind, Sergeant?"

Heath nodded with a slow grin.

"Sure thing. I was waiting for you to ask me... We found the wheelbarrow."

"Stout fella!"

"It was in that clump of trees alongside the East Road, about fifty feet this side of the pot-holes. When I got back Hennessey told me about it, and I thought I would take a look around. You know that open sandy space between the Clove and the Bird Refuge—well, I went over that ground pretty thoroughly, knowing what you had in mind, and I found a narrow wheel-track and a lot of depressions that might easily be footprints. So I guess you were right, sir."

Markham glanced severely from Heath to Vance.

"Right about what?" he asked, with annoyance.

"One of the details connected with Greeff's death," Vance answered. "But wait till I check on the things that led up to the wheelbarrow episode..."

At this moment Leland, with Bernice Stamm at his side, came through the portières of the drawing-room into the front hall. He appeared somewhat embarrassed.

"Miss Stamm and I could not stand the noise," he explained; "so we left the others in the library and came to the drawing-room. It was too sultry outdoors—the house is more bearable."

Vance appeared to dismiss the other's comments as unimportant.

"Is everybody in the library now?" he asked.

"Every one but Stamm. He has spent most of the afternoon setting up a windlass on the other side of the pool. He intends to get that fallen rock out today. He asked me to help him, but it was too hot. And, anyway, I was not in the mood for that sort of thing."

"Where is Stamm now?" Vance asked.

"He has gone down the road, I believe, to get a couple of men to operate the windlass for him."

Bernice Stamm moved toward the front stairs.

"I think I'll go to my room and lie down for a while," she said, with a curious catch in her voice.

Leland's troubled eyes followed her as she disappeared slowly up the stairs. Then he turned back to Vance.

"Can I be of any assistance?" he asked. "I probably should have helped Stamm with the rock, but the fact is there were several matters I wanted to talk over with Miss Stamm. She is taking this whole thing far more tragically than she will admit even to herself. She is really at the breaking-point; and I felt that I ought to be with her as much as possible."

"Quite so." Vance studied the man penetratingly.

"Has anything else happened here today that would tend to upset Miss Stamm?"

Leland hesitated. Then he said:

"Her mother sent for me shortly after lunch. She had seen Stamm go down to the pool, and she implored me rather hysterically to bring him back to the house. She was somewhat incoherent in her explanation of why she wanted him here. All I could get out of her was that there was some danger lurking in the pool for him,—the dragon superstition coming back into her mind, no doubt,—and after I had a talk with Mrs. Schwarz, I telephoned Doctor Holliday. He is up-stairs with her now."

Vance kept his eyes on Leland, and did not speak immediately. At length he said:

"We must ask you to remain here for a while."

Leland looked up and met Vance's gaze.

"I will be on the north terrace—if you should want me." He took a deep breath, turned quickly, and walked down the hall.

When he had closed the side door after him, Vance turned to Burke.

"Stay in the hall here till we return," he instructed the detective. "And see that no one goes down to the pool."

Burke saluted and moved away toward the stairs.

"Where's Snitkin, Sergeant?" Vance asked.

"After the wagon came for Greeff's body," Heath informed him, "I told him to wait at the East Road gate."

Vance turned toward the front door.

"That being that, I think we'll hop down to the pool. But we'll take the car as far as the little cement walk, and approach from that side."

Markham looked puzzled, but said nothing; and we followed Vance down the front steps to his car.

We drove down the East Road as far as the gate, picked up Snitkin, and then backed up to the tree-lined cement walk, where Vance halted. When we got out of the car Vance reached into the tonneau and took out the hand-bag that he had directed Currie to put there. Then he led the way down the walk to the low area of ground at the northeast corner of the pool. To our left, near the filter, was a large circular wooden windlass, well anchored in the ground, and beside it lay a coil of heavy sisal rope. But Stamm, evidently, had not yet returned.

"Stamm's a neat chap," Vance commented casually, looking at the windlass. "He's made a pretty good job of that winch. It'll take a lot of energy, though, to get that rock out of the pool. Good exercise, however—excellent for one's psychic balance."

Markham was impatient.

"Did you bring me all the way out here," he asked, "to discuss the advantages of physical exercise?"

"My dear Markham!" Vance reproved him mildly. Then he added sombrely: "It may be I've brought you on an even more foolish errand. And yet—I wonder..."

We were standing at the end of the cement walk. Vance took up his hand-bag and started across the fifteen feet or so, which divided us from the rim of the pool.

"Please stay where you are just a minute," he requested. "I have a bit of an experiment to make."

He crossed the grass to the muddy bank. When he came within a few feet of the water, he bent over, placing the hand-bag in front of him. His body partly shielded it from our view, so that none of us could quite make out what he was doing with it. This particular part of the ground, always moist from its direct contact with the water, was, at this time, unusually soft and yielding, owing to the heavy downpour of rain early in the afternoon.

From where I stood I could see Vance open the bag before him. He reached into it and took out something. Then he bent over almost to the edge of the water, and leaned forward on one hand. After a moment he drew back; and again I saw him reach into the bag. Once more he bent forward, and threw all his weight on his extended hands.

Markham moved a little to one side, in order to get a better view of Vance's activities; but apparently he was unable to see what was going on, for he shrugged impatiently, sighed deeply, and thrust his hands into his pockets with a movement of exasperation. Both Heath and Snitkin stood looking on placidly, without the slightest indication of any emotion.

Then I heard the bag snap shut. Vance knelt on it for several moments, as if inspecting the edge of the pool. Finally he stood up and placed the bag to one side. He reached in his pocket, took out a cigarette, and deliberately lighted it. Slowly he turned, looked at us hesitantly, and beckoned to us to join him.

When we reached him he pointed to the flat surface on the muddy ground, near the water, and asked in a strained voice:

"What do you see?"

We bent over the small section of ground he had indicated; and there, in the mud, were outlined two familiar demarcations. One was like the imprint of a great scaly hoof; and the other resembled the impression of a three-taloned claw.

Markham was leaning over them curiously.

"Good Heavens, Vance! What's the meaning of this? They're like the marks we saw on the bottom of the pool!"

Heath, his serenity shaken for the moment, shifted his startled gaze to Vance's face, but made no comment.

Snitkin had already knelt down in the mud and was inspecting the imprints closely.

"What do you think about them?" Vance asked him.

Snitkin did not reply immediately. He continued his examination of the two marks. Then he slowly got to his feet and nodded several times with thoughtful emphasis.

"They're the same as the ones I made copies of," he declared. "No mistaking 'em, sir." He looked inquiringly at Heath. "But I didn't see these imprints on the bank when I was making the drawings."

"They weren't here then," Vance explained. "But I wanted you to see them, nevertheless—to make sure they were the same as the others... I just made these myself."

"How did you make them—and with what?" Markham demanded angrily.

"With part of the sartorial outfit I purchased today," Vance told him. "The new gloves and the new shoes, don't y' know." Despite his smile his eyes were grave.

He picked up the hand-bag and walked back toward the cement path.

"Come, Markham," he said, "I'll show you what I mean. But we had better go back to the car. It's beastly damp here by the pool."

He entered the spacious tonneau, and we did likewise, wondering. Snitkin stood in the road by the open door, with one foot on the running-board.

Vance opened the bag and, reaching into it, drew out the most unusual pair of gloves I had ever seen. They were made of heavy rubber, with gauntlets extending about six inches above the wrists; and though they had a division for the thumb, they had only two broad tapering fingers. They looked like some monster's three-pronged talons.

"These gloves, Markham," Vance explained, "are technically known as two-fingered diving mittens. They are the United States Navy standard pattern, and are constructed in this fashion for convenience when it is necess'ry to have the use of the fingers under water. They are adapted to the most difficult types of submarine work. And it was with one of these gloves that I just made the mark on the earth there."

Markham was speechless for a moment; then he tore his fascinated gaze from the gloves and looked up at Vance.

"Do you mean to tell me it was with a pair of gloves like those that the imprints were made on the bottom of the pool!"

Vance nodded and tossed the gloves back into the bag.

"Yes, they explain the claw-marks of the dragon... And here is what made the dragon's hoof-prints in the silt of the pool."

Reaching into the bag again, he brought out a pair of enormous, strange-looking foot-gear. They had heavy solid-brass bottoms with thick leather tops; and across the instep and the ankle were wide leather straps, with huge buckles.

"Diving shoes, Markham," Vance remarked. "Also standard equipment... Look at the corrugations on the metal soles, made to prevent slipping."

He turned one of the shoes over, and there, etched in the brass, were scale-like ridges and grooves, such as are found in the tread of an automobile tire.

There was a long silence. This revelation of Vance's had started, in all of us, new processes of speculative thought. Heath's face was rigid and dour, and Snitkin stood staring at the shoes with an air of fascinated curiosity. It was Markham who first roused himself.

"Good God!" he exclaimed, in a low tone, as if expressing his feelings aloud, but without reference to any listener. "I'm beginning to see..." Then he turned his eyes quickly to Vance. "But what about the suit you were going to get?"

"I saw the suit when I purchased the shoes and gloves," Vance replied, inspecting his cigarette thoughtfully. "It really wasn't necess'ry to own it, once I had seen it, and its workability had been explained to me. But I had to make sure, don't y' know,—it was essential to find the missing integers of my theory. However, I needed the shoes and gloves to experiment with. I wanted to prove, d' ye see, the existence of the diving suit."

Markham inclined his head comprehendingly, but there was still a look of awe and incredulity in his eyes.

"I see what you mean," he murmured. "There's a diving suit and a similar pair of shoes and gloves somewhere about here..."

"Yes, yes. Somewhere hereabouts. And there's also an oxygen tank..." His voice drifted off, and his eyes became dreamy. "They must be near at hand," he added, "—somewhere on the estate."

"The dragon's outfit!" mumbled Markham, as if following some inner train of thought.

"Exactly." Vance nodded and threw his cigarette out of the car window. "And that outfit should be somewhere near the pool. There wasn't time to carry it away. It couldn't have been taken back to the house—that would have been too dangerous. And it couldn't have been left where it might have been accidentally discovered... There was design in these crimes—a careful plotting of details. Nothing haphazard, nothing fortuitous—"

He broke off suddenly and, rising quickly, stepped out of the car.

"Come, Markham! There's a chance!" There was suppressed excitement in his voice. "By Jove! it's the *only* chance. The equipment must be there—it couldn't be anywhere else. It's a hideous idea—gruesome beyond words—but maybe...maybe."

CHAPTER TWENTY

The Final Link
(Monday, August 13; 5 p.m.)

VANCE HASTENED BACK down the cement walk toward the pool, with the rest of us close behind him, not knowing where he was leading us and with only a vague idea of his object. But there was something in his tone, as well as in his dynamic action, which had taken a swift and strong hold on all of us. I believe that Markham and Heath, like myself, felt that the end of this terrible case was near, and that Vance, through some subtle contact with the truth, had found the road which led to its culmination.

Half-way down the walk Vance turned into the shrubbery at the right, motioning us to follow.

"Be careful to keep out of sight of the house," he called over his shoulder, as he headed for the vault.

When he had reached the great iron door he looked about him carefully, glanced up at the high cliff, and then, with a swift movement to his pocket, took out the vault key. Unlocking the door, he pushed it inward slowly to avoid, I surmised, any unnecessary noise. For the second time that day we entered the dank close atmosphere of the old Stamm tomb, and Vance carefully closed the door. The beam from Heath's flashlight split the darkness, and Vance took the light from the Sergeant's hand.

"I'll need that for a moment," he explained, and stepped toward the grim tier of coffins on the right.

Slowly Vance moved the light along those gruesome rows of boxes, with their corroded bronze fittings and clouded silver name-plates. He worked systematically, rubbing off the tarnish of the silver with his free hand, so that he might read the inscriptions. When he had come to the bottom tier he paused before a particularly old oak coffin and bent down.

"Sylvanus Anthony Stamm, 1790–1871," he read aloud. He ran the light along the top of the coffin and touched it at several points with his fingers. "This should be the one, I think," he murmured. "There's very little dust on it, and it's the oldest coffin here. Disintegration of the body will be far advanced and the bone structure will have crumbled, leaving more room for—other things." He turned to Heath. "Sergeant, will you and Snitkin get this coffin out on the floor. I'd like a peep in it."

Markham, who had stood at one side in the shadows watching Vance intently and doubtfully, came quickly forward.

"You can't do that, Vance!" he protested. "You can't break into a private coffin this way. You can be held legally accountable…"

"This is no time for technicalities, Markham," Vance returned in a bitter, imperious voice… "Come, Sergeant. Are you with me?"

Heath stepped forward without hesitation.

"I'm with you, sir," he said resolutely. "I think I know what we're going to find."

Markham looked squarely at Vance a moment; then moved aside and turned his back. Knowing what this unspoken acqui-escence on Markham's part meant to a man of his precise and conventional nature, I felt a great wave of admiration for him.

The coffin was moved from its rack to the floor of the vault, and Vance bent over the lid.

"Ah! The screws are gone." He took hold of the lid, and with but little effort it slid aside.

With the Sergeant's help the heavy top was removed. Beneath was the inner casket. The lid of this was also loose, and Vance easily lifted it off and placed it on the floor. Then he played the flashlight on the interior of the casket.

At first I thought the thing I saw was some unearthly creature with a huge head and a tapering body, like some illustrations I had seen of Martians. I drew in an involuntary, audible breath: I was shocked and, at the same time, frightened. More monsters! My one instinct was to rush out into the clean sunlight, away from such a hideous and terrifying sight.

"That's a duplicate of the suit I saw today, Markham," came Vance's steadying, matter-of-fact voice. He played his light down upon it. "A shallow-water diving suit—the kind used largely in pearl-fishing. There's the three-light screw helmet with its hinged face-plate... And there's the one-piece United States Navy diving dress of rubberized canvas." He bent over and touched the gray material. "Yes, yes, of course—cut down the front. That was for getting out of it quickly without unscrewing the helmet and unlacing the backs of the legs." He reached into the casket alongside the diving suit and drew forth two rubber gloves and a pair of brass-soled shoes. "And here are duplicates of the shoes and gloves I brought here with me." (They were both caked with dried mud.) "These are what made the dragon's imprints on the bottom of the pool."

Markham was gazing down into the casket, like a man stunned by a sudden and awe-inspiring revelation.

"And hidden in that coffin!" he muttered, as if to himself.

"Apparently the one safe place on the estate," Vance nodded. "And this particular coffin was chosen because of its age. There would be little more than bones left, after all these years; and with a slight pressure the frame of the chest walls would have caved in, making space for the safe disposal of this outfit." Vance paused a moment, and then went on: "This type of suit, d' ye see, doesn't require an air pump and hose connection. An oxygen tank can be clamped to the breast-plate and attached to the intake-valve of the helmet... See this?"

He pointed to the foot of the casket, and I saw, for the first time, lying on the bottom, a metal cylinder about eighteen inches long.

"That's the tank. It can be placed horizontally across the breast-plate, without interfering with the operations of the diver."

As he started to lift out the oxygen tank we heard a clinking sound, as if the tank had come in contact with another piece of metal.

Vance's face became suddenly animated.

"Ah! I wonder..."

He moved the tank to one side and reached down into the depths of that ancient coffin. When his hand came out he was holding a vicious-looking grappling-iron. It was fully two feet long and at one end were three sharp steel hooks. For a moment I did not grasp the significance of this discovery; but when Vance touched the prongs with his finger I saw that they were clotted with blood, and the horrible truth swept over me.

Holding the grappling-iron toward Markham, he said in a curiously hushed voice:

"The dragon's claws—the same that tore Montague's breast—and Greeff's."

Markham's fascinated eyes clung to the deadly instrument.

"Still—I don't quite see—"

"This grapnel was the one missing factor in the hideous problem," Vance interrupted. "Not that it would have mattered greatly, once we had found the diving suit and had explained the imprints in the pool. But it does clarify the situation, don't y' know."

He tossed the iron back into the casket and replaced the cover. At a sign from him Heath and Snitkin lifted the heavy oak lid back to the coffin and returned the ancient box, with its terrible and revelatory contents, to its original position on the lower tier.

"We're through here—for the present, at any rate," Vance said, as we passed out into the sunlight. He locked the door of the vault and dropped the key back into his pocket. "We had better be returning to the house, now that we have the solution to the crimes..."

He paused to light a cigarette; then looked grimly at the District Attorney.

"Y' see, Markham," he said, "there was, after all, a dragon involved in the case—a fiendish and resourceful dragon. He had vengeance and hate and ruthlessness in his heart. He could live under water, and he had talons of steel with which to tear his victims. But, above all, he had the shrewd calculating mind of man—and when the mind of man becomes perverted and cruel it is more vicious than that of any other creature on earth."

Markham nodded thoughtfully.

"I'm beginning to understand. But there are too many things that need explaining."

"I think I can explain them all," Vance replied, "now that the basic pattern is complete."

Heath was scowling deeply, watching Vance with a look which combined skepticism with admiration.

"Well, if you don't mind, Mr. Vance," he said apologetically, "I'd like you to explain one thing to me right now.—How did the fellow in the diving suit get out of the pool without leaving footprints? You're not going to tell me he had wings, too, are you?"

"No, Sergeant." Vance waved his hand toward the pile of lumber beside the vault. "There's the answer. The point bothered me too until this afternoon; but knowing he could have left the pool only by walking, I realized that there must inevitably be a simple and rational explanation for the absence of footprints—especially when I knew that he was weighted down and wearing heavy diving shoes. When I approached the vault a few minutes ago, the truth suddenly dawned on me." He smiled faintly. "We should have seen it long ago, for we ourselves demonstrated the method by doing exactly the same thing when we walked out over the bottom of the pool. The murderer placed one of these boards between the end of the cement walk and the edge of the pool,—the width of that stretch of flat ground is little more than the length of the timber. Then, when he had walked out of the pool over the board, he simply carried it back and threw it on the pile of lumber from which he had taken it."

"Sure!" Heath agreed with a kind of shame-faced satisfaction. "That's what made that mark on the grass that looked like a heavy suit-case had been set there."

"Quite right," nodded Vance. "It was merely the indentation made by one end of the heavy plank when the chappie in the diving suit stepped on it..."

Markham, who had been listening closely, interrupted.

"The technical details of the crime are all very well, Vance, but what of the person who perpetrated these hideous acts? We should make some definite move immediately."

Vance looked up at him sadly and shook his head.

"No, no—not immediately, Markham," he said. "The thing is too obscure and complicated. There are too many unresolved factors in it—too many things to be considered. We have caught no one red-handed; and we must, therefore, avoid precipitancy in making an arrest. Otherwise, our entire case will collapse. It's one thing to know who the culprit is and how the crimes were committed, but it's quite another thing to prove the culprit's guilt."

"How do you suggest that we go about it?"

Vance thought a moment before answering. Then he said:

"It's a delicate matter. Perhaps it would be wise to make subtle suggestions and bold innuendos that may bring forth the very admission that we need. But certainly we must not take any direct action too quickly. We must discuss the situation before making a decision. We have hours ahead of us till night-fall." He glanced at his watch. "We had better be going back to the house. We can settle the matter there and decide on the best course to pursue."

Markham acquiesced with a nod, and we set off through the shrubbery toward the car.

As we came out into the East Road a car drove up from the direction of Spuyten Duyvil, and Stamm and two other men who looked like workers got out and approached us.

"Anything new?" Stamm asked. And then, without waiting for an answer, he said: "I'm going down to get that rock out of the pool."

"We have some news for you," Vance said, "—but not here. When you've finished the job," he suggested, "come up to the house. We'll be there."

Stamm lifted his eyebrows slightly.

"Oh, all right. It'll take me only an hour or so." And he turned and disappeared down the cement path, the two workmen following him.

We drove quickly to the house. Vance, instead of entering at the front door, walked directly round the north side of the house, to the terrace overlooking the pool.

Leland was seated in a large wicker chair, smoking plac-idly and gazing out at the cliffs opposite. He barely greeted us as we came forward, and Vance, pausing only to light a fresh cigarette, sat down beside him.

"The game's up, Leland," he said in a tone which, for all its casualness, was both firm and grim. "We know the truth."

Leland's expression did not change.

"What truth?" he asked, almost as if he felt no curiosity about the matter.

"The truth about the murders of Montague and Greeff."

"I rather suspected you would find it out," he returned calmly. (I was amazed at the man's self-control.) "I saw you down at the pool a while ago. I imagine I know what you were doing there... You have visited the vault also?"

"Yes," Vance admitted. "We inspected the coffin of Sylvanus Anthony Stamm. We found the diving equipment in it—and the three-pronged grappling-iron."

"And the oxygen tank?" Leland asked, without shifting his eyes from the cliffs beyond.

Vance nodded.

"Yes, the tank too.—The whole procedure is quite clear now. Everything about the crimes, I believe, is explained."

Leland bowed his head, and with trembling fingers attempted to repack his pipe.

"In a way, I am glad," he said, in a very low voice. "Perhaps it is better—for every one."

Vance regarded the man with a look closely akin to pity.

"There's one thing I don't entirely understand, Mr. Leland," he said at length. "Why did you telephone the Homicide Bureau after Montague's disappearance? You only planted the seed of suspicion of foul play, when the episode might have passed as an accident."

Leland turned his head slowly, frowned, and appeared to weigh the question that Vance had put to him. Finally he shook his head despondently.

"I do not know—exactly—why I did that," he replied.

Vance's penetrating eyes held the man's gaze for a brief space of time. Then he asked:

"What are you going to do about it, Mr. Leland?"

Leland glanced down at his pipe, fumbled with it for a moment, and then rose.

"I think I had better go up-stairs to Miss Stamm—if you don't mind. It might be best if it were I who told her."

Vance nodded. "I believe you are right."

Leland had scarcely entered the house and closed the door when Markham sprang to his feet and started after him; but Vance stepped up quickly and put a firm restraining hand on the District Attorney's shoulder.

"Stay here, Markham," he said, with grim and commanding insistence.

"But you can't do this thing, Vance!" Markham protested, trying to throw off the other's hold. "You have no right to contravene justice this way. You've done it before—and it was outrageous!"*

"Please believe me, Markham," Vance returned sternly, "it's the best thing." Then his eyes opened wide, and a look of astonishment came into them. "Oh, my word!" he said. "You don't yet understand... Wait—wait." And he forced Markham back into his chair.

A moment later Stamm, in his bathing suit, emerged from one of the *cabañas* and crossed the coping of the filter to the windlass beyond. The two men he had brought with him from Spuyten Duyvil had already attached the rope to the drum and stood at the hand-cranks, awaiting Stamm's orders. Stamm picked up the loose end of the coiled rope and, throwing it over his shoulder, waded into the shallow water along the foot of the cliff until he came to the submerged rock. We watched him for some time looping the rope over the rock and endeavoring to dislodge it with the assistance of the men operating the winch. Twice the rope slipped, and once a stake anchoring the winch was dislodged.

It was while the men were repairing this stake that Leland returned softly to the terrace and sat down again beside Vance. His face was pale and set, and a great sadness had come into his eyes. Markham, who had started slightly when Leland appeared, now sat looking at him curiously. Leland's eyes moved indifferently toward the pool where Stamm was struggling with the heavy rope.

"Bernice has suspected the truth all along," Leland remarked to Vance, in a voice barely above a whisper... "I

---

* Markham, I believe, was referring to the opportunity that Vance had given the murderer in "The 'Canary' Murder Case" to commit suicide after he had admitted his guilt.

think, though," he added, "she feels better, now that you gentlemen understand everything... She is very brave..."

Across the sinister waters of the Dragon Pool, there came to us a curious rumbling and crackling sound, like sharp, distant thunder. As I instinctively glanced toward the cliffs I saw the entire pinnacle of the rocky projection we had examined the day before, topple and slide downward toward the spot where Stamm was standing breast-deep in the water.

The whole terrible episode happened so quickly that the details of it are, even today, somewhat confused in my mind. But as the great mass of rock slid down the cliff, a shower of small stones in its wake, I caught a fleeting picture of Stamm glancing upward and then striving frantically to get out of the path of the crashing boulder, which the rainstorm earlier in the afternoon must have loosened. But his arms had become entangled in the rope which he was attempting to fasten about the rock in the pool, and he was unable to disengage himself. I got a momentary glimpse of his panic-stricken face just before the great mass of rock caught him and pinned him beneath the waters.

Simultaneously with the terrific splash, a fearful, hysterical shriek rang out from the balcony high above our heads; and I knew that old Mrs. Stamm had witnessed the tragedy.

We all sat in stunned silence for several seconds. Then I was conscious of Leland's soft voice.

"A merciful death," he commented.

Vance took a long, deep inhalation on his cigarette.

"Merciful—and just," he said.

The two men at the windlass had entered the water and were wading rapidly toward the place where Stamm had been buried; but it was only too obvious that their efforts would be futile. The great mass of rock had caught Stamm squarely, and there could be no hope of rescue.

The first sudden shock of the catastrophe past, we rose to our feet, almost with one accord. It was then that the hall door opened and Doctor Holliday, pale and upset, lumbered out on the terrace.

"Oh, there you are, Mr. Leland." He hesitated, as if he did not know exactly how to proceed. Then he blurted out:

"Mrs. Stamm's dead. Sudden shock—she saw it happen. You had better break the news to her daughter."

CHAPTER TWENTY-ONE

The End of the Case
(Monday, August 13; 10 p.m.)

LATE THAT NIGHT Markham and Heath and I were
sitting with Vance on his roof-garden, drinking champagne and
smoking.

We had remained at the Stamm estate only a short time
after Stamm's death. Heath had stayed on to supervise the
detail work which closed the case. The pool had been drained
again, and Stamm's body had been taken from beneath the rock
boulder. It was mutilated beyond recognition. Leland, with Miss
Stamm's assistance, had taken charge of all the domestic affairs.

Vance and Markham and I had not finished dinner until
nearly ten o'clock, and shortly afterward Sergeant Heath joined
us. It was still hot and sultry, and Vance had produced a bottle
of his 1904 Pol Roger.

"An amazin' crime," he remarked, lying back lethargically
in his chair. "Amazin'—and yet simple and rational."

"That may be true," Markham returned. "But there are
many details of it which are still obscure to me."

"Once its basic scheme is clear," Vance said, "the various shapes and colors of the mosaic take their places almost automatically."

He emptied his glass of champagne.

"It was easy enough for Stamm to plan and execute the first murder. He brought together a house-party of warring elements, on any member of which suspicion might fall if criminality were proved in connection with Montague's disappearance. He felt sure his guests would go swimming in the pool and that Montague, with his colossal vanity, would take the first dive. He deliberately encouraged the heavy drinking, and he himself pretended to overindulge. But as a matter of fact, he was the only member of the party, with the possible exception of Leland and Miss Stamm, who did no drinking."

"But Vance—"

"Oh, I know. He gave the appearance of having drunk heavily all day. But that was only part of his plan. He was probably never more sober in his life than when the rest of the party left the house for the swimming pool. During the entire evening he sat on the davenport in the library, and surreptitiously poured his liquor into the jardinière holding the rubber-plant."

Markham looked up quickly.

"That was why you were so interested in the soil of that plant?"

"Exactly. Stamm had probably emptied two quarts of whisky into the pot. I took up a good bit of the soil on my finger; and it was well saturated with alcohol."

"But Doctor Holliday's report—"

"Oh, Stamm was actually in a state of acute alcoholism when the doctor examined him. You remember the quart of Scotch he ordered from Trainor, just before the others went down to the pool. When he himself came back to the library, after the murder, he undoubtedly drank the entire bottle; and when Leland found him his state of alcoholic collapse was quite genuine. Thus he gave the whole affair an air of verisimilitude."

Vance lifted the champagne from the wine cooler and poured himself another glass. When he had taken a few sips he lay back again in his chair.

"What Stamm did," he continued, "was to hide his diving outfit and the grapnel in his car in the garage earlier in the day. Then, feigning a state of almost complete drunken insensibility, he waited till every one had gone to the pool. Immediately he went to the garage, and drove—or perhaps coasted—down the East Road to the little cement path. He donned his diving suit, which he put on over his dinner clothes, and attached the oxygen tank—a matter of but a few minutes. Then he put the board in place, and entered the pool. He was reasonably sure that Montague would take the first dive; and he was able to select almost the exact spot in the pool toward which Montague would head. He had his grapnel with him, so that he could reach out in any direction and get his victim. The water in the pool is quite clear and the flood-lights would give him a good view of Montague. The technique of the crime for an experienced diver like Stamm was dashed simple."

Vance made a slight gesture with his hand.

"There can be little doubt as to exactly what happened. Montague took his dive, and Stamm, standing on the sloping basin opposite the deep channel, simply hooked him with the grappling-iron—which accounts for the wounds on Montague's chest. The force of the dive, I imagine, drove Montague's head violently against the metal oxygen tank clamped to the breastplate of Stamm's helmet, and fractured his skull. With his victim stunned and perhaps unconscious, Stamm proceeded to choke him under the water until he was quite limp. It was no great effort for Stamm to drag him to the car and throw him in. Next Stamm replaced the board, doffed his diving suit, hid it in the old coffin in the vault, and drove to the pot-holes, where he dumped Montague's body. Montague's broken bones were the result of the rough way in which Stamm chucked him into the rock pit; and the abrasions on his feet were undoubtedly caused by Stamm's dragging him over the cement walk to the parked car. Afterward Stamm drove the car back to the garage, returned cautiously to the library, and proceeded to consume the quart of whisky."

Vance took a long inhalation on his cigarette, exhaling the smoke slowly.

"It was an almost perfect alibi."

"But the time element, Vance—" Markham began.

"Stamm had plenty of time. At least fifteen minutes elapsed before the others had changed to their bathing suits; and this was twice as much time as Stamm required to coast down the hill in his car, slip into his diving suit, put the piece of lumber in place, and station himself in the pool. And, certainly, it took him not more than fifteen minutes, at the most, to replace the board, hide his diving suit, deposit his victim in the pot-hole, and return to the house."

"But he was taking a desperate chance," Markham commented.

"On the contr'ry, he was taking no chance at all. If his calculations worked out successfully, there was no way in which the plot could go awry. Stamm had all the time necess'ry; he had the equipment; and he was working out of sight of any possible witnesses. If Montague had not dived into the pool, as was his custom, it would have meant only that the murder would have to be postponed. In that case Stamm would simply have walked out of the pool, returned to the house, and bided his time."

Vance frowned wistfully and turned his head lazily toward Markham.

"There was, however, one fatal error in the calculations," he said. "Stamm was too cautious—he lacked boldness: he covered his gamble, as it were. As I have said, in planning the house-party he invited persons who had reason to want Montague out of the way, his idea being to supply the authorities with suspects in the event his scheme did not work out. But, in doing so, he overlooked the fact that some of these very people were familiar with diving apparatus and with his own under-sea work in the tropics—people who, having this information, might have figured out how the murder was committed, provided the body was found...".

"You mean," asked Markham, "that you think Leland saw through the plot from the first?"

"There can be little doubt," Vance returned, "that when Montague failed to come up from his dive, Leland strongly suspected that Stamm had committed a crime. Naturally, he was torn between his sense of justice and fair play, on the one hand, and his love for Bernice Stamm, on the other. My word, what a predicament! He compromised by telephoning to the Homicide Bureau and insisting that an investigation be instigated. He wouldn't definitely expose or accuse the brother of the woman he loved. But, as an honorable man, he couldn't bring himself to countenance what he believed to be deliberate murder. Y' know, Markham, he was infinitely relieved when I told him this afternoon that I knew the truth. But meanwhile the man had suffered no end."

"Do you think any one else suspected?" Markham asked.

"Oh, yes. Bernice Stamm suspected the truth—Leland himself told us so this afternoon. That's why the Sergeant, when he first saw her, got the impression she was not primarily worried about Montague's disappearance.—And I feel pretty sure that Tatum also guessed the truth. Don't forget, he had been on the trip to Cocos Island with Stamm and was familiar with the possibilities of diving suits. But the present situation no doubt seemed a bit fantastic to him, and he couldn't voice his suspicion because there was apparently no way of proving it.—And Greeff, too, having helped to equip some of Stamm's expeditions, undoubtedly had a fairly accurate idea as to what had happened to Montague."

"And the others also?" asked Markham.

"No, I doubt if either Mrs. McAdam or Ruby Steele really suspected the truth; but I think both of them felt that something was wrong. Ruby Steele was attracted by Montague—which accounts, perversely, for the antagonism between them. And she was jealous of Bernice Stamm, as well as of Teeny McAdam. When Montague disappeared, I have no doubt the idea of foul play did enter her mind. That's why she accused Leland: she hated him because of his superiority."

Vance paused a moment and went on.

"Mrs. McAdam's mental reactions in the matter were a bit subtler. I doubt if she entirely understood her own emotions. Unquestionably, however, she too suspected foul play. Although the fact that Montague had faded from the scene would have favored her personal ends, I imagine she had some lingerin' sentiment for the chap, and that's why she handed us Greeff and Leland as possibilities—both of whom she disliked. And I imagine also that her scream was purely emotional, while her later indifference indicated the dominance of her scheming mind over her heart. The horror of the possibility of Montague's having been murdered accounted for her violent reaction when I told her of the splash in the pool: she pictured terrible things happening to him. The old feminine heart at work again, Markham."

There were several moments of silence. Then Markham said, almost inaudibly, as if stating to himself some point in a train of thought:

"And of course the car that Leland and Greeff and Miss Stamm heard was Stamm's."

"Unquestionably," Vance returned. "The time element fitted exactly."

Markham nodded, but there was a troubled reservation in his frown.

"But still," he said, "there was that note from the Bruett woman."

"My dear Markham! There's no such person. Stamm created Ellen Bruett to account for Montague's disappearance. He was hoping that the whole affair would simply blow over as a commonplace elopement. He wrote the rendezvous note himself, and put it in Montague's pocket after he returned from the pool that night. And you remember that he indicated where we could find it, when he opened the clothes-closet door. A clever ruse, Markham; and the sound of the car on the East Road bore out the theory, though Stamm probably didn't take the sound of the car into consideration at all."

"No wonder my men couldn't find any trace of the dame," grumbled the Sergeant.

Markham was gazing at his cigar with a thoughtful abstracted look.

"I can understand the Bruett factor," he remarked at length; "but how do you account for Mrs. Stamm's uncannily accurate prophecies?"

Vance smiled mildly.

"They were not prophecies, Markham," he replied, with a sad note in his voice. "They were all based on real knowledge of what was going on, and were the pathetic attempts of an old woman to protect her son. What Mrs. Stamm didn't actually see from her window, she probably suspected; and nearly everything she said to us was deliberately calculated to divert us from the truth. That's why she sent for us at the outset."

Vance drew deeply on his cigarette again, and looked out wistfully over the tree-tops.

"Much of her talk about the dragon was insincere, although there is no question that the hallucination concerning the dragon in the pool had taken a powerful hold on her weakened mind. And this partial belief in the existence of a water-monster formed the basis of her defense of Stamm. We don't know how much she saw from her window. Personally, I think she felt instinctively that Stamm had plotted the murder of Montague, and I also think that she heard the car going down the East Road and suspected what its errand was. When she listened at the top of the stairs that first night and heard Stamm protesting, the shock produced by the realization of her fears caused her to scream and to send for us later to tell us that no one in the house was guilty of any crime."

Vance sighed.

"It was a tragic effort, Markham; and all her other efforts to mislead us were equally tragic. She attempted to build up the dragon hypothesis because she herself was not quite rational on the subject. Moreover, she knew Stamm would take the body away and hide it—which accounts for her seeming prophecy that the body would not be found in the pool. And she was able to figure out where Stamm would hide the body— in fact, she may even have been able to tell, from the sound, approximately how far down the road Stamm drove the car before returning to the garage. When she screamed at the time the pool was emptied, she was simply making a dramatic gesture to emphasize her theory that the dragon had flown off with Montague's body."

Vance stretched his legs and settled even deeper into his chair.

"Mrs. Stamm's prognostications of the second tragedy were merely another effort toward foisting the dragon theory upon us. She undoubtedly suspected that her son, having succeeded in murdering Montague, would, if the opportunity presented itself, also put Greeff out of the way. I imagine she knew all about Greeff's financial plottings, and sensed Stamm's hatred for him. She may even have seen, or heard, her son and Greeff go down toward the pool last night and have antici- pated the terrible thing that was going to happen. You recall how frantically she endeavored to bolster up her theory of the dragon when she heard of Greeff's disappearance. I had a suspicion then that she knew more than she would admit. That was why I went directly to the pot-holes to see if Greeff's body was there... Oh, yes, that tortured old woman knew of her son's guilt. When she begged Leland to bring him back into the house this afternoon, saying that some danger was lurking in the pool, it wasn't a premonition. It was only her instinctive fear that some retribution might overtake her son at the scene of his crimes."

"And it did overtake him," mumbled Markham. "A curious coincidence."

"He sure had it coming to him," put in the practical Sergeant. "But what gets me is the trouble he took to avoid leaving footprints."

"Stamm had to protect himself, Sergeant," Vance explained. "Any noticeable imprints of his diving shoes would have given away the entire plot. Therefore, he took the precaution of placing a board over that patch of ground."

"But he took no precaution against his footprints on the bottom of the pool," Markham submitted.

"True," Vance returned. "It had not occurred to him, I imagine, that the imprints he made under the water would remain; for he was certainly a frightened man when the marks of his diving shoes came to light: he was afraid they would be recognized for what they were. I admit that the truth did not occur to me at the time. But, later, a suspicion of the truth dawned on me; and that is why I wished to verify my theory by searching for a diving suit and shoes and gloves. There are but few companies that make standard diving equipment in this country, and I had little trouble in locating the firm from which Stamm had acquired his outfit."

"But what about Leland?" Markham asked. "Surely he would have recognized the tracks."

"Oh, to be sure. In fact, the moment I mentioned those strange tracks to him, he suspected immediately how they had been made; and when he saw Snitkin's drawings he knew the truth. I think he rather hoped that we also would see it, although he could not bring himself to tell us directly because of his loyalty to Bernice Stamm. Miss Stamm herself suspected the truth—you recall how upset she was when I mentioned the queer footprints to her. And Mrs. Stamm, too, knew the significance of those imprints when she heard of them. But she very cleverly turned them to her own purpose and used them to support the theory of the dragon that she was endeavorin' to instil in us."

Markham filled his glass.

"That part of it is all clear," he said, after a short silence. "But there are certain points connected with Greeff's murder that I don't yet understand."

Vance did not speak at once. First he lighted a fresh cigarette slowly and meditatively. Then he said:

"I can't make up my mind, Markham, whether Greeff's murder was planned for this particular week-end, or was suddenly decided on. But the possibility unquestionably was at the back of Stamm's mind when he planned the party. There can be no doubt that he detested Greeff and also feared him; and, with his perverted mind, he saw no way of eliminating the menace presented by Greeff except through murder. What led Stamm to his decision to do away with Greeff last night was undoubtedly the amazin' amount of dragon talk that followed the finding of the imprints on the bottom of the pool, and the claw-like tears down Montague's chest. He saw no reason why he should not continue to build up this outlandish theory of the dragon. As long as the circumstances of Montague's death appeared entirely irrational and fantastic, Stamm, no doubt, felt safe from apprehension; and in this state of false security, he sought to repeat the irrationality of Montague's death in Greeff's murder. He argued, I imagine, that if he were safe from suspicion as a result of the dragonish implications in Montague's murder, he would be equally safe from suspicion if Greeff were disposed of in a similar manner. That's why he duplicated the technique so carefully. He struck Greeff over the head to make a wound similar to the one on Montague. He then strangled Greeff, in order to reproduce the throat marks; and, that accomplished, he used the grapnel on Greeff's chest, thus reproducing the supposed dragon's claw-marks. He then carried the murder to its logical extreme—or, rather, to its *reductio ad absurdum*—by chucking the fellow into the pot-hole."

"I can see how his mind was working," Markham admitted. "But in Greeff's case he had to create the opportunity for the crime."

"Quite so. But that wasn't difficult. After Stamm's vicious outburst Saturday night, Greeff was only too glad to accept the reconciliation Stamm offered him last night in the library. You recall that Leland told us they sat for hours talking amicably before retiring. What they probably talked about was the prospect of a new expedition, and Greeff was delighted to be able to offer his help. Then, when they had gone up-stairs, Stamm undoubtedly invited Greeff into his own room for a last drink, later suggesting that they go for a walk to continue the discussion; and the two went out together. It was at that time that both Leland and Trainor heard the side door being unbolted."

Vance again sipped his champagne.

"How Stamm inveigled Greeff into the vault is something we'll never know. However, it's a point of no importance, for certainly Greeff was in a frame of mind to acquiesce in any suggestion Stamm might have made. Stamm may have told Greeff that he was able to explain Montague's death if the other would go into the vault with him. Or, it may have been a more commonplace invitation—the expression of a desire to inspect the masonry after the heavy rains. But whatever the means used by Stamm, we know that Greeff did enter the vault with him last night..."

"The gardenia, of course—and the bloodstains," Markham murmured.

"Oh, yes; it was quite evident... And after Stamm had killed Greeff and mutilated him exactly as he had mutilated Montague, he took him down to the pot-holes in the wheel-barrow, over the sandy ground along the foot of the cliff, where he would not attract the attention of any guard that might have been stationed on the East Road."

Heath gave a gratified grunt.

"And then he left the wheelbarrow in that bunch of trees, and pussy-footed back to the house."

"Exactly, Sergeant. Moreover, the grating metallic noise that Leland heard was obviously the creaking of the rusty hinges of the vault door; and the other sound which Leland described could have been nothing but the wheelbarrow. And, despite all Stamm's caution on re-entering the house, both Leland and Trainor heard him throw the bolt."

Vance sighed.

"It was not a perfect murder, Markham, but it had the elements of perfection in it. It was a bold murder, too; for if either of the murders were solved, both would be solved. It was a double gamble—the placing of two chips, instead of one, on a selected number."

Again Markham nodded sombrely.

"That part is clear enough now," he said. "But why should the key to the vault have been found in Tatum's room?"

"That was part of Stamm's fundamental mistake. As I have said, Stamm was overcautious. He didn't have the courage to carry through his plot without building bridges. He may have had the key for years, or he may have secured it recently from Mrs. Stamm's trunk. But really, it doesn't matter. Once he had used it for his purpose, he could not throw it away, for obviously he intended to remove the diving suit from the vault when the first opportunity offered. He could have hidden the key in the meantime; but if the diving suit had been discovered in the vault by some one's tearing down a wall or breaking in the door, suspicion would immediately have fallen on him, as it was his own diving suit. Therefore, in an effort to protect himself in this remote eventuality, he probably put the key first in Greeff's room, to point suspicion to Greeff. Then, when the opportunity to murder Greeff arose, Stamm planted the key in Tatum's room. Stamm liked Leland and wanted Bernice to marry him—which, incidentally, was the primary motive for his getting rid of Montague—and he certainly would not have tried to throw suspicion on Leland. You will remember that I first searched Greeff's room—I thought that the key might be there, inasmuch as there was a possibility we would think that Greeff had merely run away. But when it was not there I looked for it in Tatum's room. Luckily we found it and didn't have to break into the vault—which I would certainly have insisted upon if there had been no other means of entering."

"But what I still don't understand, Vance," Markham persisted, "is why the key should have interested you in the first place."

"Neither do I—entirely," Vance returned, "And it's much too hot tonight to indulge in psychological analyses of my mental quirks. Let's say, for brevity, that my idea about the key was mere guesswork. As you know, the vault fascinated me because of its strategic position; and I couldn't see how else the first murder could have been so neatly accomplished unless the vault had been used in some way. It was most convenient, don't y' know. But the entire matter was far from clear in my mind. In fact, it was dashed vague. However, I thought it worth determining, and that's why I went to Mrs. Stamm and demanded to know the hiding-place of the key. I frightened her into telling me, for she didn't associate the vault with Stamm's machinations. When I discovered that the key had disappeared from its hiding-place, I was more convinced than ever that it was a factor in the solution of our problem."

"But how, in the name of Heaven," asked Markham, "did you first hit upon the idea that Stamm was the guilty person? He was the only person in the house that seemed to have a good alibi."

Vance shook his head slowly.

"No, Markham old dear; he was the only member of the party who did *not* have an alibi. And it was for that reason that I had my eye on him from the first—although I admit there were other possibilities. Stamm, of course, thought that he had built up a perfect alibi, at the same time hoping that the murder would pass as a mere departure. But when Montague's murder was established, Stamm's position was really weaker than that of any of the others; for he was the only one who was not standing beside the pool at the time Montague dived in. It would have been difficult for any one of the others to have murdered Montague in the circumstances, just as it would have been impossible for Stamm to have murdered him if he had actually been in a state of acute alcoholism. It was this combination of circumstances that gave me my first inkling of the truth. Naturally, Stamm couldn't have gone to the pool with the others and still have accomplished his purpose; and, reasoning from this premise, I arrived at the conclusion that it was possible for him to have feigned drunkenness by secretly disposing of his liquor, and then made his drunkenness a reality after he had returned to the house. When I learned that he had spent the entire evening on the davenport in the library, I naturally became interested in the jardinière holding the rubber-plant at the head of the davenport."

"But, Vance," protested Markham, "if you were so certain from the first that the crime was rational and commonplace, why all the silly pother about a dragon?"

"It was not silly. There was always the remote possibility that some strange fish, or sea-monster, had been responsible for Montague's death. Even the greatest zoologists understand but little about aquatic life: it is positively amazin' how meagre our knowledge of under-water creatures really is. The breeding of the Betta, for instance, has been going on for decades, and with all our experimentation with this labyrinth family, no one knows whether the *Betta pugnax* is a nest-builder or a mouthbreeder. Mrs. Stamm was quite right when she ridiculed scientific knowledge of submarine life. And you must not forget, Markham, that Stamm was an ardent fish hunter, and that he brought back to this country all kinds of rare specimens about which practically nothing is known. Scientifically, the superstition of the pool could not be ignored. But, I admit, I did not take the matter very seriously. I clung childishly to the trodden paths, for life has a most disappointin' way of proving commonplace and rational when we are hopin' most passionately for the bizarre and supernatural. Anyway, I thought it worth while to inspect Stamm's collection of fish. But I was more or less familiar with all his exhibits; so I descended to the realm of simple, under-standable things, and tested the soil in the jardinière."

"And incidentally," Markham commented, with a slow smile, "you lingered over the fish and the other plants so as not to give Stamm any idea of what you were really after in the rubber-plant pot."

Vance smiled back.

"It may be, don't y' know... How about another magnum of Pol Roger?" And he rang for Currie.

It was less than a year after these two sinister murders at the old Dragon Pool, with their sequence of tragedies, that Leland and Bernice Stamm were married. They were both strong and, in many ways, remarkable characters; but the memory of the tragedies affected them too deeply for them to remain in Inwood. They built a home in the hills of Westchester, and went there to live. Vance and I visited them shortly after their marriage.

The old Stamm residence was never occupied again, and the estate was acquired by the city and added to what is now Inwood Hill Park. The house was torn down, and only the crumbling stones of its foundation remain. But the two square stone posts of the entrance gate, which marked the beginning of the driveway from Bolton Road, are still standing. The old Dragon Pool exists no more. The stream that fed it was diverted into Spuyten Duyvil Creek. Its semi-artificial bed has been filled in, and what was once the basin of the Dragon Pool is now overgrown with wild vegetation. It would be difficult today even to trace the course of the old stream or to determine the former boundaries of that sinister and tragic pool.

After the final tragedy and the breaking up of the century-old traditions of the Stamm estate, I often wondered what became of Trainor, the butler, when the doors of the ancient mansion had been closed for all time. Why the memory of the fellow should have remained in my mind, I cannot say; but there was in him something at once ghost-like and corporeal, something both pathetic and offensive, which made a strong impression on me. I was, therefore, glad when I recently ran into him.

Vance and I were visiting a tropical-fish shop in East 34th Street; and there, behind the counter, half hidden by the tanks, was Trainor.

He recognized Vance at once, and shook his head lugubriously as we approached him.

"I'm not doing so well with my *Scatophagus* here," he repined. "Not the proper conditions—if you know what I mean, sir."